Prais

"Ratzlaff debuts with an accomplished whodunit that combines solid prose, a winning lead, and plausible amateur sleuthing . . . This series is off to a promising start."

— Publishers Weekly

"The writer describes her writing as cozy mysteries because that's exactly how it feels. The story flows along effortlessly to its conclusion."

— Betty Lou Roselle, delcoculturevultures.com

"This debut volume of a new cozy mystery 'Native Prairie Mysteries' series has more unexpected plot twists and turns than a Kansas tornado and is a compulsive page turner of a 'whodunnit' murder mystery from start to finish."

— Midwest Book Review

THE
MOTH
WASN'T
HARMLESS

Native Prairie Mysteries
Book Two

TARA RATZLAFF

CAMEL
PRESS
Kenmore, WA

A Camel Press book published by Epicenter Press

Epicenter Press
6524 NE 181st St.
Suite 2
Kenmore, WA 98028

For more information go to:
www.Camelpress.com
www.Coffeetownpress.com
www.Epicenterpress.com
www.tararatzlaff.com

This is a work of fiction. Names, characters, places, brands, media, and incidents are either the product of the author's imagination or are used fictitiously.

Cover design by Scott Book
Design by Melissa Vail Coffman

The Moth Wasn't Harmless
Copyright © 2024 by Tara Ratzlaff

Library of Congress Control Number: 2023950854

ISBN: 978-1-684921-71-3 (Trade Paper)
ISBN: 978-1-684921-72-0 (eBook)

I would like to dedicate this book to the memories of my grandmother, Barbara Holm, who introduced me to mysteries and my aunt, Delores Andol, who gave wonderful books as gifts.

ACKNOWLEDGMENTS

I WOULD LIKE TO THANK MY PARENTS for their unwavering support, Jennifer McCord, executive editor and associate publisher of Epicenter Press, for encouraging a first-time author, and most of all my husband and daughter for being more confident in me than I am!

CHAPTER ONE

The diversity of a native prairie provides habitat for birds, reptiles, insects, and other wildlife such as white-tail deer.

I WAS SITTING AT THE KITCHEN TABLE enjoying a cup of white chocolate cappuccino, appreciating the peace and quiet of having the house all to myself early on a Sunday morning in late October, when the kitchen door burst open and my best friend, Jessica Golding, came rushing in. I couldn't even bemoan the interruption, as it was nice to see my friend returning to her positive, animated self. She'd had a difficult time last month when her long-lost brother returned home only to be murdered before they could be reunited. The whole incident had brought up a lot of bad memories and it was great to see her normal personality exerting itself.

"Do you know who the new librarian is?" She blurt out excited.

"I don't, but I assume it's someone we know or you wouldn't be this wound up," I said as I looked at the clock. "By the way what are doing here, shouldn't you be at the restaurant?" Jessica owned a restaurant in town that was known for old-fashioned home cooking, items such as meatloaf, fried chicken, meatball dinners, homemade soups, and amazing sandwiches and burgers all at reasonable prices. Her breakfasts were my favorite, in particular her omelets. The lone drawback was that it was only open Monday through Saturday, 6:00 a.m. – 2:00 p.m. Sundays she opened for a brunch buffet from 12:00 p.m. – 2:00 p.m. and typically spent the morning hours before church at the restaurant.

"If all we went through last month taught me anything it's that my staff is awesome and I can trust them to run the place. In fact, I'm taking the entire day off; besides I can't imagine the buffet will attract too many people today with the corn maze going on. I heard three different food trucks will be there as well," she said as she removed her coat and sat down at the table across from me. "Now, do you want to know who the new librarian is or not?"

Deciding to tease her a little bit, I said, "It doesn't matter to me, I don't often go there." This was a true statement. I loved to read, but preferred to buy my books as I often re-read my favorites.

She shook her finger at me, "I know you better than that. You are as nosy as I am."

"Alright, alright," I laughed at her. "No, I don't know and yes, I'd like to."

"It's Marcy Crumpet, well Marcy Bozeman now," she spit out not trying to contain her glee.

"Marcy; that's awesome!" Marcy was an old high school class-mate of ours. We had been inseparable until our senior year when Marcy inexplicably got involved with the school bully Brian. When the three of us were together we had presented quite a contrast in appearance. I was 5'7", big-boned, blonde curly hair, and un-athletic; Jessica was a petite 5'2", agile, with dark straight hair; and Marcy was a classic tall, slender, beautiful blonde. Best of all she didn't have a vain bone in her body. She had been the life of the class with her optimistic outlook on everything. She and Jessica shared that trait, but where Jessica was a little more reserved, Marcy had tended to act first and think later. Then what Jessica said registered, "She's a librarian? That doesn't fit with what I remember of her," my voice trailed off as I looked at Jessica to see if she remembered Marcy the same.

"I know, right? I was in the library yesterday afternoon after the restaurant closed and she's the same old Marcy, beautiful, cheerful, frank in speech—and all of the sudden our town library isn't such a somber place now that she's here. Although I have to admit she did look a little drawn and worried," Jessica said looking puzzled.

"How long has she been here?"

"She said they moved here about three weeks ago."

"Maybe she is tired from the move. Wait a minute; did you say her last name is Bozeman?" I asked not wanting to hear what I knew the answer was going to be.

"Yes." Marcy studied me with a knowing smile, waiting for my response.

"She married that idiot Brian?" I blurt out, my reaction not disappointing her.

"She did, right after graduation. They've been married for ten years now and have a ten-year-old son."

"That guy was the nemesis of my high school years. He was such a jerk, and not just to me, he picked on everyone. He never quit making fun of me for that time I tried out for the volleyball team and, well let's just say, it didn't go well."

Jessica giggled and said, "Nobody could believe someone as strong as you were couldn't serve a ball over the net either overhand or underhand."

"I can see the humor in it now, but at the time it was humiliating. Other people teased me too, but Brian Bozeman had a way of making his teasing nasty. Why would she ever have married him?"

"Love is a funny thing. She dated him our entire senior year, maybe she's been a good influence on him and he's changed," Jessica said optimistic as always. She got up and helped herself to a doughnut; little did she know they had been sitting open on the counter for five days.

"If my memories of Brian are accurate, I doubt it," I said as I watched her take a bite. She grimaced and spit it out into the garbage, then dropped the rest of the doughnut in Wizard's dog dish. The little dachshund; that belonged to my twenty-three year old, 6'2", curly black-haired brother Kirk, was thrilled with the unexpected treat. Of course it would have been better if it wasn't a powdered sugar doughnut as Wizard wasn't content to eat it in his dish and I watched him drag it into the living room leaving a white trail behind him. I turned back to Jessica and asked, "I wonder where Brian is going to find work?"

Continuing to pace around the kitchen, Jessica answered, "Marcy told me MM construction hired him. You know they can never find enough help."

"I'm glad they are done with my cabins." MM construction was owned by two brothers, Mitch and Mark Carboot. Dad and I had made the much-debated decision to add tourism into our farm operation and had hired them to build three 18' x 18' cabins in one of our native prairies to rent out to birders, wildlife and native prairie enthusiasts, or anyone wanting to get away from it all. We weren't known for our scenery in this part of northwestern Minnesota, as the topography was flat with broad expanses of farmland broken up by wooded farmsteads. The primary draw for any tourist was a state park with a small man-made lake seven miles away. My hope was that we would help bring a little more tourism to the area by providing the cabins. I may be biased but I think our native prairies were an oasis in the midst of the farmland. My name is Carmen Karlaff and my family and I have been operating a native grass and wildflower seed farm that my Dad, Chet, and now myself, had been operating for the past thirty-five years. My younger brother Kirk helped at times but his passion was pursuing a career in hard rock music, which was fortunate for us as his "help" wasn't always beneficial. The small town we lived about five miles from was Arvilla, with a population of 2500. Arvilla was approximately thirty miles east of the North Dakota border and twenty miles south of the Canadian border. Although I don't notice it, I've been told our close proximity to Canada gives our speech a Canadian accent. Our operation was more than a farm as not only did we grow and harvest the seed; but we, along with some excellent hired help, also cleaned our own seed, marketed it, packaged it, and shipped it all over the United States. I had been thinking about expanding our business into tourism since college. I succeeded in convincing Dad, and we made a mutual decision to build the cabins a few months ago.

"I'm sure you are for more reasons than not wanting to deal with Brian. Are you ready for your first guests coming on Friday?" Jessica asked.

"I have some last minute decorating, but the better question is, are you and Edna ready?" Edna and Jessica were the respective bakery and restaurant owners in town and were supplying food for the cabins. We were providing breakfast and dinner. Supper was on their own, with hopes they would bring some business to the two remaining places in town that offered evening meals. When the guests called for reservations I had them choose whether they wanted pre-frozen meals waiting in the freezer to thaw and heat up in the microwave at their leisure, or fresh food delivered once a day in the morning. To prevent confusion, I made sure all my advertising explained that in Northwestern Minnesota, dinner was the noon meal and supper was the evening meal. Edna would provide bakery items like doughnuts, crepes, and muffins for breakfast and Jessica would provide fresh fruit and juice. Dinner would consist of Edna's homemade buns and some type of dish Jessica would prepare that could be reheated such as lasagna.

"We have it all figured out. Are we going to meet on Thursday to do a final walk-through?" Jessica asked settling back in her chair.

"That's the plan. Now that harvest is over, my schedule is open, other than loading seed and setting the mill for each crop. What time works for you to get away from the restaurant?" I asked.

"2:00 p.m., if that works for Edna?"

"I'll talk to her and get back to you," I answered.

"Are Sam and Phil going to run your seed plant like usual?" Jessica asked.

"Yes, and I'm thankful, as I wouldn't want to be in the position of trying to hire anyone right now."

"I know. That's why I'm only open for breakfast and dinner. The existing staff is happy with that schedule and I don't need as many employees either. I know people would like us to be open in the evenings, but if you can't find help it's not worth being run ragged. I'm sure that's why MM construction hired Brian. They didn't have much choice, when you need labor sometimes any living body will do. Anyway, back to Marcy; I told her we'd have to get together for supper some evening."

"That sounds good. I'd love to see her," I agreed.

"We can talk to her this afternoon. She said she joined the committee to help the Henning's with their corn maze. You are planning on going?"

"Of course, even if I didn't want to go, I wouldn't have a choice as part of the event is on our property," I said reminding her.

"That's right, I forgot. What did you decide to do?"

"The Henning's corn maze is adjacent to our big bluestem field. Theirs is the main attraction, but we left three acres of our field and harvested it at a four foot height. The adults and older kids will have fun in the corn maze, but we thought it would be fun for the little kids to have their own maze to play in. Nick mowed a maze into it before he left. He also parked a flatbed trailer next to it so the parents could stand on it, be able to watch their kids, and shout directions if needed."

"That sounds like fun. I know the corn maze last year was frustrating for the youngsters, the parents had to go with and they wanted to do it on their own," Jessica agreed.

"I'm hoping for a good turnout. Everyone is getting sick of coming up of fundraising ideas for the pool. It was nice of the Henning's to donate the profits from this years' corn maze."

"People will show up, especially as the Eagles club donated prizes for the five fastest times through the maze along with collecting the various tokens at each branch that off-shoots to a dead end. That should encourage people to stick around until the end and buy food while they are waiting. We are hoping that this event combined with the money from the Hawaiian vacation trip raffle will help us meet our goal."

"The raffle didn't get cancelled? I thought that after Jacob's legal problems he would have reneged on the trip." Jacob was a local lawyer who had donated a Hawaiian vacation for four along with plane fare. He had been involved in the whole mess with Jessica's brother a month ago.

"We were fortunate; everything had been purchased and already turned over to the pool committee," Jessica responded.

Arvilla's town pool had cracked over the summer and expensive repairs were needed. Nobody wanted their taxes raised for a pool project, so a pool committee made up of some parents and local business owners had formed to put on a flurry of fundraising events with a raffle for a Hawaiian vacation the primary fund-raiser.

"As sad as this sounds," Jessica continued, "I think all the notoriety helped with tickets sales. We had hoped to sell one thousand tickets which in this small community would be a true miracle and had stalled out at six hundred before all the scandal with Jacob. I think once his defense team, in an effort to put a better spin on his public persona for the upcoming trial, got the word got out that Jacob had supplied the trip, it ended up being free advertising and we sold another three hundred tickets. With a great turnout today and along with the raffle we should be close to meeting our goal. The weather is even doing its best to cooperate."

"Is James coming?" I asked. James Harmen was a good friend and neighbor. He and Jessica started dating a few months ago. I was thrilled for my two best friends.

"He is, but he's going to meet me there, as they are vaccinating the cows this morning and he might be late," she answered and then went on to ask, "What about Nick? Oh, that's right, you said he was gone." Noticing my expression she asked, "What's wrong? I thought things were good with you and Nick?"

"They are, or at least they were. I'm starting to regret not leaving our relationship as co-workers." Nick Banning was our farm's foreman; we had hired him three months ago. With Dad retiring, and Kirk not interested in the farm, we needed a mechanic and someone to help me manage the farm. Agronomy was my strong suit with my mechanical abilities not sufficient to even rate. Nick was thirty-two, came from a small town in Oregon by the Willamette Valley where he had worked on a turf grass farm, and had experience with irrigation. He was also a diesel mechanic. He had some gaps in his employment history, but his references checked out with everyone having positive things to say about him. He has worked out well for us as he is knowledgeable, dependable, and a hard worker. He is also very attractive, 5'10" tall with dark brown hair, and a lean muscular build. We had admitted to each other the attraction between us, but were taking it slow. "We've had a few dates and they have all went well, but . . ." I answered and my voice trailed off.

"What's wrong?" Jessica asked.

"I don't know. It's frustrating to me that he hasn't told me much about his past. In fact other than his work references and mentioning that his home life as a teenager wasn't the best, that's all I know. He knows almost everything there is to know about me, and I know next to nothing about him. Last Tuesday he got a phone call when we were working together in the shop. He went outside to talk. I don't have a problem with that, everyone is entitled to some privacy, but when he came back in and said he'd get the maze mowed, move the trailer there, but would have to leave afterwards I got irritated. A 'family emergency' he said, but wouldn't tell me anything else. He left that night, and I haven't heard from him since. It's a good thing he had earned some paid time off or I think I'd fire him."

"You don't mean that, Carmen," Jessica exclaimed.

"No. I guess I don't," I said as I got up to wash my mug. "I'm just mad at myself."

"Why?" She asked me with eyebrows raised.

"I went against my better judgment. I should have left our relationship professional."

"Nick is a good guy, I'm sure of it. You'll have to find some patience; there must be a little bit in you somewhere." Jennifer said with a smile as she got up from the table. "Put it out of your mind and let's have a fun day."

Wizard padded back into the kitchen with powdered sugar on his muzzle and a yellow rubber ball in his mouth he was energetically squeaking.

"It looks like Wizard is ready for some activity." Jessica laughed when he dropped the ball at her feet, tail wagging. "How is it going taking care of him?"

Kirk was in Minneapolis working on getting a record album recorded. While myself, and the rest of my family and friends, had no clue what Kirk's hard rock music was about, we all had to admit for a guy who was; in as kind of way of saying it as possible, haphazard in his approach to life, he was relentless in his pursuit of a music career. Last month a record producer had made the long seven hour trip and traveled up here to northwestern Minnesota from Minneapolis to check out Kirk's band and, to everyone's surprise except Kirk's, offered them a deal. It was unfortunate for us that Kirk couldn't take Wizard to Minneapolis with him, so Dad and I were stuck taking care of him.

"He's been well behaved. I'm not sure if it's because he's getting older or if Kirk was the bad influence. I'm leaning towards Kirk," I said with a smile.

I walked over to the door and let Wizard out, making sure he left the rubber ball in the house. Our home; which Kirk, I, and Dad shared wasn't located on the actual farm premises so it was safe to let the little dog out to roam by himself without fear of getting run over by any farm equipment. I was a little defensive having to tell people that at twenty-eight years of age I lived with my dad and brother. My mom had passed away during my last year of college and when I moved back home after graduation to help farm, Dad asked me to stay, then about a year ago Dad had a major heart attack and that wasn't the right time to leave either. Lately Dad has become involved with our neighbor Karla Harmen, who is James' mother. I was beginning to believe it was time for me to start looking for my own place again.

"I'd better get going," Jessica said looking at the time on her phone. "I need to swing by the restaurant to make sure they don't need anything and then grab some warmer clothes from home to change into after church if I'm going to be standing outside all day. It's a beautiful sunny day, but the wind has a bite to it." She walked towards the door.

"Hold on, let me get Wizard in the house first, wouldn't want the little guy to get run over." I opened the door and both Wizard and my calico cat, Tabitha, raced inside.

"I'll see you later," Jessica said as she walked out to her car.

"What have you two been up to?" I asked them looking down as they both wound around my feet clearly revved up and looking for food. I got their food out of the cupboard and put it in their respective dishes. Good behavior was not the normal for Wizard, which is why it never ceased to amaze me he didn't eat Tabitha's food. Although maybe it wasn't as surprising as Tabitha was as big as he was and had claws she wasn't afraid to use. Wizard inhaled his food and trotted to his dog bed in the living room. Tabitha ate more delicately, and when finished, took the time to get a few scratches from me before heading to the living room to curl up next to Wizard. I heard a car door slam; I looked out the window and saw Dad walking towards the kitchen door carrying two one-gallon jugs of milk. I rushed over to open the door for him. "I thought you had left early for church?"

"Not yet, I had a hankering for oatmeal this morning and

discovered we were out of milk so I made a quick trip to town."
Dad answered.

"I could have picked it up." I said feeling guilty.

"I peeked in your room and you were sound asleep. I decided
to let you be, as I knew you were up late working on the bin fans
last night."

"It's been a quite a year for them, almost like they are jinxed.
We've had two fans break down and one that turns off for no
reason we can find. We were lucky to have two extra fans but I'm
working on trying to find a replacement for the possessed one.
In the meantime I have to keep checking it." Our native grass
and wildflower crops were harvested when the seed was barely
ripe and therefore it was green and wet. If the fans on the bins
didn't keep running, the seed would overheat and be ruined. If
we waited for the seed to completely ripen before harvesting, it
would all blow off and we would have nothing. Native seed was
not genetically modified to suit the timing of the harvester. The
fans ran about a month for each crop. The first few crops we harvested were now dry and ready to be cleaned at our seed facility
which we called the seed plant. Our first load would be going into
the line on Monday.

"You and Karla are planning to help me with our big bluestem
maze?" I asked with hope as I put the milk away, amazed at Dad's
ability to go to a store for one thing and leave with only that item.

"We will be there. You did put a time frame on this so we aren't
there all day I hope?"

"Yes," I said with a laugh knowing he was kidding. Dad was
social and loved being out and about. "It's from 1:00 p.m. – 4:00
p.m., which will give you and Karla plenty of time to take advantage
of the corn maze after our maze is over if you want."

"I think we might. It's been a long time since I've been in a corn
maze. Are you planning to try it?" Dad asked me.

"Of course; Jessica and James are going to go through it with me.
Jessica stopped by this morning to let me know Marcy Crumpet is

back in town. I'm hoping to see her there too, although I guess her last name is Bozeman now."

"I forgot to tell you I had heard she was back. Word is her husband Brian isn't endearing himself to anyone in town. It sounds like he's a rather boorish brute. If my memory is correct he didn't treat you too well in high school."

"There is nothing wrong with your memory," I said trying not to grit my teeth.

"One always hopes people like that change when they grow up," Dad said.

"Some people are incapable of change. I can't believe Marcy married him. I better get going," I said looking at my watch. "It is 9:30 a.m., which gives me enough time to shower, dress warm, and check the fans again before church starts at 10:30 a.m. I'll head over to the maze after church to help set up."

"When are you going to eat?" Dad asked knowing meals weren't something I missed too often.

"The taco truck is one of the food trucks they brought in. I'm hoping to get there early enough to grab a giant plate of nachos before our maze starts. You and Karla don't have to be there until 12:30 p.m.," I told him.

"I think we'll get there a little before then. I believe you'll have a line of squirming kids anxiously waiting," he said with a knowing smile.

"You may be right," I said and ran for the shower.

CHAPTER TWO

Compass plant is a 4 – 6 foot tall plant with
flowers shaped like a daisy that follow the sun.

AFTER SHOWERING AND SWINGING BY TO check the fans, which were fortunately all running, I drove as fast as I dared to church trying not to be late. It was a full house this morning, but Dad and Karla had left room in the pew for me. The vaccinating of the cattle must have gone well as James was with Jessica when they squeezed in next to me a few seconds later. I have to admit my mind wandered during the sermon, but I did pick up the gist of not judging others, lest you be judged. I made a mental note to try and cut Brian some slack. Maybe he had a terrible childhood and that's why he had acted the way he did. I snuck out without visiting when church was over and raced to the maze. When I arrived I was shocked to find the field Henning's had set aside for parking was full. I eventually found a spot and jogged to our maze. Dad and Karla joined me as I was dragging a table and a couple chairs over from the break room. We set it up at the start of the maze for them to sit at as they sold tickets. We also put up some stakes with ropes to shape a line and I put up an umbrella so Dad and Karla could be in the shade. Dad had been correct; there was a large group of kids who were jumping around with already stressed-out-looking parents trying to hang on to them. I could see the corn maze had started and was running a steady stream of adults and teens through the maze. While I was excited by the good turnout, I was even more amazed by the decorations. There were bundled up cornstalks, with assorted pumpkins and gourds surrounding each bundle placed all around the mazes, ticket stands, and even by the food trucks and picnic tables. Someone had also gone to the trouble of setting up three animated witches surrounding a black cauldron that was smoking. I was standing wondering what else I needed to do when someone poked my shoulder. I turned around to find Melanie behind me holding a roll of tickets. Melanie was a short, petite, angelic-looking woman around forty years of age. She had been around town for as long as I could remember. Bright-colored clothing was what she was known for and she didn't disappoint today with a blinding yellow tunic sweater covered with orange pumpkins and golden orange leggings. I wasn't sure it matched, but she nailed the fall theme. She ran a meditation studio but must have an alternate source of income as I've never talked to anyone that goes to it.

"Here are the tickets for your maze," she said handing them to me. She then asked, "How do you like the decorations?"

"They look great, did you do it all?"

"I did; Edna, Jessica, and Marcy also helped."

"You guys did an excellent job." To be honest I was quite surprised. She tended to be on the eccentric side with her over-the-top concern for butterflies, bees, and other insects, but no one complained too much as she put in many volunteer hours and was very active in the community.

Her next words confirmed her bug eccentricity when she said, "I do so hope the meditation cleansing I did last night will help keep the bugs away. These outdoor activities are always a concern for the well being of the insects."

"At least this late in the year the butterflies will have already migrated," I said not knowing how else to respond. Changing the subject I asked, "Have you seen Marcy? She's an old high school classmate and I was hoping to see her."

"She's around here somewhere with her wonderful, polite son, and her brute of a husband," Melanie said with a grimace. "They moved in to a house on the same block as mine. Her husband has such a black aura."

"It sounds like Brian hasn't changed."

"I forgot all you guys went to school together. He isn't a stellar example of the quality of students that the high school is known to produce. Marcy and her son however are a delight. I'll never know what attracts two people to each other, but then again I didn't do a very good job with my ex-husband either. I married a man younger than me hoping I would be able to mold him, but even that didn't work," she laughed. "Anyway, you have your tickets," she looked at her watch, "you're scheduled to start in ten minutes. Have fun."

She walked away, leaving me rather stunned. I had no idea she was capable of such organization. Any of my previous encounters with her had led me to believe she was scatter-brained, but I should have known better from all the volunteer organizations she chaired or co-chaired. I shook my head and walked over to where Dad and Karla were sitting. They had been dating for about six months now and were well suited for each other. Karla was a few years younger than Dad's sixty-three. Dad had a full head of hair now turning grey, which tended to be on the curly side, and had a thicker build like myself. Karla's straight hair was just beginning to turn grey. She was wiry, fit, and not letting age stop her from going full steam on her and James' cattle farm near our home.

"Quite a turnout, isn't it?" Karla said as I walked up to them.

"It is," Sheriff Poole agreed startling me as he must have been right behind me and I hadn't noticed. He was a stocky man standing around 5'4" with thinning black hair and the start of a stomach paunch. He had a prickly demeanor and we had butted heads last summer when Jessica was a suspect in the murder of her brother, but I felt we had come to an understanding by the time it was resolved. He was looking friendly today. "I hope there are no bodies to find in the maze," he said as he winked and walked away. The sheriff was a retired patrol officer from Minneapolis, and had moved back home around the same time the previous sheriff died of pancreatic cancer. He threw his name in the hat for the election and to no one's surprise he won as his sole opponent was the seventy-eight year old town drunk, who has run in every sheriff's election for the last twenty years on a campaign platform of no more drunk and disorder arrests if he was elected.

I shook my head at his attempt at humor. Karla laughed as she asked, "What would you like us to do?"

"I need one of you to sell tickets and one of you to give out prizes when they get out of the maze. The exit for the maze is next to the entrance so you'll both be able to sit at the table. I'll be up on our trailer helping parents yell directions to their kids if they have problems. I don't want anyone to have any meltdowns. Mazes can be scary, but I think being able to look up and see their parents should alleviate that."

"I'm glad you provided chairs," Karla said with a smile and wink. "We are kind of old you know, and wouldn't want to stand for the entire time."

"Of course," I answered chuckling to myself, knowing full well she could outwork me on most days. I'm sure she was looking out for Dad, as while he had improved significantly from his heart attack over a year ago, the surgery and subsequent recovery had taken a lot out of him.

They moved to their station at the table and I climbed up on the trailer. Dad started selling tickets and more parents joined me on the trailer. For the next three hours it was pure chaos. It was fun but exhausting, which I imagine being a parent would be like twenty-four hours a day. When it was over Dad and Karla decided to skip the corn maze and head home. I wandered over to find

Jessica and James. I spotted them visiting with people by the taco truck and walked that way, my stomach growling as I hadn't had time to get my plate of nachos before our maze started. As I walked up to them, a tall woman looked up, shrieked, and headed my way with arms out. As she grabbed me in a hug I figured out it was Marcy.

"You haven't changed a bit," she hollered while jumping up and down holding on to me. "It's so nice to see you!" she said over and over.

I worked to extract myself, stepped back, and smiled at her, "You haven't changed either, as exuberant as ever." Other than the exuberance, it wasn't an actual true statement. While yet beautiful, I could see strain in her face.

"Meet my son, Charlie," she said as she pulled me over to where James and Jessica were standing next to a thin, blond-haired boy, with his mother's features. "Charlie this is Carmen, she went to high school with your Dad and I."

"Nice to meet you," he said meeting my eyes direct, not staring at the ground like so many kids his age do.

"It's nice to meet you also. Are you enjoying living here?"

"Yeah, I've met quite a few kids already. Everyone has been nice."

"As a matter of fact, he spent most of the afternoon in the maze with Judith's son," Marcy interjected. Judith was the town dentist and a member of Jessica's book club. "They had to leave, but we decided to hang around to hear the results of who was the fastest through the maze."

"It's going to be me," said a gruff voice behind me.

I turned around and to my misfortune came face to chest with my high school nemesis Brian. Other than a well developed stomach paunch he hadn't changed much, 6'3", brawny with a full head of brown hair.

"Well if it isn't star volleyball player Carmen. Getting those serves over the net yet?" he asked poking me in the shoulder.

"Very funny Brian, it's nice to see you," I said trying to be civil. I moved aside so Brian could stand next to his wife. As I did I noticed Charlie move behind his mother as if trying to get away from his father.

Brian scanned the crowd, smiled when he spotted someone, and said in his booming voice, "Tom Hartz, hey, nerdy Tom; I couldn't believe my ears when I heard you owned the lumberyard. The other team manager George, what was his last name? Oh yeah, George Munson. I heard he works for you Jessica, as a girly cook which makes sense, but Tom, you surprised me. I said there was no way, little, scrawny, football team manager Tom could own and operate anything as masculine as the lumberyard." He punched Tom in the stomach and laughed heartily when Tom gasped and bent over.

"You never did grow up did you Brian," Tom said when he caught his breath.

"Brian, what are you doing?" Marcy yelled at him. "Tom, I'm so sorry."

"You don't need to apologize, Marcy. I think I'll get some food later," he said as he walked away.

"You always were a coward," Brian yelled after him.

We all stood there with our mouths open. James took off and caught up with Tom. I turned to Brian and said, "Why are you such a jerk?"

"Can't you people take a joke?" He shook his head and started to walk away saying over his shoulder, "Meet me at the car at 6:00 p.m. Marcy. I can't leave until I get my prize."

After he left, we all stood looking at each other, uncomfortable, and not sure what to say, when Marcy at last broke the silence. "Charlie why don't you take this and go get us some hot chocolate." She handed him money and he took off as fast as his legs would take him.

"I am so sorry guys, I tried to leave him; I've had enough. Charlie and I were going to move in with my folks, but no sooner had we got here when Brian showed up and told me he had bought us a house and promised he could change. He said that moving back home would give us all a fresh start. It was foolish of me but I gave him a chance, knowing I shouldn't, and we moved into the old Cooper house on 1st Avenue. The only good thing that's happened is in this small of a community, Brian's rudeness is more obvious and I think Charlie is even getting embarrassed by him. It will make the divorce I've decided to proceed with so much easier on him if he can see that his dad isn't perfect. Brian used to be his hero. I'm hoping Brian will let us have the house without a fight. I can make the payments without him. I'm used to that. He never holds on to a job for any length of time and I've become used to doing without his income."

Jessica and I didn't know what to say. What possessed you to marry him in the first place didn't seem like the right thing to say. Jessica interjected into the silence, "We'll be here for you no matter what happens," and hugged Marcy. James returned to stand by us.

"Is Tom okay?" Marcy asked.

"Yes, although he's mad. He wishes he had stood up to him, but I told him it wouldn't have done any good." Being 6'2", broad-shouldered with muscles built from wrangling cows and building fences; I was sure James had never backed down to anyone in his life, proving what a great guy he was to commiserate with Tom and make him feel better about not confronting Brian.

"No, when it comes to people like him, you never win. They are oblivious to how their actions can hurt anyone else," said a voice from an older couple that walked up to us with a boy that looked to be about Charlie's age.

"How are you folks doing?" Jessica asked.

"We are wonderful. We were enjoying the day very much until we overheard that jerk. I'm sorry he's your husband dear," said the elderly woman looking straight at Marcy.

Jessica looked at me, her eyes twinkling; I assumed thinking the same thing I was, that this conversation just kept getting more uncomfortable.

"This is Frank and Alice Fenmore and their grandchild Billy, who is Charlie's best friend," Marcy said introducing them.

Jessica chimed in, "The Fenmore's are my best afternoon pie customers."

"That's true, we don't miss many afternoons at your restaurant for pie," Alice continued, "We stop in and have a piece most days while we wait to pick Billy up after school."

"Sometimes they bring me a piece too," said Billy. "It's really good. My favorite is your lemon meringue."

"Thank you," said Jessica giving Billy a handshake.

We let the Fenmore family go ahead of us in line and as I waited I looked around and noticed George Munson visiting with a tall, handsome, physically fit, shaved-head man in his late forties. Contrary to Brian's opinion of George, he was a valued employee at Jessica's restaurant. He was an all-around jack-of-all-trades, not only helping her cook, but he also cleaned tables, washed dishes, and waited tables when needed. He even filled in for Jessica when she needed time off. She often said he could run the restaurant better than she could. I stepped out of the line, instinctively heading closer to them when both men started getting red in the face and the mystery man moved closer to George, towering over him and I overheard him say, "If you have any proof it would be in your best interest to give it to me." George stumbled backwards and replied, "I warned you not to come back to town." George turned around and rushed away. The man looked up; saw our group in line and his face turned white. James tapped me on the shoulder as it was our turn at last to place our food order. Once we got our food and found a table we sat down to eat. I looked around but the man had disappeared. The Fenmore's declined to sit with us and said they were going to get some kettle corn.

"What is the story with the Fenmore's? Did they adopt Billy?" I asked wondering as while I had seen Mr. Fenmore around town on occasion I wasn't aware they had a child that young.

"Their daughter, Callie, got pregnant in her senior year of high school. I don't know if you remember her, I think she was younger than us." Jessica said.

"I vaguely remember a Callie; I think she was a year younger. A very quiet girl if I'm thinking of the right person," I said trying to remember.

"That sounds like her. Anyway, a short time after giving birth she died in a car accident. They've been raising their grandson ever since."

"That's awful!" I exclaimed. "I must have been gone at college already as I don't have any memory of that. What about Billy's dad?"

"If anyone knows who the father is they aren't saying. Rumor around town was that George was the father as he followed Callie around like a puppy and doted on her. I don't believe it though. Not only does Billy look nothing like him but George isn't the type of person to not acknowledge his son," Jessica insisted.

"It is strange that no one in this small of a town knows," Marcy commented.

"Other than the color of his hair and his chin; which is distinctive, Billy resembles his Grandfather. If it was someone local you wouldn't notice a resemblance unless they were standing next to him," I commented.

Charlie returned walking carefully carrying the hot chocolates for him and his mother.

"Thanks dear," Marcy said scooting over for him to sit down with us.

He sat down, un-wrapped the taco his mother handed him, and inhaled it. When he finished the taco and his hot chocolate he looked up and asked, "Is it okay if I go find some of my friends?"

"Be sure to meet your dad and myself by the car at 6:00 p.m.," Marcy told him.

"I will," he said and took off running.

"I hope he's going to be okay," Marcy said watching him run off. "He looks like a well-adjusted kid," I told her.

"He is, so far anyway. I hope he'll handle the divorce okay." She got up and dumped her mostly untouched food in the garbage. "It was nice seeing you guys again. Are you up to meeting me for supper tomorrow for a girl's night out?" she asked.

I nodded as Jessica answered, "That sounds great, but unless we want to eat at the Dairy Queen we'll have to head to Parkville for a restaurant. Arvilla doesn't have anything else open on a Monday night. How does that sound?"

"It sounds good to me," Marcy answered. "Is Michael's restaurant open yet?"

"It is," I chimed in. "Should we all ride together?"

"I can't," Marcy answered, "but I'll meet you there at 7:00 p.m."

"I have to drive separate also," Jessica responded. "I'll be there picking up supplies for my restaurant, but seven works for me."

"I'll see you then," Marcy said and walked away.

There was silence at the table as we ate until James asked, "Have you heard from Nick?"

"No," I answered with a bite to my tone. I saw Jessica nudge James.

"Are things not going well?" He asked looking at her, surprised by her nudge.

I sighed, resigned to dealing with the question. James had been my friend as long as I could remember. We had grown up playing together as kids, our farms less than a half mile away as the crow flies, and had stayed good friends as adults. Most of the town assumed we would be married some day, but neither of us felt that way about the other. I was thrilled when he and Jessica started dating a few months ago. They were perfect for each other, although sometimes, like today, I felt like a fifth wheel around them. "When he's here things go well, but anytime anything about his past comes up, he clams up. I could have dealt with that, after all we just started dating; he doesn't need to share his entire life with me right away. However when he leaves work and takes off for a "problem" without clueing me in; then yes, I'm kind of upset."

"Maybe he'll explain it all when he gets back," James said looking in alarm at Jessica, clearly wishing he hadn't brought Nick into the conversation.

"I hope so, because at this point in our relationship I can afford for us to not be dating without too much damage to my heart, but the farm would take a hit if he left. That's enough on that topic," I said crumpling up my wrappers. "Are you guys ready to check out this maze?"

"We sure are." Jessica grabbed the tray with all our wrappers and dumped them in the garbage as we walked over to buy our tickets.

We got in line behind Karen Olson who along with her husband Paul owned the theatre in town.

Karen turned and said to us, "I saw you guys talking to Marcy and Brian earlier. I was glad she came back. She's good in the library, but I could have done without her husband."

"I don't disagree, but how has he gotten on your bad side?" I asked.

"I never have liked him. He terrorized my brother, George, in high school, and now Brian has focused on my husband and his job as a football coach. Paul coaches the junior high and varsity football teams. As the school is short on numbers this year they are letting the sixth graders participate on the junior high team. Brian showed up at Charlie's first practice and thought he was going to be the coach. He started yelling at the kids and told the quarterback he wouldn't be the quarterback for long, that Charlie was going to be the starting quarterback. Paul shut him down, as if a ten year old would be ready for that, but not before he got called a bunch of derogatory names in front of the kids and also told he didn't know anything about football and should welcome Brian's expertise. He told Paul he should be more welcoming towards his advice, otherwise he would just replace him as coach. I guess he thinks that because he was a football star in high school he is supposed to be an expert."

"Sounds like he hasn't made himself very dear to the community so far," Jessica said.

"The best contribution to the community he could make would be to drop dead." She covered her mouth and said, "I can't believe I said that. Now if this was a television movie we'd find his body in the maze and I'd be blamed."

"I don't think you'd be the sole suspect," I said laughing.

We had been inching closer to the entrance of the maze and at last it was our turn.

The oldest Henning boy, Clayton, handed us a piece of paper along with a pencil and said, "Write your name on your ticket, and I'll put your start time on it. There are twenty-one numbered areas in the maze that are marked with a riddle. Solve each riddle, mark down your answer on the corresponding line and grab a matching token from the bucket. When you are done make sure your ticket is marked with your finish time when you exit. There will be prizes for the five fastest times. You can go through the maze as many times as you want, but only the first time can be counted towards winning a prize. Do you have any questions?"

We didn't have any, "Hand me your tickets please." He wrote the time on them, handed them back to us and said "Good luck," as he moved aside to let us in.

"This will be fun," Jessica said. "Do you guys care if we get a prize, because I'd kind of like to take my time and stroll through instead of racing?"

"Not rushing around sounds perfect," I said. "What do you think James?"

"That is fine with me. Which direction should we go first?" James asked as once we entered the maze we could see we had five different paths to choose from. We started on the one heading to the North, and I can say in all honesty that was the last time I knew what direction we were going. The Henning's had done an excellent job. The riddles were hard, yet solvable, and even if we had wanted to rush through it, I don't think we could have completed it any faster. We got turned around often, walking by the same riddles many times before finding the last one after searching twenty minutes.

When we emerged from the maze and had the finish times put on our tickets the enjoyment of the day was interrupted by yet another Brian incident. He had the same man I had seen with George cornered by the prize stand. Brian was sticking his finger repeatedly in the man's chest, saying, "Don't even think you can tell me what to do with the information I have." James started to walk over to them to help but before he got there Brian strode away and the man turned and hurried in the opposite direction.

"Who was that?" I asked when James returned.

"That was Coach Janning," James answered.

"I thought he looked familiar. Why is he in town, didn't he move away around ten years ago?" I asked.

"He's in town to be inducted into the school hall of fame for coaching Arvilla's only football team that ever advanced to the state tournament. They are having a ceremony for him sometime next week."

"What's Brian's problem with him I wonder?" Jessica asked.

"Who knows, Brian is being his usual self, a jerk," I said. "But I also saw George arguing with the coach earlier."

"That is strange; George is the most mild-mannered person I know," Jessica said.

Deciding to put my nosiness to rest, I said, "Let's not waste any more of this beautiful day worrying about Brian. I see they have the times posted. I know we aren't in the running but let's go see who is in the lead."

We walked over to the board that was propped up by the exit and looked to see whose names were in the lead. They had been crossing off names as faster times were posted. As expected, our time was nowhere near the leaders, but I was happy to see Brian's name had been knocked off the leader board. I noticed that Gary, our head roguer on the summer weeding crew, was in the top five along with Billy Fenmore and three other names I didn't recognize. They must have been local high school kids as I recognized the last names but not the first names.

"I guess it isn't very nice of me to be happy that Brian won't win a prize?" I asked James and Jessica not hiding my glee.

"I was thinking the same thing," James agreed.

Jessica just smiled. Sometimes she was too nice of a person. But thinking two's company and three's a crowd; I decided to make myself scarce. James and Jessica didn't get a lot of time alone together and it was time to let them have a true date night without me. "That was fun, but I better get going. I need to check in at the seed plant."

"See you Monday night," Jessica said as I walked away. I waved and walked towards my pickup. It felt glorious to get into the shelter of the pickup and turn on the heater. I hadn't realized how cold it had gotten as the day progressed. I cranked the heat, turned on my seat warmer and drove for the seed plant.

CHAPTER THREE

*The root of blue giant hyssop, a perennial mint,
was used medicinally by American Indians.*

I DECIDED TO SWING BY AND CHECK the fans again. After checking the seed for dryness in several bins I determined all the fans with the exception of the purple prairie clover bin could be turned off for the season. I left for the seed plant. Phil and Sam had worked on the new dust control system at the seed plant on Friday which I wanted to check out, they also loaded a wagon full of blue grama, and I planned to run some of it through our, what is technically known as a air screen seed cleaner, but we refer to simply as a mill and then check a seed sample. If I could get everything on the mill set correctly, they could start cleaning seed Monday morning without having to wait for me to get there. Blue grama wasn't the usual crop we cleaned first but a couple of our customers were in desperate need of it for seeding projects yet this fall. There was a shortage from other suppliers due to the drought, so if we could deliver some in the next week we'd get a quick infusion of cash heading into the winter season, which would be welcome as the majority of our income doesn't come in until the summer months after our seed is planted in the spring by customers. Our crops were used primarily for conservation programs; things like roadside plantings, gravel pit reclamation projects, replanting after wild fires, conservation reserve programs, commonly known as CRP, and prairie restoration plantings. It was a niche market with not many farmers wanting to tackle it. Raising native grass and wildflower seed involved a lot of physical labor as our crops don't flow out of combine hoppers or bins and a lot of hand shoveling is needed. We also hire a crew of roguers to hand-weed fields in the summer, as you can't use herbicides to remove certain weeds out of native grass and wildflowers fields without killing the crops also. The next problem was if you were successful in growing and harvesting it, then you run into the problem of finding a place willing to clean the seed. We solved that by investing into our own seed cleaning facility. To ensure quality, all seed was required to have a seed test to make it legal to sell. There were several private and university laboratories that would test the seed samples for a fee. Seed can't be sold without a test showing its germination and purity and that there were no noxious weeds in the seed lots.

I enjoyed being in the seed plant by myself without the noise of the mill running. Sam and Phil did a great job keeping the place clean and today was no exception. There wasn't a speck of dust or dirt on the floor. I pulled over the freestanding ladder and climbed up to inspect the new chute on the dust removal system. Everything looked great, not that I expected anything less from them. They had worked here so long they knew how everything worked as well as I did. I turned the system on and kept adjusting the seed mill until I was sure the seed coming out was good. I let the mill run long enough to get a few thirty pound bags, and then I grabbed a sample. I shut down the mill and went back to the break room to run my own version of a seed test. It doesn't take the place of the seed laboratory results, but it gives me a good idea if the mill is set correct before we run any more seed through it. The results were good; everything was ready for the guys on Monday morning. I left a note for Sam and Phil by the coffee maker. It was only 9:30 p.m., but after standing outside for most of the day I was cold and tired. Despite the cranked heater, I shivered the entire way home and was looking forward to a nice long, hot bath with a good cozy mystery. But my plans would have to wait as when I walked in the kitchen door, Dad and Karla were sitting at the table. They looked up with smiles on their face, and as much as I wanted to head straight for the tub it would be rude to ignore them.

"That was fun today," Karla said. "Thank you for asking me to help."

"Thank you. I don't know what I would have done without you both."

"There is some hot chocolate on the stove if you want to warm up; you look froze," Dad said.

"It got cold fast once the sun started to set. I hadn't noticed it while we were in the corn maze, but when we got out the wind had picked up and chilled me to the bone. It's not a good sign that winter hasn't even started and I'm already cold."

"It takes a few days for the body to adjust to the cold," Dad said laughing at me.

"I did stop by the bin site and turn off all the fans except for the purple prairie clover," I told Dad.

"That will help the electric bill," Dad responded.

"How was the turnout for the corn maze?" Karla asked. "We must have had around 150 kids go through our maze."

"I don't know, but there was a steady stream of people any time I looked over at it, and it was going strong even at the tail end when we went through it. The food trucks were busy too. They have to be very close to raising enough to complete the pool repairs."

"Who won the maze?" Dad asked.

"I didn't stick around long enough to find out. I checked to make sure Brian Bozeman wasn't one of the finalists on the list and then left."

"He is a piece of work isn't he?" Karla said and continued, "I've seen him in town a couple of times and I don't think he's been doing anything except alienating anyone he talks to."

I helped myself to some hot chocolate, grabbed some mini marshmallows from the cupboard, and joined them at the kitchen table. As I put my legs under the table they bumped into something. I looked down. Wizard was passed out on Dad's feet. "Has he been out?"

"He had a fun afternoon. I took him with over to Karla's when we got back from the maze and he ran around with her dog, Butch, while she checked on some calves. I figured it would wear him out and miraculously he didn't find any cow-pies to roll in."

"It looks like it was a mission accomplished. Has Tabitha been around?"

"She went outside when I picked up Wizard before I went over to Karla's."

"I'll call for her before I go to bed." Tabitha was an indoor/outdoor cat. She didn't suffer much either way. We don't see a lot of her in the summer as she enjoys being outside, but when the temperatures start dropping, the house becomes more appealing. She had a heated garage with food that she shared with her friend Clyde if she preferred to stay outside. She and Clyde, our tom cat, got along well. Clyde had a distrust of the house and I've never been able to get him inside. We have one other outdoor phantom cat that has a separate spot in another building. He was feral for the most part. Someone must have dropped him off as he showed up here about a year ago already neutered. We make sure he has a warm place to sleep and plenty of food. He is the best mouser and loves to leave mouse body parts for us to find. I assume he wants us to know he is earning his keep.

I stretched, yawned, and said, "I'm going to go soak in the bathtub right now and read the latest book from my favorite author." I swallowed the last of my hot chocolate and stood up. "I'll let Wizard out one last time. Goodnight guys."

"It's time for me to go too," Karla said.

I nudged Wizard with my toe, trying to get out of the way so Dad and Karla could say good night without me watching. Who was I kidding, getting away was more for me. I was thrilled for them but I have to admit I found it hard at times to see Dad with someone other than mom. "Come on Wizard." He didn't move; I called again, "Wizard come." He lifted his head and opened one eye.

"Come on boy, you need to go out." He stood up, shook himself, and ambled towards the door. I opened it, let him out, stuck my head out the door, and hollered for Tabitha. She came up the steps and looked at me with an expression of what are you yelling at me for? She then sashayed into the house. Wizard followed and they both trailed me up the stairs to my bedroom where they piled on the bed. It looked like I would have to fight for space when I got out of the tub. I grabbed my book from the nightstand and headed for a nice long hot soak in bubbles.

I WOKE UP MONDAY MORNING TEN MINUTES before my alarm was set to go off. Even more surprising, I felt well rested. This was a good thing as Jessica and I were getting together with Marcy tonight and it would be a late night. Tabitha continued to snooze but at some point in the night she had moved over to the pile of clothes I had left on the floor. I would have some work to do to get the cat hair off before I washed them. She opened one eye when she heard my closet door open, but must have decided moving wasn't worth the effort and closed it again. I dressed and hurried downstairs. With a few extra minutes in my schedule I was looking forward to making some eggs for breakfast instead of cereal. I walked in the kitchen and found Dad sitting at the table paging through a cook book.

"What are you doing Dad?" I asked giving his shoulders a hug.

"I have to admit I'm sick of my usual recipes and was hoping to find something new and easy to cook for supper. It's selfish of me, but these types of things are when your mom being gone hits home. She was an awesome cook."

"I miss her too." I said swallowing a lump of grief.

"You think you've dealt with your grief and unexpectedly something hits you. For the most part I feel like although I haven't forgotten, I am at least doing well, it has been almost ten years after all. Karla and I are enjoying each other's company. I've gotten active again with some senior citizen groups, but every once in a while the grief hits again."

I sat down next to him, "Mom left a big hole, but she would be happy we are moving on."

"I have no doubt of that. She'd be proud of how well we are all doing, but," he pushed back his chair, "it doesn't solve what meat to take out for supper."

I wiped away the tears that had started coming out of my eyes, and said, "You don't need to worry about me for supper, I'm going out with Marcy and Jessica."

"That sounds like a good idea for Karla and me also," Dad said closing the cookbook with a thud.

"Have you heard from Kirk lately?" I asked Dad as we ate our breakfast.

"He called yesterday after Karla and I got home from the maze. He said things are going well. The producer's assistant, who is the primary person they are working with, has been a bit of a handful, but Kirk thinks they are recording some quality songs."

"I'm excited for him, but I wish it was music I enjoyed listening to."

"You and me both. I think I'll take a walk after breakfast, do you have time to join me?"

"I'll make time. Wizard could use some activity too." He thumped his tail at the mention of his name.

Dad and I cleaned up the kitchen, put on tennis shoes, grabbed our coats, hats and mittens, and went out the door with Wizard following at our heels. Tabitha snuck out at the same time. We had a trail mowed along a row of trees between two of our fields that was easy walking.

"How are you going to handle Nick when he comes back?" Dad asked after we'd been walking a few minutes hunched up against the cold brisk morning.

"I don't know. I guess I'll have to let him take the lead. I'm sure he wasn't lying when he said it was an emergency but it doesn't explain or excuse why he hasn't even called me."

"I'm not going to lie, it doesn't make any sense to me either, but I do trust my instincts and Nick is good man," Dad said trying to reassure me.

I grudgingly said, "I think he is too, but this disappearing act isn't helping to affirm that."

"We have no clue how much garbage is in his background. I would bet it's something he's embarrassed about. Be patient; if you like him, give him some space," was Dad's advice.

"I feel like that's what I'm doing already. I haven't bothered him at all."

"Maybe you should be," Dad said.

I stopped and looked at him, "What do you mean?"

"Nick isn't a stupid man, he knows how bad it is he left, and the longer it drags on it doesn't get any easier to call you. If the reason he's gone is something he's ashamed of he may feel like he can't call you."

I thought about what Dad said and replied, "I guess that makes sense. Maybe I'll try and give him a call tonight. But I'm not sure I'm ready to be the nice one, he's the one that left with no explanation."

"It's something to think about anyway," Dad stated.

Wizard started barking at something ahead of us. "I hope he didn't find a skunk." I sniffed the air, no odor yet. He kept barking as we walked towards the noise. We found him with his nose down a hole, alternately digging and barking as he tried in vain to catch a gopher.

"It's not going to happen boy, with your short legs you can't dig that fast." I picked him up. "I'm sure the gopher is long gone and has found his way out of a different branch of his hole." Wizard squirmed in my arms for a couple of seconds then realized it was a losing battle. We turned around and head for home. After we got a little farther away from the hole I put Wizard down so he could walk again. He raced ahead of us, nose to the ground hoping for something else fun to go after. I picked him up again before I let him in the house so I could wipe off his feet with a towel we kept by the door and then set him down in the kitchen where he rushed over to get a drink out of his water dish.

"I'd better get going," I said to dad as he settled in his recliner to read his newspaper.

CHAPTER FOUR

*The best place to store wildflower seeds
is in the refrigerator until you plant them.*

I~T DIDN'T FREEZE LAST NIGHT SO NO SCRAPING~ of vehicle windows was necessary, but the temperature was cold. My pickup thermometer showed thirty-eight degrees Fahrenheit. It wouldn't be too much longer before we saw some snow.

My phone rang as I was buckling my seatbelt. It was Jessica. "I'm worried about George," she said without even saying hello.

"Why is that?" I asked her knowing by the sound of her voice something was wrong.

"He didn't show up for work this morning, never even called; that is not like George."

"That is odd. Did you call him?"

"I called him several times and I even called the sheriff. George never answered and the sheriff wasn't interested. He said George is an adult and can disappear for a few days if he wants to, but I'm concerned, I know he wouldn't miss work unless something was drastically wrong."

"Did you check his house?"

"I can't get away from the restaurant. Could you do a favor for me and swing by George's house sometime today to check if he's there?" she asked.

"I will, but he must have had some sort of an emergency," I said thinking about the argument I'd seen between him and Coach Janning.

"I assume so, but it isn't like him to not call. You don't suppose Brian pulled some sort of prank on him?" Jessica wondered.

"It wouldn't surprise me."

"I hope I hear something from him soon. I'm not worried about the restaurant. Shirley, Phyllis's sister, was in town visiting and is filling in for him, but I am worried about him." Phyllis was Jessica's longtime waitress and known for her legendary memory and never having to write down an order.

"I'll stop by his place sometime today," I replied.

"Thanks Carmen, I have to go, the restaurant is filling up," Jessica said and hung up.

I puzzled about where George might be on my way to the seed plant and parked next to Phil's car. It never ceased to amaze me that Phil, who had to be at least six and half feet tall with a full head of curly black hair that gave him another two inches of height, drove a tiny VW bug. It was entertaining to watch him fold and unfold himself to get in and out of it; it was fortunate he was stick-thin. The mill was humming when I opened the door. I didn't notice yesterday but walking in today with the mill running, I could tell the improvements to the dust control system made a tremendous difference. Phil and Sam looked up when the door opened. I gestured towards the little insulated room we had installed in the building where you could visit without shouting to hear each other.

"You must have worked yesterday. I saw your note," Sam said when they joined me in the room. Sam was a small, stocky, incredibly strong man in his early sixties with a balding head, and about a foot and a half shorter than Phil. Phil had more experience running the mill and handling any mixing needed for seed orders while Sam was better suited for the manual labor like loading seed, and making up the seed pallets for shipping. They got along well and I hope to never have to replace them.

"I was here last night for a couple of hours tinkering with it to get it right for the blue grama. Is everything working well?"

"It is. We should have no problem getting a pallet ready to ship by the end of the week. What about a seed test?" Phil asked.

"I got a sample yesterday and will get it in the mail for overnight delivery to the seed lab when I go home at noon."

"I guess there isn't anything for us to do, but keep cleaning seed," Phil said.

"Have I told you often enough how much I appreciate you guys?"

"Every year, all winter long." Phil laughed, he knew how I disliked being stuck running the mill when one or both of them wasn't able to work.

"I'll say it again anyway. Thank you! I'm going over to the break room to start getting the computer inventory program set up for this year's crops. After dinner I have to meet up with MM construction at the cabins to do the final walk-through. If you have any problems call me on my cellphone." I walked out of the building and over to the break room. I should have picked up some rolls or bars for them to eat during their break. I made a mental note to pick some up at dinner as I'd be in town to mail the seed samples anyway. I was hoping I'd have enough time to swing by George's house too. I turned on the computer and opened our seed inventory program. It took me until 11:30 a.m. to get all the new crops entered along with their seed lot numbers, plus updating all the seed lots that were leftover from the previous season. It was a tedious process as not only did we have our own crops, but in order to make seed mixes we had to buy from other growers the different grasses and wildflowers we didn't produce. At any given time I was keeping track of sixty different seed lots in quantities from ounces for the wildflower seeds to thousands of pounds for the grasses. I finished, saved my entries, stood up, and stretched. I thought about walking back to the seed plant, but decided that they would have let me know if there were any problems. I put the seed sample in an envelope with an address label and left for town to mail it, hoping with any luck I'd have time to swing by George's.

As I pulled up in front of the post office, Melanie was coming out dressed in her normal flamboyant colors, fuchsia, and red today. She stopped when she saw me and said, "I'm looking forward to a lot of new customers when your cabins are up and running."

She had talked me into putting brochures in the cabins advertising her meditation studio. I was confident nobody was going to rush into town to squeeze meditation in when on vacation, but you never know and it got her to stop bothering me about it.

"How much profit did the mazes make on Saturday?" I asked her.

"We cleared over $4500.00."

"That's fantastic!"

"Yes it is; even better I looked over both mazes after everyone was gone and I didn't spot any squashed insects; of course I can't account for the tiny ones."

Her comment once again enforced my opinion that she was the ultimate conservationist. I was an animal lover but I have to admit I didn't spend near as much time thinking about insect welfare. I was having a tough time reconciling the take-charge, in-control Melanie I had seen in action on Saturday with the Melanie I had previously known as being kind, but at times strange, and always flamboyant.

"How long is it until the cabins are ready for guests?" she asked me.

"I am meeting with Mitch and Mark to do the final walk-through this afternoon. Our first guests are coming on Friday. We only made one cabin available for the first weekend, kind of a soft opening. When we are up and running next spring we are requiring week long stays."

"I wish you had let me help with the decorating. You need colors that promote peace and tranquility. There is a real science behind how you arrange the furniture to create the best aura."

I couldn't help but laugh. "This isn't a fancy hotel. The furniture consists of a queen bed, bunk beds, a couple of rocker recliners, and a kitchen table and chairs. The people that will be renting these cabins are coming for the peace that Mother Nature offers, not the décor of the cabin. I do appreciate your thoughts, but at this time I feel rustic cabin décor is the way to go."

"You have to do what you need to but you can call me when you decide to go a different way." She waved and walked down the street, long bright fuchsia coat streaming out behind her, touching the top of her shiny silver boots. I shook my head and went in the post office to mail my sample. When that was done, I walked down the block to Edna's bakery. Realizing I needed to hurry in order to stop by George's and meet Mitch and Mark on time, I moved to where she had prepackaged assortments of goodies for sale. I picked out a box with assorted donuts and long johns, and made my way to the cash register. I was lucky; there were just two people ahead of me.

"Are we on for Thursday afternoon to go out to the cabin and get it prepped for your first guests?" She asked when it was my turn to pay. Edna Forting was about eight years older than Jessica and I. We got to know her when we played in a sand volleyball league with her. She was six feet tall, fit, and athletic which astounded me, considering she ran a bakery. I would be obese in short time if I was around bakery goods all day long. Jessica and I didn't stay on the same team with her for too long as we weren't a good fit for Edna's competitive nature. I think quitting as quick as we did, enabled us to remain friends.

"Yes. In fact I'm heading to meet with Mitch and Mark for the final walk-through this afternoon."

"You already decorated and furnished them, why do you need a walk-through?" Edna asked.

"They insisted. They are also planning to bring the final bill."

"Now it makes sense," Edna said laughing. "They want to make sure that they get paid."

"Perhaps I should bring them some goodies too," I said looking behind me to make sure there was nobody waiting.

"Let me get it," Edna said. "I know their favorites."

"Thanks," I said as she moved away to put a dozen doughnuts in a bag.

She handed them to me and rang up the total.

"Does 2:00 p.m. work for you on Thursday?" I asked her. "I know Jessica said that was a good time for her to sneak away from the restaurant."

Edna thought for a moment and said, "That will work for me too. There isn't any school on Thursday and Friday, and the teenager who works for me will be here to fill in."

"I'll see you then. I better get moving, thanks again." I said as I rushed out the door and started running down the street to my pickup. As I got to my pickup I heard someone calling my name. I turned around and saw Frank and Alice Fenmore waving as they walked towards me.

"We didn't get a chance to thank you the day of the maze for helping with it. It was such a nice activity for the whole town," Alice said smiling at me.

"Thank you, but there were a lot of people that gave of their time to make it happen," I replied.

"We've been trying to make a point of thanking everyone who was involved. The pool is one of Billy's favorite places in the summer and we are so glad the community is coming together to save it." Alice continued, "It was such a nice day, and everyone had so much fun; even Billy was tired out when he got home and that doesn't happen very often. It was a good turnout too. I hope they got enough to fix the pool."

"I heard they are a few hundred dollars short." She opened her mouth to say something else and I hated to be rude but I had to interrupt her, "I'm sorry to rush you, but I am late for an appointment. Have a great day. Again, I'm sorry but I have to go."

"That's fine dear," Alice said as they both waved.

I got in my pickup and they continued to walk down the street. George lived on the same street as Steve Crumpet, Tom Hartz, and Paul & Karen Olson. His home was the smallest on the block, but it was a well-kept one story house with a two car garage. I parked and got out to peer in the garage windows. His vehicle was in the garage. I walked to the front door and was putting my hands up to the window to try and peek in, when the door opened a crack. I hollered for George and when there was no answer I stepped in. The door opened to a tiny, yellow, cheerfully-decorated kitchen. The kitchen table, with an overturned chair lying beside it, was sitting in a windowed breakfast nook next to a kitchen counter. There was a smashed glass serving dish of some type and a puddle of blood on the floor, and then my gaze turned to the open doorway leading in to what looked like a living room and I saw a leg. I rushed in the room and saw George laying face up with his forehead a bloody mess. I immediately called 911. I started to feel dizzy but steadied myself when I heard the 911 operator answer. I gave them the location and details. They asked if he was alive; I knelt to see if I could find a pulse. Although I couldn't be sure if I was feeling my own pulse throbbing in my fingers as I felt his neck I relayed that he appeared to have a faint pulse. They said the ambulance was on its way. I sat down next to George, picked up his hand and held it as I talked to him and told him help was coming. I heard sirens and the poor luck of the day continued when Sheriff Poole walked in with the EMT's. The sheriff helped me to my feet and led me out of the house, mumbling about me being nothing but trouble as he did.

"Did you touch anything?" He asked me when we got outside.

"Just the door when it opened as I tried to peek in the window.

I did check for a pulse when I called 911 and I held his hand until the ambulance and you arrived. Is he going to be okay?"

"I don't know," the sheriff answered as the EMT's wheeled George out of the house and in to the ambulance. "Why were you here anyway?"

"Jessica asked me to stop by. He didn't show up for work today and she was worried about him."

"She called me too. I thought she was overreacting, but it looks like she was correct in being concerned. I called for the crime scene technicians to come. I'll wait here until they do."

"Is it okay if I leave?" I asked as my stomach started to roll. I couldn't believe I was once again on the premises of another crime scene.

"Go ahead. If I have any questions I know where to find you." I started to walk away and stopped when he said, "Carmen, I know I can't keep you from telling Jessica but can you keep this between yourselves until I notify his family?" He paused then asked, "Any chance you happen to know who any family members are?"

I thought for a moment, "Karen Olson is George's older sister. As far as I know that's it, I believe their mother passed away a few years ago, but I'm not sure about the dad. I'm sure Jessica would know."

"Thanks, I give her a call," he said.

I sat in my pickup for a few minutes trying to collect my thoughts before I called Jessica. She was horrified and said she'd rush right over to the hospital. I looked at the time and realized I was going to be late to meet with Mitch and Mark. I drove as fast as I dared, which wasn't very fast as my hands were shaking and I ended up being fifteen minutes late. Although they were used to me by now; and would be more astonished if I was on time. I grabbed the bag of doughnuts, which no longer smelled good to me, and walked up to them. "Here's a peace offering for my lateness." I said as I handed them the bag, wanting desperately to share what I had just gone through.

"That wasn't necessary Carmen, but we won't turn them down," Mitch said taking them from me.

"I was going to be on time, but Frank and Alice Fenmore stopped me in town," I said using the Fenmore's as my excuse.

They smiled and Mitch said, "They are a sweet couple, but Alice can talk your ear off. They have my admiration though; it has to be tough for them raising a grandson at their age. But enough of that, on to happier things, are you ready to check out the cabins?"

"You do realize I've already furnished and decorated them?" I said with a shaky laugh.

They both looked at me with concern but must have decided to ignore my strange demeanor as Mitch said, "We know, but time got away from us and we didn't get the formalities done before you set everything up."

"I was kind of hoping you had forgotten and the final invoice was overlooked," I said, making a concentrated effort to act normal.

"Not a chance," Mark said chuckling, as we walked over to the closest cabin and I opened the door.

The first thing that hit me was the clean scent of the knotty pine that MM construction had installed on the walls brightening up the cabin yet leaving them feeling cozy. When we had moved the furniture in and decorated, the interior doors on the bedroom and the bathroom weren't installed yet. So sometime between then and now they had finished. I felt myself start to relax as I looked around. "It looks great guys. You did a fabulous job and it's just what I had envisioned."

"We should check out the other two cabins," Mark suggested.

We walked over to the other two. I flushed the toilets, turned on the faucets, and opened and closed the doors. The heat was already on, so I knew the furnaces were working. When finished we walked back to our pickups.

"Are you happy with them?" Mitch asked.

"Do I get a discount if I say no?" I replied.

"Sorry," Mitch laughed as he handed me the spare keys and the bill.

I was nervous to look at it, but I took a deep breath and grabbed the paper out of the envelope and unfolded it. I gave a little shout of excitement when I saw that it was the exact amount it was supposed to be. "This is the amount remaining after I gave you the down payment. I find it hard to believe that there were no overruns. Isn't that kind of standard for a contractor?" I teased them, knowing that MM construction prided themselves on their commitment to their estimates, which between that and their excellent work is why they were in such high demand. I grabbed my checkbook out of the glove compartment.

"I heard you guys hired Brian Bozeman," I said wondering if Brian could have been responsible for hurting George as I hunted for a pen. "How is he working out for you?"

"We had our doubts, but it's tough to find workers, and for all his faults he is a good worker." Mitch said.

"Mitch isn't there yet, but I've had my fill of him. It would help if he could keep his mouth shut," Mark added.

"He does have a problem with that," I agreed.

"We'll have to talk with him soon or we are going to lose the rest of our employees. He appears to enjoy tormenting people. So far we've been able to use him as a finishing guy. That way he's the last person on site, finishing up the odds and ends, and working when everyone else has moved on to the next job," Mark said.

"How is that working?"

"As well as it can. He gets the job done and it keeps him from having to interact with any of the other workers. It will be more difficult this winter though as our work will be indoors. We have two houses we built this fall and have to finish the interiors. We won't be able to keep him separate from other workers at that point. If he can't shape up, we'll have to let him go. He's good, but he's not worth losing the rest of our crew."

"Good luck with that, I knew him in high school and he doesn't appear to have changed at all in the last ten years so I doubt you can change him now." I ripped the check out and handed it to them saying, "thanks again."

We got in our pickups. I let Mitch and Mark leave before me. I got out of my pickup again and walked back to the cabins. I wanted to look at them all on my own and take a few minutes to compose myself before I went home to get ready for supper, although Jessica may not be up to going out anymore. As I looked around, I was ecstatic that the cabins had turned out so much better than I dreamed. I had reservations lined up for spring, and I wanted people to love the experience. With everything on-line a couple of negative comments could sink my venture in no time at all. I had taken out a sizable loan to build them and hoped I wouldn't regret it. After about fifteen minutes; I went back to my pickup, decided I had enough time to stop by the seed plant to make sure everything was going well, drop off the box of bakery goodies and make another attempt at trying to act normal.

An hour later I was on my way home. Phil and Sam hadn't needed anything and hadn't noticed anything amiss about me. I got home to a quiet house with the exception of Wizard barking his welcome. I let him out; noticed Tabitha was in the far corner of the yard hunting. She made no move indicating she wanted inside. I called Jessica to check on George and find out if she was up to going out. She told me George was stable, his sister Karen was with him, but the doctors had no idea when he might regain consciousness. I made sure to let her know 2:00 p.m. Thursday worked for Edna too. She related she was already in Parkville picking up her supplies and was looking forward to a distracting evening out. I assured her that I felt the same. I let Wizard back in and went upstairs to shower and change.

CHAPTER FIVE

A moist, firm seedbed and a shallow planting depth of
1/8 – 1/4 inch is ideal for planting native seed.

I WANTED TO DRESS-UP FOR SUPPER with Marcy and Jessica, but after looking out the window and seeing the wind whipping the trees around and the last few leaves lose their fight to cling on I decided against it. Instead I put on a comfortable pair of jeans that I could wear with some dressy brown boots and a warm bulky sweater. I did opt for a nice necklace and earrings which would have to suffice for my feelings of wanting to be fancy as I rarely wore jewelry. Wizard was stretched out sleeping on Dad's recliner, and wouldn't even lift his head when I called. I left him there, hoping he wouldn't decide to chew up the arm of the chair. Tabitha was waiting by the door when I opened it, and rushed in. I took a few seconds to fill up her dish, grabbed my purse and keys, and went out to my pickup. As I was getting in I remembered I hadn't checked on Nick's cat yet today. I ran back in the house, grabbed a can of food and sped to Nick's, thankful it was on the way to the restaurant. I pulled up in front of Nick's house and his enormous black short-haired cat poked his head out of the shelter Nick had set up for him with a heat lamp. I checked that his heated water dish was full, filled the dish of dry food, and emptied the can of soft food into his other dish. I scratched him a few times and apologized that I couldn't stay longer. He didn't act like he minded too much when I left. After all the rushing around and the horror of the day, the hour drive to Parkville was relaxing.

I pulled up in front of Michael's at the same time as Jessica. I caught her before we walked in and asked, knowing it was a pointless question as I had just talked to her an hour ago, "Did you hear any updates on George?"

"Only that he hasn't gained consciousness yet. Sheriff Poole asked me if I knew who George's relatives are. All I knew was that his mom passed away a few years ago, his dad was in the nursing home with dementia but he may have passed away, and Karen Olson is his sister. I think he might have been dating someone, but I don't know who. Was it horrible at his house?"

"It didn't look good. It was obvious a struggle happened."

Jessica put her hand over her mouth and said, "Oh, no, poor George."

I put my hand on her shoulder and said, "I'm so sorry. I know you've grown close to George in the years you've worked together at the restaurant." George was one year younger than us. I didn't know him well other than that he was shy with a cheerful and good-natured personality if you engaged with him. "Do you have any idea why someone would have attacked him?"

"No, he's been normal at work. He hasn't acted like anything was wrong. I can't believe this happened to him."

"He'll be okay."

Jessica took a deep breath and said, "I hope you're right. We'd better go in, I'm sure Marcy is waiting for us. It's going to be hard to obey the sheriff and not say anything about George."

I agreed and we walked in together. Marcy was waiting for us on a bench in the entry. She stood up when she saw us and rushed over to give us a hug.

"It's so good to see you both. I've been looking forward to this. I already gave them our name for a table. I didn't think having to wait for a table would ever happen in this area of the world, but I guess Parkville is growing. They said it would be a few minutes," she blurted out in one long breath.

"I don't think our population is growing, at least not bringing in new people, but we do seem to be hanging on to more of our young people. More and more people are able to do jobs online enabling them to either move back home or never leave," Jessica told her as we sat down next to her. She continued with a laugh, "Of course the wait could also be due to the fact that there are few restaurants open anymore."

"Whatever the reason, it doesn't matter to me. I am thrilled to be home. It feels like a dream come true, and Charlie is enjoying it here also. He's made a lot of good friends already. When we lived in Minneapolis he didn't get to know anybody. He had a couple friends, but with no one living close to us and most of the parents working, they never got to see each other outside of school hours. It's great that they can walk to each other's homes here."

The hostess called Marcy's name, we stood up and the hostess led us to our booth. Jessica slid in next to Marcy, so I made room on my side for us to stash our coats and purses. The waiter showed up with the menus and asked us what we would like to drink. Marcy and Jessica decided to have glasses of white wine, while I stuck to water. I was planning on ordering my entrée without regard to calories and I thought I'd at least be good with my beverage. He left to get our drinks and conversation stopped as we looked through the menu. We closed our menus when he returned.

"Are you ladies ready to order?" he asked.

"I think so," I said, as I looked at Marcy and Jessica. They both nodded.

"What can I get for you?" He asked pulling his pad out of his pocket.

"I'll have the salmon, with a tossed salad, and a baked potato," Jessica said.

"Same for me," Marcy said, "but I'd rather have asparagus instead of the tossed salad."

The waiter looked at me. I had been trying to decide between the barbecue ribs or the salmon, and decided to go with the flow. "I'll take the salmon also, but I'd like mashed potatoes and a Caesar side salad."

"Thank you ladies, I'll be back in a bit with some rolls and a hors d'oeuvre tray." He walked away.

We burst into laughter; Jessica sighed and said, "When did we become ladies?"

"Time flies doesn't it?" Marcy said, and continued, "I know I said it before, but it is so nice to see you both. I visited some with Jessica at the library and I know she owns the restaurant in town and is dating James Harmen, what a nice guy," she nudged Jessica with her elbow, "but what about you Carmen, what's up with you?"

I settled back into the booth, "Long story short, I got a degree in agronomy and then came back to run the family farm."

"I thought you always said in high school you didn't want to farm," Marcy said, not letting me get by with my short version.

"To be honest, I didn't; but I felt like I didn't have a choice as Kirk had zero interest, while I at least enjoyed some aspects of the farm, and Dad needed someone to take over. Dad wisely made me go to college and gave me the freedom to make my own decisions. I started out as a business major at the University of North Dakota, in Grand Forks, but envisioning a future in dress clothes didn't appeal to me. I then transferred to the Crookston Campus of the University of Minnesota where I got my agronomy degree with a minor in business. Eventually I discovered I wanted to come back to the farm. I guess I realized when you have a vested interest in the farm, and you aren't being forced to work for your dad, it becomes more personal and now I can't imagine doing anything else. It doesn't hurt that our farm is unique by raising native grasses and wildflowers and not conventional crops, I've found that I do love it."

"Is there a significant other in your life?" Marcy asked.

I must have looked a little sad, as she immediately said, "I'm sorry, I didn't mean to pry."

"It's not that, I have found a pretty special person, but something is going on in his personal life, so, it's a bit complicated right now."

"Take your time, that's an old married women's advice to you, I married way too fast and I've lived to regret it."

As she brought it up I couldn't help but say, "I was stunned when I heard you had married Brian." I stopped talking when I saw Jessica looking at me like I had lost my mind. "I'm sorry; it wasn't my place to say anything."

"No it's okay. It's nothing I haven't thought myself for the last ten years. I dated him in high school because I was the homecoming queen and he was the football star. It felt like it was the thing to do. It didn't help that I ended up pregnant, and my parents insisted I get married. I knew better, but I was eighteen and too young to realize there were other paths I could have taken."

"It's too bad we quit hanging around together our senior year. Maybe we could have helped," I said.

"I blame Brian for that. I was too young to realize I was being manipulated and isolated by him," Marcy said.

"We're so sorry. It was our fault too. We should have tried harder to keep in touch with you," Jessica said putting her hand on Marcy's arm.

"It hasn't been that bad, for the most part Brian has been good to me, just not to other people. He has tried hard to be a good dad to Charlie, but," she stopped.

"He's not abusive?" Jessica asked.

"No, Charlie is more of a scholar than an athlete and they struggle to find things in common. I think Charlie feels he isn't good enough for his dad."

"That's tough for a kid to deal with," I said.

"It's been better here. Charlie got on the football team, which he couldn't in Minneapolis. They had so many kids they have tryouts and he'd never make the team."

"Does he want to be on the football team, or is he doing it for his dad?" I asked her.

"Oh yes, he loves being on the team, but he's not aggressive. He doesn't care if he gets to play. He enjoys being part of the group. Of course that doesn't help, Brian already has made of pill of himself with the coach, hounding him to play Charlie more, and trying to be part of the coaching staff. To be frank, I'm tired of it all, everything is a huge drama. Brian has to be the center of attention and the only way he knows how to get attention is by being loud and belligerent. I lost two jobs in Minneapolis because he'd somehow imagine a reason to be all big and threatening to my bosses any time I'd slip and say if something wasn't going well at work. He'd claim he was doing it for me, but I think it bothered him that my jobs paid better than his and he'd do anything he could to get me fired. I took this job knowing Brian didn't ever want to come back here. I told Brian I was moving back home, hoping he wouldn't come with. I moved in with my parents, got Charlie enrolled in school, and hired a divorce lawyer to draw up papers. But when I gave them to Brian, he wouldn't sign them. He said Charlie needed a dad and he was buying a house and wanted us to be a family. I told him I didn't think anything would change, but I decided to give him yet another chance and we moved in with him. It's now been three weeks and he's worse than ever."

"What are you going to do?" Jessica asked.

"I had the divorce lawyer update the papers and he put them in the mail to me. I should get them tomorrow."

"Does Brian know?" I asked.

"Yes, I told him this morning before I left for work," she said with a firm look in her eyes.

"How did he take it?" Jessica asked curiously.

"He surprised me by taking it well. I'm not sure he believes it will happen. As I was leaving he said, "You'll change your mind when the town is applauding me.""

"What did that mean?" I wondered out loud.

"I have no idea. He always has some grand scheme that never works out."

The waiter showed up with our salads, buns, the hors d'oeuvre tray and the conversation stopped for a few minutes.

After we had some food in our stomachs to take the edge off our appetites Jessica said, "If you need us for anything, let us know."

"For sure," I agreed.

Marcy got a little red in the face, like she was trying not to cry and said, "I appreciate it."

The waiter came with our entrées. "Are you done with your salads?" he asked.

We handed him our salad bowls, and I asked, "Could you leave the buns and hors d'oeuvre tray please? We haven't finished them yet."

He smiled at us and said, "Not a problem. Enjoy your meal."

We dug in.

"Everything is so good," I said after a few minutes. I grabbed another roll and a couple of olives off the hors d'oeuvre tray.

"Not only is it delicious on its own, but not having to cook it myself makes it fabulous," Marcy said. "It gets tiring being in charge of all the meals for a family."

"It sure does, especially when you are cooking for the entire town," Jessica piped up and we all laughed.

Marcy's phone rang, she answered, and her face paled in an instant. "What's wrong?" Jessica asked when she hung up.

"That was the Sheriff's Department. Brian has been picked up and is under arrest for the assault of George Munson and the murder of Coach Janning."

Jessica and I stared at her dumbfounded until I said, "What did you just say?"

Marcy looked completely flustered as she gathered her purse and coat. "I don't have any idea what is going on, they just said Brian was found dazed and confused next to Coach Janning's body. I don't have any idea what George has to do with it, but I need to get home before Charlie hears about this and then get to the Sheriff's Department."

"Would you like one of us to come with you?" I asked.

"No, thank you both, but I need to go." She rushed out of the restaurant.

Jessica and I left after paying for our meals and Marcy's. With everything that had gone on today, and thinking how fast life could change, Nick was on my mind as I drove home. Dad was asleep and Tabitha was sitting on my bed waiting for me. I sat down next to her, took out my phone and stared at it trying to decide if I should call Nick or not. I couldn't figure out if I was scared that he'd answer or scared that he wouldn't answer. I made myself dial.

The phone rang two times before Nick answered. "Hello Carmen."

I felt my tension and anger dissipate at the sound of his voice, "How are you doing Nick?"

"Much better now that I've heard from you," he said with a sigh.

"Anything I can help with?" I asked hoping he would share something of what was going on.

"I wish you could, but its better you aren't involved. I miss you Carmen and I wish I could let you know why I'm here, but it isn't my story to tell. I have some very messed up family members and they needed my help. I should be back soon. You do want me to come back?" He asked as his voice trailed off.

"Of course I do," I answered. I took a deep breath and then changing the subject said, "The kids thoroughly enjoyed the maze you mowed in the big bluestem field. In fact the whole day was a success, today, however was another story." We spent the next twenty minutes talking about Marcy, Brian, the assault on George and the murder of Coach Janning. Yes, I knew the sheriff had told me not to tell anyone about George, but Nick wasn't here to blab it to anyone else and I needed to talk to someone. It felt good to reconnect with Nick. After we hung up I crawled back into bed, plumped my pillow, made room for Tabitha, and after wondering how Marcy was doing I finally fell asleep.

CHAPTER SIX

Prairie larkspur is a pale blue wildflower that is toxic to cattle.

AFTER TOSSING AND TURNING ALL NIGHT I was jolted awake by the alarm clock. Tabitha flew out of the bed. She stood by my bedroom door, hair on her back raised, and tail standing straight up until I turned off the alarm. I lay back down as I considered last night. I couldn't imagine what reason Brian would have for killing Coach Janning or for assaulting George and I hoped this wouldn't mess up Marcy and Charlie's lives. I got out of bed, looked out the window and saw it was cloudy with a few snowflakes dancing in the wind. It looked cold and depressing. Winter was coming. It was time, but I had hoped for a few more rain showers to help with the drought before the snow and freeze-up started. I did enjoy winter once there was a foot or two of snow on the ground but I didn't enjoy the time between the switch of seasons. If it was going to be cold there may as well be snow so at least you could find enjoyable things to do like cross-country skiing or snowshoeing. It was time to get moving, I had wasted enough time staring at the weather. It was only Tuesday with a lot of week to go. Sam and Phil should be finishing the first bin of blue grama today, and we could get the first shipment ready. Tabitha followed me downstairs to the kitchen, forgiving me for the rude noise that had woke her up. Dad was sitting at the table feeding pieces of bacon to a happy Wizard who was on the floor next to him with his tail wagging as fast as it could go.

"I thought we weren't supposed to be encouraging him to beg," I said as I stood in the doorway.

Dad must not have heard me come downstairs as he jerked and said, "It's tough to refuse him."

"Kirk's not going to be very happy when he gets home and finds his dog spoiled and five pounds heavier," I said trying to keep a straight face.

"You and I both know Kirk isn't any better when it comes to training this dog," Dad said.

I laughed, "I know, but it was fun to catch you doing something you shouldn't be. It isn't often a daughter gets that opportunity."

"And that's how it should be," he said as he fed the last piece of bacon to Wizard. "Speaking of Kirk he called last night and said he might be home in about two weeks."

"That's good news," I answered as I made some toast.

"How was your evening?" Dad asked.

"It was great until Marcy got a phone call informing her Brian was under arrest for assaulting George Munson and the murder of Coach Janning."

I had debated if I could tell Dad about George. I knew Dad wouldn't say anything to anyone, but I thought I should at least try to stay on the sheriff's good side, but decided I didn't care. I told him I had found George, he was in the hospital unconscious, and that I had no idea what had happened between Coach Janning and Brian.

Dad was shocked and asked, "Are you okay? Finding George had to be traumatic."

I considered for a few seconds and answered, "It was horrible, but it helped he was alive and knowing I found him and got medical attention for him makes it better."

Dad had more questions but soon realized I had no further information than what I had already told him and wound down by cautioning me, "Try to keep your nose out of it, please."

"I'll try," I said, hoping I wasn't lying.

"Would you have any time to run into town today?" Dad asked deliberately changing the subject.

"I should, why, what do you need?"

"Tom from the lumberyard called and the new screen door for the back porch is in. Could you pick it up for me?"

"I can. I'll grab it before I go to the seed plant."

"Thanks Carmen. I'd better get going. Karla and James wanted some help moving cattle in from the pastures before snow comes," he said as he stood up. "Wizard hasn't been out yet."

"I'll take care of it. It looks cold out there today, make sure you dress warm."

He rolled his eyes at me, but I noticed he grabbed his scarf as well as his hat and gloves when he walked out the door.

I finished up my toast and let Wizard outside. Tabitha sniffed the cold air and walked back towards the living room. While Wizard did his business, I filled his and Tabitha's food and water dishes, cleaned up the kitchen, and took out some steaks to thaw for supper. I opened the door and found Wizard waiting to come in. He charged into the living room no doubt to join Tabitha on the couch. I took a few minutes to call the seed plant.

Phil answered with his customary brusqueness, "Phil here."

"Good morning Phil. Do you need any parts from town?"

"The new chute for the dust control is shaking. We could use another clamp to make sure it holds."

"I have to run to town on an errand for Dad so I'll pick that up too. Are you going to finish that bin of blue grama today?"

"I'd say this afternoon; around 1:00 p.m. is my best guess."

"Okay, when I get there we'll get the next wagon loaded while Sam gets the shipment ready. I'll see you later."

I took a chance and called the sheriff to find out if he would tell me why Brian was suspected of assaulting George and killing Coach Janning.

The sheriff answered on the first ring, "Good morning Carmen."

"I'm sorry to bother you . . ."

He interrupted me and said, "You're wondering why I arrested Brian Bozeman."

I guess the sheriff knew me. "Why did you?"

"He was seen running from George's house."

"Have you notified George's family yet?" I asked assuming he must have as Jessica had said his sister, Karen, was at the hospital.

"His sister, Karen Olson, is the only living family he has."

"Did she have any idea what might have happened?" I asked him wondering how much longer he was going to tolerate my nosiness.

"All she knew was that George had been agitated the last couple of days, but she didn't know why and couldn't think of anyone who might want to hurt him."

"Can you share anything about Coach Janning's murder?" I asked, knowing I was pushing my luck.

His voice trailed off and he said, "Carmen, I know better than to think you'll stay out of this." He paused and then giving a sigh like he came to an unfavorable decision he continued, "Brian didn't show up at the MM Construction office to turn in his company issued pickup at the end of Monday's work day. When Mitch and Mark drove to the worksite to check on him they found Coach Janning dead, face down in cement, and Brian lying off to the side holding his head and semi-conscious. He was dazed, very confused, and babbling; however Brian has already been released."

"What? How is that even possible?" I asked confused.

"In regards to George's assault, Brian claims he found George like that and was scared and ran out."

I harrumphed, "A likely story. If he was so scared, why didn't he call someone to help?"

"I don't disagree, but you can't arrest someone for being a less than desirable person. The crime scene technicians tell me based on the blood splatter whoever attacked George would have blood on their cloths and Brian didn't have any of George's blood on his clothing."

"Maybe he got rid of them."

"We have him on a neighbor's security camera running down George's driveway wearing the same clothes we found him in by Coach Janning's body."

"Why wasn't he kept in jail for the coach's murder?"

"The sheriff said, "We don't have definite answers yet, but it appears Brian was knocked out first and the coach was killed after."

"How can you be sure of that?"

"Brian was working on the cement slab, but he must have finished as he had taken his coveralls off."

"What does that have to do with anything?"

"Let me finish," the sheriff said irritated now.

"Sorry," I said feeling chastised.

The sheriff continued, "The coach was found dead face down in the cement, and Brian was found about ten feet away. We assumed at first the two of them had fought, and Brian collapsed from his injuries after killing the coach. Yet Brian had a couple cement fingerprints on his shoulder, which they noticed right away as he had clean clothes on. If he hadn't changed out of his dirty coveralls, we might not have noticed them. The fingerprints matched Coach Janning, plus there were two spots in the cement where it looked like the coach had previously fallen. One spot was a section showing somebody had sat in the cement, along with handprints where they had pushed off to get up. Those prints match the coach. The second spot was where the coach was found. It appears to the crime scene technicians Brian shoved the coach, who in turn fell on his backside into the cement. Then either the coach knocked out Brian or the unknown assailant did. We are assuming the coach did, and at that point he put his hand on Brian's shoulder to check if he was okay. After he checked on Brian we think he started to walk away, the murderer clobbered him and he fell, face first in the cement."

"Couldn't he have been hit by Brian and then belatedly died from his injury and fell in the cement?" I asked.

"The autopsy report findings say the blow that killed Coach Janning would have killed him immediately. There is no way he would have been able to stumble away. Our working theory right now is that Brian was the actual target and somehow Coach Janning got in the way."

"Why would they have left Brian alive?" I wondered.

"Maybe they didn't know he was alive, maybe they got interrupted by someone, or maybe the coach was the actual target, at this point we don't know anything for sure other than that Brian couldn't have administered the fatal blow that killed the coach. Either way, I had to let Brian go, but I'm not convinced in any way that he isn't involved in this somehow. When I questioned him I could tell he was hiding something. I cautioned him to not leave town and that he's still under suspicion. I'm hoping George will wake up soon so he can tell us what happened to him as it must have some bearing on the murder. Again Carmen, I know you won't listen, but be careful. I know you like to detect but someone did some serious damage to George and killed Coach Janning."

I paused and said, "I don't plan on looking into this, last time I did it was because you accused my best friend of murder."

"Good, see to it that you stay out of this," he said and hung up.

I grabbed my keys, locked the door, and with reluctance left the nice warm house. The snowflakes had stopped falling. There wasn't anything but a dusting on the roads, but the biting cold wind was relentless. I was pleased to note it was a north wind, meaning the bin site would be sheltered for loading seed. We would have to tarp the wagon for the drive to the seed plant. Native grass seed was very light and could blow out of the wagon if not covered. A good friend of ours who is mechanically inclined had developed a vacuum to load seed for us that was adapted to not break or smash seed. We used to have to shovel it out of the bin into a conveyor that would move the seed from the bin to the wagon, but now we had two hoses attached to a big tank that would vacuum the seed out of the bin and then we'd use a tractor to dump the tank into the wagon. It was a bit more time consuming, but much less labor intensive.

I pulled up in front of the hardware store, parked and walked in the door. The front counter was empty, but I could hear loud voices coming from the hallway. I checked the shelves, didn't see the clamp I needed so I peeked around the counter and saw Brian Bozeman and Steve Crumpet, Marcy's brother, who was the owner of the store, standing in the hallway arguing. I couldn't make out what they were saying but it didn't take a genius to figure out they were mad. Steve poked Brian in the shoulder and moved towards him, but looked up and saw me. He said something to Brian and then started walking towards me while Brian stormed out the back door. You would think getting arrested for murder would mellow him out for at least a day.

"Good morning Carmen," Steve said when he got close to me, visibly trying to calm himself. "Sorry you had to witness that. I'm glad to have Marcy home, but I could have done without that idiot husband of hers. It didn't help that MM Construction is building a storage shed for me and they hired him. Not only do I have to see him here, in addition to when I visit Marcy and Charlie, but even worse that idiot sheriff let him off for the murder of Coach Janning."

"I don't think anyone is happy to have Brian back," I answered, realizing the sheriff had only shared the crime scene evidence exonerating Brian with me. "Did Brian say why he was released?" I asked wondering what Brian's version would be.

"He only smirked when I asked him. He was a jerk when I played football with him in high school and he hasn't changed since becoming my brother-in-law. I hope Marcy gets that divorce sooner rather than later."

"She had supper with Jessica and myself last night and mentioned she was planning on it. I hate to see a family broke up, but maybe in this case it's for the best. What were you fighting with him about?" As soon as I said it, I wondered if I had gone too far. It wasn't any of my business but I was known for my nosiness.

"He's convinced I'm the one who talked Marcy into wanting a divorce."

"Did you?" I asked being intrusive once again.

"I should have years ago, but I always felt it wasn't my place to say anything. With Marcy living so far away, I didn't know if things were as bad as I thought they might be. I didn't see them more than once a year and I guess I hoped she was happy. I figured my view of him was biased from knowing him in high school, and I assumed or maybe just hoped, he had matured. I have to admit he is good with Charlie." He stopped and said, "Enough wasting of my time on him for the day. What can I help you with Carmen?"

"I need a six inch clamp, I did look but didn't see one anywhere."

"I've been doing some rearranging, let me look." He was back a few seconds later with the clamp, "Is this what you needed?"

"It is; can you put it on the farm account?"

"I will," Steve replied, already typing it in his computer as I left.

The next stop was the lumberyard. When I drove in the parking lot I saw Brian. He was sitting in his pickup and it looked like he was arguing with someone on the phone. I shook my head as I wondered what it would be like if every day was one big argument with everyone you came into contact with. Tom Hartz was on the phone when I walked in. He looked agitated when he hung up and noticed me.

"Are you okay?" I asked him.

"Not really, I asked MM Construction to not send Brian here anymore, but he just called to say he was here to pick up an order. I can't believe Brian is walking around free when the coach is dead. I can't get Brian out of my life, he made my high school years awful and now he's back again." He started to tear up. "I'm sorry Carmen; Coach Janning was like a father to me. I regret not keeping in touch with him over the years, but if it wasn't for him I would never have survived being the football manager, besides James, the coach was the only one who ever stood up for me." He attempted to get himself under control and asked, "What can I help you with?"

"Dad said the screen door he ordered was in."

"It is, you can take your pickup around to the back of the building, I'll have the door waiting and we'll slide it right in."

"Do you want me to pay now, or will you be billing us?"

"I'll double check, but I think your dad paid when he ordered it." He went over to his computer and pressed some keys. "Here it is, and yes it's paid for."

"Okay thanks, I'll bring my pickup around to your back door." I drove around to the back where Tom was waiting with the door. I helped him shove it in the back of my pickup, and made sure it was tied down. It was only 10:00 a.m. so I decided to stop by the library and see how Marcy was doing. Last night had to have been traumatic. As I pulled up to the library I noticed there weren't too many cars around. That gave me hope she'd have some time to talk in private. I parked my pickup and hurried in the library. There wasn't any protection from the cold wind as the library had lost most of its trees to Dutch Elm disease a few years ago. They'd planted a row of trees, but they had a long way to go before they were big enough to offer any protection from bad weather. As I scurried into the library I spotted Marcy in conversation with an elderly gentleman who had a few wisps of hair putting up a valiant last stand before complete baldness. He looked to be in his eighties but with the aid of his cane was standing straight and tall. I walked towards both of them, stopping a few feet away waiting for them to finish their conversation.

Marcy looked up and spotted me, "Carmen, it's good to see you. This is Mr. Kleb. He is not only my best customer, but he's my favorite." Mr. Kleb blushed as he extended his hand out to me.

"It's nice to meet you Mr. Kleb. Do you live here in town?" I asked as I didn't recognize the name and in a small town like Arvilla, while not knowing everyone personally, I was familiar with most last names.

"My wife, Nora, was from here, so when we decided to retire about fifteen years ago we moved here."

"What is her name?" I asked him thinking I might recognize it.

"Her maiden name was Danielson. She didn't have any family left here by the time we moved back but Nora encouraged me to be active in the community. I tried the school board for a while, but didn't enjoy it. So instead we focused on helping our church, but she passed away four years after we moved here and I quit volunteering. I would have been very lonely if not for this library. It has a forward-thinking board, with a lot of activities to participate in. I was a little worried after Maggie, the previous librarian, left but Marcy has continued the programs and has several ideas for some new ones. But I do wish she would get rid of her bothersome husband, he's been here a few times and doesn't give off a good vibe." He stopped talking and looked at Marcy.

I also looked at Marcy with question marks in my eyes.

She looked at both of us and laughed, "Mr. Kleb tells it like it is. I was just telling him I let Brian know last night he wasn't going to change my mind, the divorce was happening, and he had to find a place to live by Friday. Being arrested for assault and murder, even mistakenly, drove home the point that I want nothing further to do with him. Mr. Kleb gets so upset when Brian comes in here; I wanted him to be aware that Brian may cause some disturbances this week while he tries to change my mind in case Mr. Kleb would rather stay home."

"Do you think he'll get violent?" I asked

"No, Brian is more bluster and loudness than action; but he was mad, both at the sheriff for arresting him and me for insisting on a divorce. I hope MM construction keeps him busy at least during library hours."

"You are welcome to stay with my dad and me if you want," I offered.

"I told her the same thing," Mr. Kleb said. "I have a four bedroom house with lots of room."

"Thank you both for your offers, but Charlie and I will be fine. Brian has never been violent, just revels in verbal nastiness to others."

"Stupid man," I heard Mr. Kleb mutter, as he turned to walk away.

"What can I do for you Carmen?" Marcy asked.

"Nothing. You ran out quite fast after the sheriff called you last night, it had to be a tough night and I wanted to check on you. The sheriff told me Brian was released but I did see him at the hardware store this morning. It looked like he was giving Steve a hard time, and Steve said you told Brian the divorce was happening; I wanted to make sure you were okay."

"Thank you Carmen, that was nice of you, but as you can see, I'm fine. Can I interest you in a book?" She asked, clearly trying to change the subject.

I went along with her and asked, "Do you have anything new by Krista Davis?"

"I do. Follow me." I followed her to the section of the library where they displayed the new published books. She pointed at it. "I'll have to check the waiting list to make sure no one else has been waiting for it, I'm assuming not as we tend to catch that before we put the book out." I followed her to the checkout counter and watched as she scanned it.

"Nope, you are in luck." She handed me the book, smiled and said, "Thanks for your concern Carmen, but I got this handled. Brian won't be a problem for too much longer."

"I hope you're right, remember Jessica, James and me are willing to help you in any way we can."

"I know you will and I appreciate that." She handed me the book and said, "Enjoy."

As I strode toward the door, I noticed Mr. Kleb sitting at a table reading a newspaper. He nodded at me as I walked by. I put on my gloves and rushed to the pickup. I got in, turned on the seat warmers, and cranked the heat. I had enough time to call in a to-go order for dinner and swing by Jessica's restaurant to pick it up. I realized Jessica must be busy cooking when Phyllis answered the phone. I ordered a club sandwich and some chips to-go. Phyllis said it would be fifteen minutes before the food would be ready, giving me enough time to swing by the post office and pick up some priority mail stamps and envelopes to have on hand for mailing in seed samples. It was my lucky day and there wasn't a line in the post office. I was able to whiz in and out and made it in time to get my sandwich and homemade chips before they got cold. I inhaled the food as I drove to the seed plant. I wished I had picked up some water, so when I parked by the break room I ran in and got a bottle of water from the refrigerator we kept stocked with drinks. After taking a long drink I closed the bottle and put on my coveralls before I walked over to the seed plant. As I entered I saw Phil shutting down the mill. He turned and spotted me.

"You are right on time Carmen. Sam is working on the paperwork for the shipment and after he's done he'll start shrink-wrapping the pallets. Give me a minute to sew up this last bag and we can go load the seed."

"Does it work to take my pickup or do you have yours hooked up to the wagon already?"

"I do. If you could take my pickup and the wagon over to the bin site, I'll follow you with the tractor and vacuum."

I walked back out and grabbed gloves, hat, and a dust mask out of my pickup. As I walked behind the seed plant where Phil's pickup was parked I checked to make sure he had a tarp for the wagon in the back of his pickup before I took off. Twenty-five miles per hour was the top towing speed for the wagon which sometimes caused angry drivers to be backed up behind me on the highway if there was too much traffic to pass. US Highway 59 runs north-south through the middle of our farm and at times has a lot of traffic as it is a direct route to Canada. When I got to the bin site I parked the wagon and waited for Phil to come with the tractor. He pulled in about five minutes after I did.

"This is the one part of this farms' operation that I enjoy the least," I said to Phil as he walked up to me, putting on his gloves, and a mask for dust.

"It's not so bad. Although I don't like messing with indiangrass, that stuff makes my skin itch if it gets under my clothes."

"I discovered if you use duct tape to seal the bottom of your coveralls tight to your boots it helps," I told him.

"I'll have to remember that when we start loading indiangrass," Phil said as he climbed into the bin. I put on my mask and followed right behind him. An hour and a half later we emerged dusty and stiff from bending over holding the hoses. Phil took care of emptying the vacuum into the wagon while I checked my phone for any messages. Dad had left a text that he wouldn't be home for supper, as Karla was feeding him and she wanted me to know I was invited also. I checked my phone. It was only 3:30 p.m. I should have plenty of time before supper to get this load back to the seed plant and do any adjusting to the mill that might be needed. I answered Dad that I could make it by six, asked him to put the steaks I had left out either back into the fridge or take them with to Karla's, and that I would see them later. I also sent a text to Karla to thank her for the invitation.

"Can we leave the tractor here?" Phil asked as he walked up to me after emptying the vacuum.

"Might as well, there isn't any significant snow in the immediate forecast, and we'll be back here tomorrow to load the next lot. I'll hop in with you and you can drive your own pickup back to the seed plant. Did your family enjoy the corn maze this weekend?" I asked Phil as we drove.

"The kids did. I spent more time visiting with people and I

never did get through the maze myself. There was a good turnout."

"It helped that the weather cooperated. I heard from Melanie that they just about met the pool fundraising goal. What did Donna say?" Phil's wife, Donna, was on the pool committee.

"They did. Donna thought a bake sale or holding a dance for the teenagers and charging admittance would take care of the remaining balance. She'll be glad when the fundraising is over. It's taken up a lot of her time."

"I'm sure it has," I agreed.

"Say, do you know who Brian Bozeman is?" Phil asked.

"I don't like to admit knowing him but, yes," I answered remembering Phil and Donna didn't grow up here. "Did he manage to offend you too? I've been running into a lot of people who have been upset with him."

"Not me, but I was visiting with the coach they are inducting into the hall of fame at the maze on Sunday and this Brian dude interrupted us and harassed the coach."

"What did he do?"

"He pushed me out of the way, got in the coach's face, shoved a finger in his chest, laughed, and said you are running out of time."

"What did that mean?" I asked.

"I have no idea, but the coach paled, turned, and walked away as fast as he could. Brian snorted and walked away."

"It doesn't make any sense to me. Brian was my high school nemesis, in fact almost everyone's nemesis. He and his wife Marcy, who's the new librarian by the way, just moved back to town a few weeks ago. Marcy told Jessica and me she's planning to divorce him. I hope it happens soon and he doesn't decide to stick around town."

"Where does he work?" Phil asked.

"MM Construction hired him. When I asked Mitch about it, he said they weren't thrilled about it but like everyone else they need help and were desperate. Although unless Brian changes it didn't sound like he'd be employed there much longer. He's been causing problems with the other employees." After debating with myself for a few seconds I said, "You should let the sheriff know what you saw."

"Why is that?"

"Yesterday George Munson was assaulted and is in the hospital unconscious, then sometime in the early evening Coach Janning was killed and Brian found nearby."

Phil was stunned then said, "I hadn't heard any of that. Do they know what happened?"

"No, Brian was a suspect for a short time, but has been released."

We pulled up in front of the seed plant. Phil honked; Sam must have been watching as the overhead door opened for us to drive right in. Before leaving the seed plant I called the sheriff, got his answering machine and passed on what Phil had told me. I left the seed plant with enough time to get to Karla's by six without even having to speed. It helped that having worn coveralls all day my clothes weren't dirty so I didn't need to run home and change clothes.

CHAPTER SEVEN

Hummingbirds enjoy the nectar found in the
tubular spurs of the wildflower columbine.

JAMES WAS WALKING TO THE FRONT DOOR at the same time as I pulled in to their yard. He saw me and waited at the door. As I got closer I noticed he looked tired. James and his mom ran a 600 head cattle ranch along with a hay business. He'd told me before that he was going to have to hire some help soon, as his mom, Karla, was starting to consider retiring.

"Did you have a long day?" I asked him.

"Aren't they all?" He answered with a smile.

"Do you enjoy it?" I asked knowing what the answer would be.

"I loved every minute of it," he laughed and held the door for me. "Jessica told me about George and you finding him; are you doing okay?"

I took a deep breath, blew it out slowly and said, "I think so. It helps that he was alive, but it wasn't very pleasant to see. I hope he wakes up soon and can tell us what happened."

We took off our coats and boots in the entryway and walked towards the kitchen. I could hear Dad and Karla talking. They looked up from the table where they'd been peeling some carrots when we walked in.

"Hey guys," Karla said. "You are right on time to peel potatoes."

"Not me." James said, "I need to go heat up the grill for those steaks I see on the counter."

"Tough luck," Dad said, "I already did that."

"Ha ha," I laughed and handed James a potato as I sat down next to Dad and started peeling. "Did you guys hear about Brian getting released from jail?" I asked knowing Dad would have told Karla and James about Coach Janning being murdered. I figured the sheriff couldn't get too mad at me; the news had to have spread all around town by now anyway.

They stopped what they were doing and looked at me questioningly until Dad offered, "Is that good or bad?"

"There was no evidence to hold him. In fact the sheriff thinks Brian may have been the intended victim instead of the coach, but he didn't have any opinions on who hurt George or why."

They looked at each other in silence until Karla said, "I can't think of anyone who would want to hurt George or the coach, but the list of people who don't like Brian wouldn't be a short one."

"I feel bad for the coach, he left town around ten years ago and was only back for his induction into the Arvilla High School Hall of Fame. To think he got killed because he happened to be in the wrong spot at the wrong time," Dad said.

"The sheriff was confident Brian knows something. I hope George regains consciousness soon and is able to tell us what happened to him. I would assume his assault must have some connection to what happened to Coach Janning and Brian."

"While Jessica is thankful for Phyllis's sister Alice's help while George is in the hospital, she's missing him and it would be devastating if he can't come back. I wish there was some way I could help her," James said shaking his head.

At that Karla burst out laughing, "I'm sorry son, but while you have many skills, cooking is not one of them."

We all laughed, setting the tone for an enjoyable evening and a fine meal of steak, mashed potatoes and sautéed carrots, until James had to ask about Nick.

"Have you heard from Nick?"

"He's supposed to be back to work tomorrow. On that note, I'd better get going, I need to swing by his place, I didn't get there earlier today and I need to check on his cat. I'll see you later Dad. Thanks for supper Karla and James."

James walked me out to my pickup. As I was getting in he said, "I don't know if this helps but I do remember seeing George and Brian talking quite animatedly last week. I watched to make sure everything was okay as it was unusual for George to be so upset. When they saw me, they stopped and Brian started to walk away. George said something to him, but I couldn't hear what he said; whatever it was Brian turned, smirked at him, and walked away. I asked George if everything was alright, and he said it was nothing."

"Do you think the sheriff is wrong and Brian did hurt him?"

"I have no idea, you're the amateur detective. I'm just giving you the facts ma'am," he answered.

"It's interesting information. Thanks again for a fun evening." I got in my pickup and drove to Nick's.

I turned into Nick's driveway and was surprised to see lights on. As I got closer to the house I could see Nick's pickup parked on the other side of the garage. Nick was standing on his porch holding his cat. I pulled up next to his pickup and got out trying not to act awkward.

"Was he out of food?" I asked as I walked up to them. Seeing Nick again in person made it difficult to remain aloof. I wanted nothing more than to be in his arms.

"No, he had plenty, he was just was missing some attention," he answered.

"I tried, but he wasn't too interested in me," I replied trying to fight my attraction to Nick by reminding myself he had a personal life that I knew nothing about.

"He's kind of a one-person cat," Nick said. We stood there in silence staring at each other until Nick said, "I'm sorry Carmen. I know you've been upset with me and you are not wrong to feel that way. I hope I'm not asking too much, but I need a little more time and then I can explain everything."

I looked at the ground while I considered, and said, "I'll do my best Nick, but secrets are not the best way to start a relationship." My phone rang; I looked at it and was surprised to see that it was Marcy. "I better get this," I told Nick as I swiped the answer button and said, "Hello Marcy."

"Thank goodness I found you," Marcy said. "My brother, Steve, mentioned you helped the sheriff solve a murder not that long ago."

"Yes," I said with hesitation.

"Do you think you could help the sheriff again?"

"I don't think he views it as helping, more like bothering him," I replied confused as to why she was asking me.

"Brian informed me this evening that he wasn't moving out until Coach Janning's murder is solved as the sheriff told him he couldn't leave town. I told him that didn't mean he couldn't live elsewhere and he replied he wasn't signing a lease anywhere as the minute the sheriff found the real culprit he was leaving Arvilla forever. Charlie is also taking it hard that Brian was arrested."

"He was released though."

"I know that, but in the social media world of kids, it's blowing up that Charlie is the son of a murderer. A few kids weren't very nice to him at school today. I've tried to call the sheriff several times to see if he could put out some sort of press release detailing Brian's innocence, but I think he's avoiding my calls," she paused and continued, "I may have vigorously chewed him out when Brian was arrested. I've talked to a few people around town and they've said you have a way of finding things out that the sheriff doesn't."

"It's more like my nosiness causes me to ask a lot of questions."

"Please Carmen, can you try?" Marcy pleaded.

"I'll try, but I'm not sure I'll have much luck," I said trying to tamper her expectations.

"Thanks Carmen. Moving here has been so good for Charlie and I would hate to see it turn into a nightmare."

"The sheriff does think Brian knows more than he's saying about what happened when the coach was murdered; possibly even George's assault too. You could work on finding out what that is." I saw Nick's eyebrows rise when I said this.

"I will," Marcy said in a determined voice as she hung up.

"Are you getting involved in an investigation again?" Nick asked.

"I guess so. The sheriff isn't going to be happy." As I said it I realized I needed to tell Sheriff Poole what James had shared with me, "In fact I'd better call him now." Nick waited as I called the sheriff and told him James had seen Brian and George arguing last week.

There was a long pause and then the sheriff sighed and said, "I'll keep that in mind. Thanks Carmen." He abruptly hung up.

"How do you keep getting mixed up in this stuff?" Nick asked.

"I don't know," I shrugged. "My friends keep asking for help, I can't say no." Of course knowing my love of mysteries and my inherent nosiness; if I was honest with myself, I knew I wouldn't have been able to resist looking into it whether or not anyone asked me.

"Will I see you at work tomorrow?" I asked him as I walked towards my pickup.

"Of course you will Carmen. I missed you. My feelings for you and my enjoyment of the job haven't changed. I hope you aren't giving up on me?" Nick asked, looking at me, brown eyes pleading.

I stopped, turned around, looked at him, and said, "I don't want to give up what we've started either. I guess since you put me before the job on your list of enjoyments I'll have to try," I said trying to add some levity to the situation. I'm not sure who moved first but suddenly we were in each other's arms sharing a deeply satisfying kiss. When we broke apart I shakily asked, "Will you be able to bowl with Jessica, James, and I tomorrow night?"

"I wouldn't miss it. See you tomorrow Carmen," Nick said as I reluctantly got in the pickup. I looked in the rear view mirror as I drove out of his yard. He hadn't moved and was standing there watching me drive away.

When I arrived home I didn't see any lights on. Dad must already be in bed. I walked in the door and got mugged by Wizard. I opened the back door for him to go outside. He had been penned up for too long as he took several laps around the fenced yard running as fast as his little legs would take him before squatting to take care of his business. I stepped out and sat down on a bench. The moon was full and other than the chill it was a beautiful night. The air was calm and it felt good to sit in silence. Tabitha came out of the shadows to sit next to me, taking advantage of Wizard not demanding my attention. I scratched her head and in typical cat fashion, she turned her back to me and started cleaning her nether regions. Wizard tired of the yard and came scurrying over to me. I stood up and we went in the house. I held the door for Tabitha but she took one look and jumped off the steps. She was going to enjoy the last of the few nice fall nights. She moved towards the garage where I could see Clyde sitting. I followed Wizard into the house and looked around to see if any damage had been done by him while Dad and I had been gone, but I couldn't find anything. He had either behaved or Dad had cleaned it up. I had to admit Wizard might be outgrowing his puppy stage, although when my brother Kirk called, I would be sure to let him know that he must have been the problem as Wizard's behavior had improved by leaps and bounds since Kirk had left. I made sure Wizard had water in his dish, and I climbed the stairs for bed.

Tired as I was, sleep didn't come; I tossed and turned for about an hour. I wasn't so sure I believed Brian wasn't responsible for what had happened to George and Coach Janning, but it did make more sense that someone wanted Brian dead instead of the coach. Maybe I could talk to Mitch from MM Construction. He might know something. Brian worked for him, plus the murder happened at his work site. I also knew the sheriff would be talking to Mitch too, if he hadn't already. I was hoping for the latter as it wouldn't be good if he and I ran into Mitch at the same time. The last thing I remembered was looking at the clock and seeing it was 1:30 a.m. and realizing I wasn't going to be very good at bowling tomorrow night or rather today.

CHAPTER EIGHT

*Big bluestem is also known as turkeyfoot due to its
three parted flower cluster that resembles a turkey's foot.*

I WOKE UP WEDNESDAY MORNING TO A PAW tapping my face. I squinted through one eye and focused on Tabitha's whiskered face. Dad must have let her inside this morning. I rolled over and tried to see the clock through blurry eyes. When I was able to focus both my eyes and see the time I jolted awake. It was 9:00 a.m. I hadn't overslept like this in years. My cellphone must have been left downstairs or it would have woke me up as I was supposed to have been at the seed plant by 7:30 a.m. to help Phil and Sam get the small mill set up for the prairie blazing star. One of our long-time customers had called late yesterday afternoon in dire need of some seed so we decided to get the small three-screen seed mill we used for specialty crops working. Sam could operate it while Phil finished the blue grama on the main four-screen mill. Prairie blazing star was one of our more high value crops and it would be nice to get some cleaned, shipped, and paid for. Nick would be wondering where I was too, although maybe it was good for him to wonder where I was for a change. I realized I wanted him to go through what I went through when he left. I shook my head, now was not the time to figure things out about Nick and me. I scrambled out of bed, took a quick shower, threw on my clothes, and raced downstairs, skidding to a halt at the site of Wizard wagging his tail next to a shredded throw pillow from the living room.

I groaned, and said "Wizard what have you done?"

The kitchen door opened and Dad walked in. "What are you doing here so late in the morning?" he asked.

"I overslept, and Wizard took advantage of it," I said pointing at the mess.

Dad surprised me by laughing. When he saw me looking at him, he said, "What? He's cute, and to be fair he has been left alone quite a bit the last couple of days. It'll be good when Kirk gets back to take care of him."

"Any idea of when that is?" I asked as I grabbed a broom and started sweeping up the mess.

"He called last night and said for the most part things were going well. As I mentioned before he's not too crazy about one of the producers. Kirk said he hasn't showed up a few times at the studio when he was supposed to, causing a lot of unnecessary down time for the band."

"That's too bad, but speaking of down time, I'd better get going." I grabbed my cellphone and ran out the door.

"What about breakfast?" I heard Dad holler.

"No time," I shouted back as I hopped in my pickup.

As I sped towards the seed plant, I remembered I wanted to talk to Mitch and called him on the hands-free app on my phone.

"Hi Carmen," he said when he answered the phone. "Let me guess you've got some questions about what happened to Brian."

"What makes you think that?" I asked him chuckling.

"Because I know you, I know you like mysteries, I know you are nosy, and I know you are friends with Marcy, plus I know the cabins are complete so it wouldn't be a question about them. Also the sheriff just left and he warned me not to talk to you."

"Does that mean I can't meet you somewhere today?" I asked.

"Refusing to speak to someone when they come looking for me isn't very neighbor-like is it?" He asked, his voice sounding like he was smiling.

"Where might I find you this afternoon for a neighbor-like visit?" I asked playing along.

"I'll be in my office as the sheriff has our work site shut down for the moment while they process the crime scene."

"Thanks Mitch. I'll see you later." I pulled up in front of the seed plant and saw Phil outside on a ladder working on the tube that funnels our waste seed out of the building into a trailer. He looked up, waved, finished whatever he was doing, got down, and walked my way.

"Aren't you a little late, boss lady?" He asked with a grin.

"I could lie and say I was busy on the phone or something, but I have to admit I overslept."

"I guess we'll excuse you this time, but next time you do realize we have to dock your pay."

"Aren't you a witty one this morning?" I laughed.

"Don't you mean this afternoon?"

"You are funny. If you're done let's get busy in the seed plant."

"Yes sir, boss," Phil said with a smile as he held the door for me.

Sam looked up from where he was adjusting the little mill when we walked in. "It's about time you showed up," he hollered.

"I think I need to be late more often, so you guys would get used to it," I answered him as I rolled my eyes. "So how far along are you?"

"I loaded half a wagon of prairie blazing star into the system. We tried a run with the number ten screen, but it looked like too much good seed was going through, so I was changing the sieve for this one," he said pointing to the sieve he had placed in the mill. "I did look in your seed cleaning book, and the number ten was what we used the last time with this mill for the blazing star. I think we need to downsize the sieve openings this year."

We kept a detailed book for all the seed lots we cleaned with notes of what did and didn't work along with crop condition. "I'm glad you checked the book. I'm sure it was your idea, we all know Phil doesn't remember anything from year to year," I said deciding to give Phil back some of his own grief.

"Hey now, you know if you didn't have me around here nothing would get done right," Phil said.

"That is true. You guys are both excellent at this and I appreciate the work you do," I said in all sincerity. The seed plant wasn't a fun place to spend your winter. We had limited windows and although we had made great improvements over the years to make things run more smooth it could be a boring job watching a mill run. Some of the crops like little bluestem you might get one thirty-five pound bag an hour of finished product. There were many boring days. Phil and Sam did well as they got along and had fun together and if you weren't lazy there was always something to do to keep busy. They worked for a road construction company in the summer and were happy when it was time to clean seed as there was no overtime required unless they wanted it and weekends off to take advantage of all that northern Minnesota had to offer in the winter months like snowmobiling and ice fishing.

While Phil went back to cleaning the blue grama, Sam and I spent the rest of the morning getting the little mill set up for the prairie blazing star. Things were running smooth when I stood up, stretched my back, checked my phone for the time, and said, "It is noon guys, and everything is set. I only wish we had more seed. Between the drought, and the moth damage we didn't have near the amount of seed we have had in the past."

"I thought you sprayed for the moth?" Phil asked.

"I did, but when everything happened with Jessica's brother being murdered I lost track of a few things and a second batch of moths moved in. It was too late in the summer for them to do a lot of damage, but some of the caterpillars hatched and munched a few seed heads before I caught it and sprayed again."

"Any chance it's a lesson you'll learn to not get involved in murder investigations; both for the sake of the farm, and your personal safety?" Sam asked knowing I had put myself in danger trying to clear Jessica's name.

"Don't worry, I have no intention of trying to find anymore killers," I said crossing my fingers in my mind as I thought about my promise to help Marcy. "Anyway, I hope you get enough prairie blazing star cleaned by tomorrow so we can get a shipment ready."

"We'll do our best," Sam answered.

I said goodbye to them both and went out to my pickup. I hadn't had time to pack a dinner this morning and having missed breakfast I was starving. I decided I'd call Jessica's restaurant and see if I could get her dinner special to go, better yet, I wasn't in that much of a hurry, I'd call and see if Mitch would take me up on an offer of a free dinner as payment for picking his brain. I needed to talk to Jessica also. I recognized that subconsciously I was avoiding Nick. As I was dialing Mitch, I chastised myself as this was the exact reason you don't date people you work with.

"Hello Mitch. I was wondering if it's not too late; would you like to meet me for dinner at Jessica's restaurant, I'll buy?" I asked when he answered on the first ring.

"That sounds a lot better than the bologna sandwich I'm holding at present. What time?"

"I should be there in about ten minutes if that works for you?"

"Sounds good, I'll meet you there."

I pulled up in front of the restaurant, not surprised that parking was nonexistent. Jessica's home cooking kept her restaurant packed. I parked around the corner next to the hardware store and jogged to the restaurant realizing as I looked down at my jeans, that I wasn't all that clean. I shrugged and decided most of the diners knew I farmed for a living and wouldn't be surprised by how I looked. As I opened the front door I saw Mitch walking down the sidewalk; I waited for him before I went in.

"Thanks for the offer of free dinner," he said when he caught up to me.

"Thanks for agreeing to talk to me."

"Well it's been kind of boring around here as of late. It will be fun to see Sheriff Poole and you going at again," he said as he nudged me.

"Did the sheriff explicitly tell you that you couldn't talk to me?" I asked Mitch as we stood looking for a place to sit.

"He did," Mitch answered smiling.

"You've got to be kidding. I thought after the whole fiasco with Jacob was over, we ended on somewhat good terms."

"I'm giving you grief," he said with a big smile. "He did however instruct me not to share any detail of the crime scene to anyone, but I don't classify you as just anyone."

"I appreciate it, but maybe I'll scan the crowd quick to make sure he's not here," I said while looking around.

"I already checked. I'm not stupid. I tend to speed every now and then and I don't need the sheriff on my bad side. So what do you want to know?" He asked when we sat down in an open booth.

"I told Marcy I'd try and find out whatever I could. I don't know if you are aware but she's trying to get a divorce and Brian is using this mess to delay things."

"I had heard him mention his wife wanted a divorce. I thought that was smart on her part," Mitch said with a grin.

I continued, "Their son Charlie is also being teased by other kids that his dad is a murderer, so I'm trying to help her."

Phyllis brought us water and menus as I said, "Brian was seen having an animated discussion with George who is in the hospital as I'm sure you know. You can understand why I've got some questions about Brian."

Mitch thought for a moment and volunteered, "Brian is a piece of work. But as Mark and I told you before, he is a good worker, but doesn't relate well with others. I have never noticed him being physical with anyone; irritating people is his favorite activity. Mark thinks I'm a fool and we should fire him. We compromised and decided to find jobs that kept Brian away from the other workers as much as possible. He told us he appreciated it, he preferred being by himself."

"Is that why he was by himself when the murder happened?"

"Yes. We had poured the cement for the storage shed Steve is putting up behind the hardware store and all that was left was to trowel the cement for another hour or two and then clean up all the tools. Mark and I had been working on some bids, not paying attention to the clock. When we finished we realized Brian had never turned his pickup in for the day. We drove out to the site and found Coach Janning face down in the cement and Brian lying moaning off to the side. Mark pulled the coach out of the cement while I went to Brian. Unfortunately the coach was dead. Mark called 911 while I sat with Brian."

"Did he say anything?" I asked.

"I wasn't sure, he was dazed, confused, and muttering a bunch of gibberish; but I thought he muttered Charlie once. The sheriff said it was the name of Brian's son, so I don't think that was noteworthy."

"Could he have been faking getting knocked out? The sheriff thinks he was knocked out before the coach was killed, giving him an alibi for the Coach Janning's murder."

"I don't see how. He had a nasty gash on the side of his face from something hitting him, and I'm positive he came to only as we arrived."

"Did you see anyone else hanging around or notice any other vehicles?"

"I wasn't paying attention. There were cars around, after all we were working in town, but nothing stands out. The sheriff did ask all these questions though."

"I know, but if you can put up with my rambling, I'm hoping you'll remember something you didn't before." Phyllis came to take our order. We both ordered the Rueben sandwich, and for about a half second I tried to resist ordering fries with it, but as usual I caved. It is tough to resist fries.

After she left I resumed, "What about earlier in the day or even the week? Did Brian talk about the coach, George, or anything that might have been bothering him?"

"No. Brian didn't talk much, except of course when he was picking on someone or when they were doing something wrong. Honestly if he wasn't such a jerk in how he went about it, most times he was right." Mitch shook his head.

"There must have been something decent in him; after all Marcy married him," I said.

"I know he was hoping to change her mind about the divorce, he commented once that if he could get her to wait a little bit everything was going to change."

"What did he mean by that?" I wondered.

"I'm not sure, when I asked him he mumbled something about old mistakes having a way of coming to light in positive ways, and boy was he going to benefit from those mistakes."

"That sounds kind of interesting, strange, but interesting. I wonder if Marcy would know what that was about. Anything else you can think of that he might have said?"

"He was pretty hard on Mr. Kleb on Monday, but you can't suspect an eighty something year old man to have anything to do with this," Mitch said.

"I doubt it, but what did Brian do to Mr. Kleb?"

"Monday morning Brian needed to stop by the library to drop off a school book Charlie had left in his pickup. Marcy was going to drop it off at the school on her dinner break. I was waiting in the pickup with the window down. When Brian came out, Mr. Kleb was following him, shaking his finger at him. Brian yelled some obscenity at him, called him a pathetic old man, laughed at him and walked back to the pickup. When he got in I chewed him out for treating Mr. Kleb with so little respect."

"Did he act apologetic?"

"Not in the least. He said Kleb should mind his own business."

"I'll have to ask Marcy; maybe she knows what it was about. Do you have any idea why the coach would have even been there?" I asked.

"No idea. He must have walked there, because I don't remember seeing his pickup anywhere."

Phyllis brought us our food. Mitch must have been as hungry as I was. All conversation stopped as we inhaled our meals. When we both pushed our empty plates away in contentment, Mitch frowned a little.

"What are you thinking?" I asked.

"I just remembered Brian's pickup was at the worksite."

"Yes. Why is that strange? You said that was why you guys went to check on him because he was late bringing the pickup back."

"Not his work pickup, his red personal pickup."

"That doesn't make any sense," I said.

"No, it doesn't. Maybe someone else in town has a pickup that looks like his, after all a lot of people have similar vehicles. Most farmers including James Harmen and even some of the town residents like Paul Olson drive red extended cab pickups. Mr. Janning, the Fenmore's, Chloe Johnson, and Phil drive white SUV's; even you drive the same kind of pickup as my dad, Mark, and at least two others. I know because I've learned to wave at everyone, otherwise I snub someone I know."

"Do you think what happened to George might be connected to Coach Janning's murder?"

"It would be quite strange if two violent incidents that happened in this town on the same day weren't connected." Mitch pondered for a bit and said, "I can't say as I've ever seen George anywhere but here at the restaurant. He must have some sort of a social life but I don't know what it would be. You'll have to ask his sister, Karen." Mitch put his crumpled napkin on his plate and said, "Thanks for dinner Carmen, but that's all I've got for you. Can you think of anything else you want to ask? I have to admit your rambling got me to remember a few things. Maybe you should work for the sheriff."

"No thanks. First of all I'm busy enough, and second I'm sure the sheriff would resign if I joined his department."

"True." He stood up and said, "Thanks again for dinner."

As he left Jessica walked up to the table. "I thought I saw you, but I didn't have a chance to get over here until now. It's been a crazy busy day, I'm really missing George," Jessica said as she slid into the booth taking Mitch's spot.

"It looked like it; all the tables and booths were full. My sandwich was great."

"That's good. What were you doing with Mitch?" She asked.

"I'm trying to help Marcy. Brian is using the coach's murder to delay the divorce and she's worried about how Charlie is handling this. I decided I'd talk to Mitch to see if he knew anything. I also took the opportunity to ask him if he knew anything about George."

"Any luck?" Jessica asked looking at me as if expecting me to have solved the coach's murder and who hurt George already, loyal friend that she is.

"I learned a few helpful things, maybe, but nothing that makes much sense. Mitch didn't have any idea; do you know who George hung around with outside of work that I could talk to? The sheriff said his sister, Karen, didn't have any idea why this might have happened to him."

Jessica's brow wrinkled up as she thought and then said, "I can't recall George ever mentioning another person. I'm realizing I knew nothing about him outside of work, which makes me feel awful. I never even asked him about his personal life. He was just George, always on time, always friendly, helpful, good-natured, and happy." She sniffed and wiped her eyes.

"He's going to be okay." Trying to distract her I asked, "Are we on for bowling tonight?"

She pulled herself together and answered, "You bet. I'm looking forward to it. Now that Nick is replacing your brother, we might have a chance of being a decent bowling team. Kirk is comedic relief for sure, but taking bowling serious he does not."

"Now you are kind of scaring me. I never thought our goal was to be a serious bowling team." Jessica was not a competitive person.

"I don't normally care, but Chloe Johnson—you know her, she owns the grocery store in town—has been a little too interested in James as of late. Ever since her last boyfriend broke up with her and moved away she's been calling James for help with various domestic things. The last time he was at her house she wanted him to bowl on her team, 'as it must be so frustrating for him to bowl with frail little Jessica,'" she said imitating Chloe's voice. "So yes; I want to demolish her team tonight."

"Okay, okay. I'll do my best to try tonight. But you don't have anything to worry about, James hasn't got eyes for anyone but you, his problem is he's too nice to say no to anyone. I'd better get back to the farm. I need to check in with Nick."

"How is that going?" Jessica asked as she stood up.

"Awkward, but we're working through it." I slid out of the booth. "I'll see you tonight." I left money on the table for a tip and walked up to the till where Shirley was filling in, to pay for Mitch and my meals.

CHAPTER NINE

Chippewa Indians used the root of big bluestem
as a diuretic and to alleviate stomach pains.

As I walked out of the restaurant, I heard my voice being called. I turned and saw Melanie coming my way.

"Carmen, wait up," she yelled waving at me to get my attention.

I stopped and waited for her to catch up to me. "What can I do for you?" I asked when she joined me.

"Marcy asked me to find you. She said she couldn't reach you on your phone."

I took my phone out of my pocket and looked at it. I had several missed calls and text messages. "I was meeting with Mitch and I had my ringer shut off. What's going on?" I asked as I turned on my ringer.

"The sheriff is looking for Charlie."

"Why would he be doing that?" I asked, although I thought I might know why. Mitch thought he had seen their personal vehicle, but it couldn't have been Charlie, he wasn't old enough to drive.

"She has no idea, and the sheriff wouldn't tell her. He showed up at the library and demanded that she come with him to pull Charlie out of school. She wants you to call her."

"I will. Before I do; you get out in the community a lot more than I do. Can you tell me who some friends of George's are? I'd like to talk to them."

"As I'm sure you've already found out, George is a quiet person. He doesn't get out much but when I did see him some place other than Jessica's restaurant he would be with Frankie Tate."

"Thanks for the information, Melanie. Does Frankie work at the dental office yet?" I asked as the last time I saw Frankie, she had been scheduling my next yearly appointment.

"No, she's in the process of starting her own mobile pet grooming business," Melanie answered proving once again she had her thumb on the pulse of the community.

"I'll look her up. I better call Marcy; thanks for finding me Melanie." I said goodbye and got in my pickup where I could call Marcy in privacy. She answered on the second ring.

"Carmen, thank goodness," she said sounding panicked.

"What's going on?"

"We're at the Sheriff's Department, waiting for that bonehead to question Charlie. They have him in a room by himself."

"They can't do that, he's a minor." I said wondering what the sheriff was up to as I was certain he knew better.

"I know. I told them, but they didn't listen. They said they wouldn't question him until I was present, but they didn't want us to have time together to fabricate a story."

"He doesn't think Charlie hurt his own dad?"

"I guess there was a witness who saw Charlie at the scene around the time of the accident."

"That isn't good. Do you have a lawyer?"

"No, I don't. Do you know who to call?"

"I don't, but I will make some phone calls and find someone who does. In the meantime, I don't believe you have to say anything until you have a lawyer present."

"But I want to talk to Sheriff Poole. I want to find out what he thinks Charlie could have done."

"I understand, but don't let Charlie say anything. Have you had a chance to ask him yourself if he was there?"

"Oh Carmen, I'm so flustered, we got him out of school and the sheriff was with us the whole time. I didn't dare ask Charlie anything with the sheriff present. Even if Charlie was near the scene there is no way he would have hurt anyone, especially his father," Marcy spoke fast, taking a big breath when she finished.

"Let me get off the phone and I'll make some calls and see what I can find out about a lawyer. Is there anything else I can do for you?"

"Could you go over to the library and get my coat, purse, and keys. I didn't think to grab anything when the sheriff took me to get Charlie."

"Not a problem. I'll bring them to you in a little bit, and with any luck find you a lawyer too."

"Thank you so much Carmen," she said as she hung up, sounding a little calmer.

Not knowing who else to call, I tried Dad's cellphone number.

He picked up on the first ring. "Good afternoon Carmen."

"Hi Dad," I explained what was going on and asked him if he knew any lawyers.

"I don't, but I happen to be sitting in front of my computer. I'll do some searching and get back to you as soon as possible."

We used to have a lawyer in town, but he'd had some serious legal problems of his own and was at present in jail, awaiting his own trial, which I was thankful for, as I'd helped put him there.

"Thanks Dad, keep me posted." I hung up, put my pickup in gear and drove to the library.

When I walked in Mr. Kleb, and Beth, a retired school teacher who filled in when needed, were at the circulation desk talking in hushed tones. They looked up when I stopped at the desk.

"Marcy asked me to bring her coat, purse, and keys to her," I told them in response to their questioning looks.

"Let me grab them out of her office," Beth said. She got up and walked over to an office door next to the circulation desk.

After staring at each other for a few minutes I asked, "How are you doing Mr. Kleb?"

"I'll be better when Marcy gets back," he said with a frown on his face.

I was glad Beth was quick and already back with Marcy's things, as Mr. Kleb looked ready to chew someone out.

"What's going on Carmen?" Beth asked. "The sheriff whizzed in looking as pompous as only he can, told Marcy she had to come with him right now, and didn't give her any time to even think. It was fortunate I was here to renew some books, so I could take her place or she would have had to close the library. Doesn't he realize we don't have any other staff here besides the librarian?"

"I know he's abrupt but if I learned anything about him from our earlier interactions he does try, and to be fair, he is investigating a murder."

"I don't care. If Marcy was going to kill someone it would have been Brian not Coach Janning," Beth stated.

"I agree, but right now I think the sheriff is more interested in Charlie," I said as I watched their mouths drop open.

"Why would they think that?" Beth asked.

"Someone saw Charlie in the area at the time of the incident. The sheriff had Marcy come with him to get Charlie out of school and bring him to the Sheriff's Department for questioning. I'm trying to find a lawyer for her. Do either of you happen to know of one?"

They both shook their heads no.

"If you think of one please let me or Marcy know. I better get her stuff over to her. Do you think you could plan on working here tomorrow, Beth? I can't speak for Marcy but I think she would be relieved if she knew someone was here so she could have time to take care of things."

"I can. Let Marcy know we are thinking of her and Charlie."

"I will," I said as I walked out. As I left the library my cellphone rang. I answered, hoping Dad had some good news.

"Hey Dad, did you have any luck finding a lawyer?"

"Sort of."

"What does that mean?"

"The nearest criminal lawyer I could find was in Parkville, and he doesn't have time to come here today."

"But tomorrow will be too late," I said interrupting him.

"Let me finish. He is willing to do a Zoom meeting with them. The catch is; he only has time at 3:00 p.m."

I looked at my phone, it was 2:20 p.m. "Okay. Thanks Dad, I'll see if I can get the sheriff to agree to a Zoom meeting."

"I don't think he has much choice. First he's questioning a minor, and second if anyone requests a lawyer he doesn't have any choice but to be accommodating."

"I'm on my way over to the Sheriff's Department right now. Did the lawyer give you his information to connect for the Zoom meeting?"

"He did. I'll text the information to you and then I'll call him back to let him know to expect to hear from you."

"Thanks Dad." I hung up, rushed to my pickup, and tried to drive within the speed limit back to the Sheriff's Department. Marcy was sitting in the waiting room. She stood up and met me by the door when I came in.

"Thank you for getting my stuff," she said when I handed everything to her.

"I have even better news. We have a lawyer for you."

"Is he coming soon?" She asked; her voice hopeful.

"Well that may be a little bit of a problem," I started to explain but I stopped when the sheriff walked out of his office.

"Marcy, you can come back now." Sheriff Poole motioned for her to come his way.

"Just a minute sheriff," I said.

He looked at me, "Don't tell me you are involved in this too.

Look I don't like questioning a kid about this either, but it has to be done."

"I know sheriff, but they do have a right to have an attorney present." I said hoping I was correct.

"Yes, but I don't see one." He stated the obvious.

"You are in luck; he can't be here in person, but he wants the questioning to take place via Zoom," I informed him.

The sheriff looked at me and shook his head as I walked over to him with my phone to give him the information. I explained things to both he and Marcy. Marcy gave me a hug as I asked her, "Do you need anything else, like a ride home?"

She said, "You've done enough, Melanie said she'd give us a ride. Thank you so much Carmen."

"It was no problem. Dad found him. I'm glad we could help." I hugged her back and whispered in her ear, "I'll keep looking into this. I'm sure Charlie had nothing to do with this." I went back outside and checked my phone. I had missed a call from Nick. I assume he was wondering what had happened to me. I decided rather than calling him back I would drive to the shop. As I pulled away from the Sheriff's Department I saw Mr. Kleb walking in. Marcy must have made a real connection with him to be so concerned about her.

As I drove to the shop I wished the day hadn't gotten so messed up. I knew it was going much worse for Marcy and Charlie, but after parting in relative normalcy last night, it felt like the delay in getting to the shop was going to make it awkward again to see Nick. I pulled up to the shop and parked next to his pickup. I took a deep breath and walked inside. Nick looked up when he heard the shop door shut.

"I've been trying to call you. I hope you aren't trying to avoid me?" He asked with hesitation.

"No." I smiled, glad to hear he was feeling the same as I was. "I had dinner with Mitch and then I got sidetracked with the whole Marcy and Brian situation."

"You had dinner with Mitch?" He asked with a funny look on his face.

"Yes," I said. "I'm trying to look into things for Marcy and I wanted to talk to Mitch as Brian works for him and it was at his job site that everything happened."

"Oh," he said and looked down.

I realized he might be jealous. Mitch was a handsome, successful businessman. It never occurred to me to think of him that way as our only interaction was business and he was almost twelve years older than me.

"What did you find out?" Nick asked.

"Not much, other than confirming Brian hasn't changed much from who he was in high school. Mitch did say Brian had mentioned knowing or remembering a mistake from the past that was going to benefit him, but Mitch didn't have any idea what he meant. As I was leaving the restaurant, Melanie caught me and said Marcy was trying to find me. I'd had my phone on mute, so I wasn't avoiding anyone. Then things got hectic and I never got time to call." I went on to tell Nick about the sheriff picking up Charlie and my trying to find a lawyer for them. I finished talking and asked, "So what was it you needed when you called?"

"Nothing very serious after hearing what you've been going through, but I've been trying to get the snow blower for the tractor up and running and I'm not having any luck. You might have to consider replacing it."

"Are you sure? That's an expense I was hoping to avoid although I knew we were on borrowed time already last year. Kirk ran it last and I remember him saying he had a tough time getting the last snow drift blown. It never got looked at as spring came so soon last year and I forgot about it when we got busy with burning, seed mixing, and shipping."

"He shouldn't have finished that last drift. It looks like some pins sheared off and wrecked the inside," Nick said.

Kirk was less mechanical than I was, at least I knew when

something was wrong and would stop before things were destroyed. I couldn't fix anything, but I did my best to keep things from getting worse. Kirk tended to wear head phones while he jammed to music and rarely heard the warning signs when something mechanical was going wrong with equipment. Not for the first time, I thought how glad I was that music was his passion and not farming.

"Can you get any parts to fix it?" I asked hoping the answer would be yes.

"I checked, and yes I can get them, but I also priced some new snow blowers at the same time," Nick answered.

"That doesn't sound good."

"The parts are cheaper, but the real kicker is they won't be available for two months."

"It will snow before then," I said with a sinking heart. Between the shop, seed plant, bin sites, our home, and a few of our elderly neighbor's driveways, we plowed a lot of snow.

"I know. That's why I asked about the price and availability of a new one. They have one for sale right now and it would fit the new tractor you bought last year."

We had purchased the tractor last year. It was smaller and easier to move with a trailer instead of putting miles on it driving between places. It worked wonderful for mowing this summer as we were able to load up the mower and tractor instead of wasting time driving a tractor fifteen miles per hour down the highway, safer too. People don't like getting caught behind slow-moving farm equipment on highways.

"It would be handy," I said considering it.

Nick moved in for the final selling point, "It attaches to the front of the tractor; you won't have to look backwards all the time to blow snow."

"Now that would be awesome." I often ended up with a headache after spending the day blowing snow, looking backwards. "Let me run the numbers and I'll get back to you."

Nick handed me the piece of paper where he had written all the costs and said, "It sounded like they had a few other people asking about it, so if possible, don't take too much time to decide."

"I should be able to take a look at it quick before supper. I'll let you know as soon as I finish. You are planning on bowling with us tonight?" I asked him, hating my voice for sounding like I was pleading.

"If it is okay with you, I'd like to."

I felt what little I had left of my defenses crumble. I couldn't act aloof; it wasn't in my genetic makeup, and I came to the conclusion I wanted a personal relationship with Nick. I would have to take a leap of faith and trust him.

"I think it would be great. Be forewarned though, Jessica is on a serious mission to beat Chloe Johnson's team."

"Who is Chloe Johnson and why is it so important to Jessica to beat her team?" Nick asked with a puzzled look on his face.

"Chloe owns the grocery store in town—I'm sure you've met her."

"Is she the attractive brunette with the curvy figure?" Nick asked me with a grin.

"Yes, that's her, but don't let Jessica hear you describe her as attractive. She's about the same age as Jessica and I but we don't know her too well other than by reputation. She's known to be a man-hunter." I explained to him about Chloe flirting with James.

He laughed, "Jessica has nothing to worry about. James is crazy about her."

"That's what I told her. I don't think she is worried about James straying, she's mad at Chloe for daring to flirt with him."

"I thought this was a small town, how is it possible you don't know Chloe better?" Nick wondered.

"Chloe is from a little town called Newstad, about fifteen miles south of Arvilla. During the time we were in high school they had their own school, but combined with us for extra-curricular activities as Newstad didn't have enough students to support their own. We never got to know her as we weren't in any of the same activities and I think she was a grade or two behind us. What I know of her as an adult isn't the best. Other than an occasional disparaging comment, she tends to ignore women. That in itself is no big deal, but she focuses a lot of her time and effort on the men in town, married or not. She hasn't endeared herself to many people. Even so, I was glad she bought Arvilla's grocery store a few years ago, as it had been for sale and no one wanted it. I would have hated for it to close permanently."

"That's true; a town needs a grocery store. I've seen the sign for Newstad when I'm on my way to Parkville. There isn't much there to denote a town." Nick said.

"No, just a couple of houses and some abandoned buildings. If you look to the east you can see the old school."

"I think I did notice it. You can let Jessica know I will bowl my absolute best. Do you want me to pick you up or meet you at the bowling alley?" Nick asked.

"It would be great if you wouldn't mind picking me up. The bowling alley parking lot is packed on league night. One less vehicle there would be appreciated."

"What time?" Nick asked looking happy I had agreed to ride with him.

"6:30 p.m. should be fine. We have a couple pizzas after we're done bowling, but you might want to grab a sandwich or something before you pick me up as it gets late by the time we finish. I'd better get going," I said looking at my phone and seeing it was 4:30 p.m. "I want to get home to look over this estimate and decide if we have the money for a new snow blower. See you later," I said as I walked out of the shop.

Before going home I swung by the bin site and shut off the last fan. I stood enjoying the silence for few minutes and then got back into my pickup. Dad wasn't home and I started towards my office, but realized by Wizard's unsubtle clues of winding around my feet, he must need to go outside. Tabitha was sitting on the deck railing and I gave her some attention while Wizard ran around. When he was finished we came back inside with Tabitha electing to stay outside. Wizard followed me to the office, curled up on his dog bed, and started chewing on a toy. He was starting to behave better I thought until I noticed Dad's shredded slipper, and decided maybe not. I started money-crunching. After about forty minutes I decided we could swing it. Most of our extra cash had been used up on the cabins, but if I put off updating any of the farm pickups until next year, the snow blower could fit into the budget. I mentally crossed my fingers and hoped we didn't have any other serious equipment breakdowns. I took a look at the clock and realized I'd better hustle if I wanted to change clothes before Nick got here. Dad walked in the door as I started up the steps.

"No time to talk, it's bowling tonight and I need to get changed. Nick is picking me up. Wizard's been out," I hollered as I ran upstairs, "also, it looks like you might need some new slippers." I smiled as I heard Dad swear.

I was changed and waiting by the kitchen door when Nick pulled in the driveway. I couldn't wait to tell Nick he could order the new snow blower.

CHAPTER TEN

*The wildflower, Culver's Root, has spires of white flowers
and when mature can reach heights of six feet.*

T HE RIDE TO THE BOWLING ALLEY was comfortable between us
as Nick and I discussed various topics such as the snow blower,
the weather, and the many different antics of our pets. He told me
he was taking his adopted tom cat in to get neutered on Friday
morning and hoped he'd get forgiven. It was a relaxed fun drive
with a lot of laughter and no talk of investigations. The parking lot
was packed as I predicted when we got to the bowling alley. He
maneuvered into a tight spot towards the back door. I saw James's
pickup as we walked through the parking lot. He and Jessica were
putting on their shoes, saw us, and waved when we walked in.

"I never thought to ask, I can rent shoes can't I?" Nick asked.

"You can, I have to also. I've never felt the need to own a pair of
bowling shoes," I answered smiling.

We walked up to the counter where I was surprised to see Frank
Fenmore working.

"Hi Frank. When did you start working here?"

"When my grandson Billy decided he was going to be the

world's next greatest bowler. I decided it was a better use of time to be working than sitting here wasting time while I waited for him. It turns out I enjoy it. I know I'm retired, but it can get kind of boring sitting around the house all day. This gets me out of the house and provides some socialization."

"It's nice to see you. I'm glad you found something enjoyable to do." Nick and I asked for our shoe sizes, Frank found them, sprayed them with disinfectant, and handed them to us. We walked over to join James and Jessica.

"Hi guys," James said, as he stood up to give us room on the bench to sit down and put on our shoes.

"Did Marcy get a hold of you this afternoon?" Jessica asked.

"Yes. Melanie found me and let me know about the sheriff wanting to question Charlie."

"I mean after that," Jessica said.

"No, did something else happen?"

"She and Charlie stopped by the restaurant and asked me to let you know Mr. Kleb confessed to killing Coach Janning and hitting Brian. She was taking Charlie to a movie tonight to distract him for a bit and wasn't sure if she would catch you. She wanted me to tell you she was thankful for all your help."

"Mr. Kleb? That doesn't make any sense. What possible reason would he have for killing Coach Janning?"

"I don't know," Jessica replied as she shrugged. "Marcy said she would call you tomorrow if she hadn't caught up to you before."

Nick looked at me, "What are you thinking, Nancy Drew?"

I fought the urge to stick my tongue out at him and said, "I'm not sure, it doesn't make any sense. Mr. Kleb is a little frail old man. I could maybe understand him trying to attack Brian, as he is fiercely loyal to Marcy, but what reason would he have to kill Coach Janning or assault George?"

"People do strange things all the time," James interjected.

"Maybe Brian was attacking Coach Janning and Mr. Kleb tried to help," Nick said.

"That sounds more probable, but it doesn't explain George. Oh well," I shook off my thoughts, "it's time to bowl. I'm sure Marcy will have more information for me tomorrow. At least she and Charlie are off the hook."

Nick, Jessica and I picked out our bowling balls. James was a more dedicated bowler and had his own ball.

"Who do we play tonight, is it Chloe's team?" I asked with a grin deliberately prodding Jessica.

"Yes it is, and I expect you all to treat this very serious tonight," Jessica said with a determined look on her face.

James looked at her in surprise. "What's gotten in to you?"

Nick and I burst into laughter. When I could talk I said, "Jessica has taken a little offense in regards to Chloe's blatant flirting with you."

"What do you mean?" James face was clueless.

"Every time we go to the grocery store Chloe sprints out of her office making sure to be hovering around the checkout line to talk to you," Jessica retorted.

"She's trying to run a successful business. I'm sure she does the same thing for everyone. It can't be easy running a small town grocery store, when everyone heads to the larger grocery store in Parkville," James said trying to defend Chloe, which I could have told him wasn't wise.

Jessica put her hands on her hips and addressed Nick and I, "Do you guys ever see Chloe when you are in the grocery store?"

"I don't," I admitted.

"I do," Nick said with hesitation.

"Maybe it's not just James she's after," I said to Jessica with a wink.

"I wouldn't put it past her. She had no problem letting me know the other day when she picked up a to-go order from the restaurant that it was a shame my working so hard left me so skinny that I didn't have any curves. 'After all James is a farm boy and would want a curvy strong wife,'" Jessica said imitating Chloe's high pitched voice. "I wanted to show her how strong I was by tossing her out of my restaurant."

We all laughed, and James put his arm around Jessica, "No worries honey, you are not only beautiful and intelligent, but best of all you are perfect for me. Now Nick, he could do better than Carmen."

"Thanks a lot," I said slugging James, while Nick grinned. "Let's get bowling and show man-hunting Chloe what a couple of strong intelligent women can do."

It was a close game, but somehow we managed to pull it off, in no small part thanks to Nick. As with everything else I had witnessed him do, he was an excellent bowler and along with Jessica's renewed interest in bowling her best, we squeaked out a win over Chloe's top of the league team.

"I'd like to protest," Chloe said to us as we turned in our shoes, "replacing your brother with Nick wasn't a fair swap, but the pleasure of watching these two bowl for an evening was worth losing," she said with what she thought was a seductive look at Nick and James.

Jessica and I managed to hold in our laughter until we sat down at a table. We burst out in guffaws, while the guys shrugged and went to get some food.

"That was fun," I said.

"What, winning or a nice evening with Nick?" Jessica asked with a smirk.

"Both," I said after a pause.

"I'm glad. You guys are good for each other. Did you get to talk to him?"

"I did. He said he needs some time. Against my better judgment I've decided to let it be. I hope I don't regret it, both for my sake and for the farm's sake."

"It'll be okay. Nick is a good guy."

"So everyone keeps saying." I leaned back in my chair and looked around the room scanning to see who all was out and about tonight. Besides the usual bowling crowd there were quite a few extra people in the alley tonight taking advantage of one of the two places left in town that offered food in the evening. When the guys came back with two pepperoni pizzas and a pitcher of coke, I heard a cheer go up from one of the back tables. I looked over and saw a bunch of guys a few years older than us standing up toasting.

"What's that about?" I asked Nick and James as they had walked by that table.

"It's a bunch of Coach Janning's old players. They're having some sort of memorial for him. The school postponed the hall of fame induction ceremony for the coach in light of his death so some decided to gather tonight in honor of him." James said. "I never did understand the big hullabaloo for the coach. He only coached for five years and except for the one year they won the regional championship and advanced to state he had losing seasons." He shrugged and continued, "I guess it was a big deal as it was the only time in our school's history that we advanced to the state tournament."

As he finished talking another roar went up and at the same time I saw Mr. Fenmore glare at the table and shake his head. "Why is he mad?" I wondered to myself, I thought.

"Why is who mad?" Nick asked.

"Mr. Fenmore glared at that table," I answered him.

"Maybe they're making too much noise," Nick suggested.

"I would guess it's more in regards to who they are toasting," James said overhearing us.

"What do you mean?" I asked him.

"I don't know the details, but when Dad was a substitute at the school I remember him saying Mr. Fenmore, who was a teacher in the school, didn't have much good to say about the coach."

"I wonder why. He never had any kids play football did he?" Jessica asked.

"No. Fenmore and Janning were neighbors, so Dad assumed something had happened between them as neighbors."

"I'll have to talk to him; he might know a reason why someone would have killed Coach Janning if Brian wasn't the target."

"Did you forget Mr. Kleb already confessed?" James said. "You don't have to stick your mystery-loving nose into this case."

"Yes," Jessica said. "While I'm eternally grateful for the help you gave me, you did almost get killed."

"I know," I said. "But I can't believe Mr. Kleb murdered anyone. Anyway, this pizza looks great and I'm starving." Everyone agreed and we dug in. I filed away in my mind tracking down Frankie tomorrow and needing to talk to Mr. Fenmore sometime also. I couldn't see anyone, even Sheriff Poole, believing Mr. Kleb was capable of killing Coach Janning, and I couldn't walk away from this yet. No matter how much I didn't want to, sooner or later I was going to have to question Brian too. I yawned.

"It's getting late for me also," Jessica commented as she started to gather up our garbage.

"I'll get it," Nick said taking the empty pizza pans and piling our stuff on it.

As he walked away, James asked, "It looks like things are going okay for the two of you?"

"He asked me for some time. So for the present I'm going to pretend he never left."

"How long is that going to last?" James asked, knowing I had zero patience.

"Long enough I hope," I said with a grimace.

We got up to leave when Nick came back to the table. As we grabbed our coats and started out the door, Steve, Marcy's brother, came in.

"Hello Steve." I stopped him while everyone else went out the door and asked, "How is Marcy doing?"

"Okay, in spite of everything. I don't know how our idiot sheriff ever thought Charlie could have anything to do with a murder. Thank goodness Mr. Kleb confessed or Charlie would be in jail."

"I don't believe frail Mr. Kleb committed murder. Do you think he did?" I asked him wondering what he thought.

"No. There is no way Kleb is responsible. I'm sure Brian killed the coach, it's too bad the coach hadn't managed to finish off Brian before Brian did him in."

"Did you see anything? After all, this happened behind your hardware store," I pushed.

"Brian was there by himself when I left work. I did see the coach walk up. I wish I would have stayed, maybe I could have stopped them from fighting."

"Did either of them appear upset or anything?"

"No. Although, the coach did have a puzzled look on his face, I said hi, but he must not have heard me."

"Did you tell the sheriff this?" I asked him.

"I told him I saw the coach."

"Maybe I'll stop by the Sheriff's Department tomorrow and talk to him," I said.

"Tell him to let Kleb go. Brian did this plain and simple. He should never have been let out of jail."

I walked away thinking if it was Brian dead, we wouldn't have to look any further than Steve. I wonder if it was possible Brian was harassing George and maybe the coach met with Brian to defend George. If I remembered correctly George was a manager for the football team. It could be George and the coach had a close relationship, except I did see them arguing at the corn maze. It was another question for Frankie when I talked to her. Steve had such animosity for Brian he could have tried to kill him if he saw Brian kill the coach. I shrugged; my thoughts were going in circles getting nowhere. I got out to the parking lot where Nick was waiting for me.

"Sorry to make you wait," I told him.

"It's not a problem. I knew you were sleuthing again, you can't help yourself," he said as he smiled. "Did you find out anything?"

"Not much, it would make a lot more sense if Brian was the one dead," I sighed.

Nick nodded and said, "I wanted to say thanks for including me on the bowling team. It was a fun night."

"I'm glad you enjoyed it. Jessica and James like you and Jessica was thrilled you are a better bowler than Kirk," I said with a laugh.

"It was kind of fun to see how worked up she was. Prior to this evening I thought she was a bit too nice."

"She has a backbone. She'll protect her own, but where she differs from most people is she can forgive, and doesn't hold any grudges."

"A rare characteristic to have," Nick said looking thoughtful.

"She's a good person and a loyal friend," I said.

We both stood in silence by the pickup until Nick said, "I guess it's time to get going."

We got into the pickup, buckled our seatbelts, and Nick reached over and grabbed my hand. I hesitated for a couple seconds and then I unbuckled mine and moved over next to him on the seat and I felt Nick's body relax.

"I am sorry," he said as I buckled into the bench seat next to him.

"Let's not go there tonight. You asked me to give you some time, and I will."

"Thank you," he said.

We talked about work the rest of the way to my place and Nick gave me a soft kiss on my cheek before I got out of the pickup. I waved goodbye as he drove out of the yard. Lights were on in the house, Dad must be awake. Tabitha was waiting outside by the door.

"You must have decided it's too cold to spend the night outside tonight," I said to her as she prepared to blast in the door when it was opened. I could hear the television from the den and peeked in. Dad and Wizard were sound asleep in his recliner. Wizard looked up and barked when he saw me and Dad jerked awake.

"Did you have a good night?" he asked.

"Yes it was fun, and we won. Nick is a definite improvement over Kirk."

"That isn't surprising. Kirk's mind is busy thinking about music and his body follows. But I'm glad his obsession is paying off for him at last."

"I am too. What did you do tonight?" I asked Dad.

"Nothing much, I talked to Karla a little bit on the phone and watched some television. It was kind of boring, but it felt good. I've been pretty busy lately for an old retired man."

"You are retired, but you aren't old. And you love being busy."

"I know," he said with a smile, "but it did feel good to relax tonight. Maybe it's the weather, it certainly is getting colder."

"Winter and five feet of snow will be here before you know it. Speaking of snow, the old snow blower is broke down and Nick found a front-mounted snow blower for us to buy."

"It doesn't surprise me; the old one has had it. It is over thirty years old."

"I guess we got our money's worth out of it," I said amazed it had lasted as long as it did.

"It has had its fair share of repairs over the years, but has performed well for us. Is it doable to buy a new one?" Dad asked.

"I crunched the numbers this afternoon and it shouldn't be a problem. We'll hold off on replacing one of the work pickups until next year."

"That's good. It'll be nice to have a front mount, so you don't have to look backwards and end up with a sore neck. I'm glad you took over blowing snow, I don't miss it. Although with a new one, I might have to convince you to let me give it a try."

"I'll take you up on your offer the next time it is twenty-five degrees below zero."

"No thanks," he said, dislodging Wizard when he got up out of the chair. "It is time for me to go to bed."

"That sounds good to me too. I'll see you in the morning Dad."

"Good night," Dad said as he left for his bedroom with Wizard following him.

CHAPTER ELEVEN

*Native prairies are characterized by a lack of
trees and shrubs and have an abundance of grasses.*

I WOKE UP BEFORE MY ALARM WENT OFF on Thursday morning. I used the unexpected extra time to enjoy the luxury of lying in the warmth of my bed for a few minutes while I reviewed the day ahead. I had to swing by the shop and check with Nick to make sure he ordered the snow blower. I should also go to the seed plant and help Sam with a shipment that had to go out this afternoon, and at 2:00 p.m. I was meeting with Edna and Jessica at the cabins. It was hard to believe it was reality and we were going to have someone staying in them. I was excited to see how it went and before the guests left I planned to question them to get their opinion about what did and did not work. I also had to find time to track down Frankie. I'd have to save questioning Mr. Fenmore and Brian for another day. I glanced at the clock, and saw I had used up the extra time I gained by waking up early and now I was late. I'd be grabbing a quick breakfast again. I could smell blueberry muffins. Dad must be baking. They would be perfect to grab and go. I dressed as fast as I could and rushed downstairs.

Tabitha and Wizard were both sitting as close to Dad as they could get, hoping for something to miraculously fall off his plate. He looked up from his newspaper when I walked in the kitchen. "Good morning, I made blueberry muffins."

"Thanks, I could smell them upstairs. I'm late as usual so I was hoping breakfast would be something portable." I grabbed a paper towel, put a blueberry muffin on it, and ran out the door shouting, "Thanks, Dad." I started to get in my pickup and realized I had forgotten my coffee and turned back towards the house, where Dad met me at the door with my coffee cup.

"Forget something?" He asked with a smirk.

"You are a life saver, thanks again." Then I ran for my pickup.

I pulled into the shop and got out of my pickup wiping muffin crumbs off my sweatshirt. Nick was busy looking at something on the work bench and hadn't heard me come in.

"What are you looking at?" I said when I was right behind him, smiling when he jumped.

"Obviously I didn't hear you come in. I got the recoil fixed on this leaf blower."

"Do you need any help with anything?" I asked him, hoping not as I didn't have much time.

"No, I don't have anything pressing, just some odd and end repair jobs," he said putting the leaf blower back on the wall. "I'll be ordering the snow blower as soon as the salesman gets in around nine."

"Great! I'm on my way to the seed plant to help Sam with a shipment. I won't be back the rest of the day. After I leave the seed plant I'm meeting with Edna and Jessica at the cabins. If you need anything let me know. Melanie told me she knew Frankie Tate was a friend of George's and I'd like to visit with her yet today too." I stopped to take a breath and Nick and I locked eyes. I fought the undeniable pull between us, regretting we were at work and realizing I was falling hard for Nick.

"Any chance you let the sheriff know this information?" Nick asked stepping away from me interrupting the moment.

"I'm only talking to her. If she knows anything pertinent I'll pass it on to the sheriff."

He looked at me, doubting whether he could believe me and said, "Okay, but Carmen, please be safe," as he picked up a chainsaw that had quit working last spring.

"I will." I left the shop and drove to the seed plant. When I walked in the mill was running and Phil was sewing up a bag of seed. He waved when I walked in. I waved back and headed towards the back of the building where we did the shipping. Sam was looking at his paperwork when I joined him.

"Good morning Carmen," he said when he saw me. "I don't think we can ship everything on the packing list."

"Why can't we?" I asked. Our best customer from southern Minnesota was taking the rest of last years' crops of purple prairie clover, leadplant, big bluestem, and a couple bags of this years' blue grama crop.

"This years' blue grama crop doesn't have a seed test back yet. Do you know if it's done?"

"It should be. I'll give the lab a call and find out what happened." I stepped in to the little office to make the phone call. When the mill was running it was loud and the little office we put inside the seed plant offered some buffer from the noise. I was on hold about two minutes, before someone picked up. She checked on the lot, said it was done but could see the test hadn't been emailed, apologized for their oversight, and told me she'd send it at once.

I hung up and let Sam know it was coming. He got on the forklift while I got the shipping labels made. He set out some pallets to stack the seed bags on. It was a big shipment of nine thousand pounds of seed. A couple hours later we had it stacked and shrink-wrapped on ten pallets. It was 12:30 p.m. by the time we were finished. Sam grabbed his dinner, and we both walked over to the break room. Phil shut down the mill and joined us a few minutes later.

"Did you bring something to eat?" Phil asked.

"No, as usual I was running late this morning and didn't take the time. But I'll be heading into town soon and I'll get something there."

"Are you sure? I do have an extra sandwich. Donna always packs me too much."

"No, I'm alright, thanks though. What has Donna been up to these days, I haven't seen her since the corn maze?"

"She keeps busy with the kids. We'll be glad when Joseph gets his driver's license; between his and Kristy's activities all Donna gets done is drive them places. She's anxious to get back to her home-made soap making business."

"Is Joseph in football?" I vaguely remembered Phil saying something about it awhile ago.

"Yes, he should be able to enjoy it a little better now."

"What do you mean?" I asked.

"Paul Olsen succeeded in getting Brian banned from showing up at practice. The practices should get back to being productive and fun."

"Brian wasn't one of the coaches, was he?" I asked, knowing he wasn't but hoping I could prod Phil into sharing some more information about Brian.

"No, but he showed up at every practice, hounding Paul and insisting that his son Charlie should be the junior varsity starting quarterback. Brian harassed the kids, always hollering at them, telling them they weren't working hard enough. He kept telling Paul he might as well quit, as it was just a matter of time before he had the head coaching job. He was a real jerk. Joseph said Charlie didn't even want to be the quarterback, and was embarrassed by his dad."

"How did Paul handle it? I would have been so mad at him usurping me."

"Joseph said it looked like Paul was going to attack Brian, he was so mad at him. Joseph said he would have helped. I let him know that would not have been a wise idea. Not only would the school have suspended him, but he would have been in big trouble at home too. Brian must have gotten on Paul's last nerve, because after that practice he got the school board to support banning Brian."

"Why did Paul put up with it at all? I would have quit and let Brian have the job?"

"I think he needs the money."

"The salary of a high school football coach can't pay that much money?"

"It doesn't but the theater isn't bringing in a ton of money either. I heard the coaching job pays around $4000.00 per year. His wife, Karen, had some health issues last year and I think they have some sizeable medical bills. I imagine every little bit helps."

"I didn't know; why wasn't there a benefit for them?" The community of Arvilla was good to organize benefits for people who had money difficulties from medical expenses.

Phil shrugged, "I'm not sure. I'm guessing since they aren't members of a church or any civic organizations, nobody organized it."

Sam spoke up, "What about the football team?"

"You're right Sam, we should have done something," Phil answered. "I'll talk to Donna, I'm sure we can get something planned for them."

"That would be great, let me know what you come up with. I would imagine there are others who may want to help," Sam said finishing off his dinner.

"Paul is George's brother-in-law, I wonder if the spat between Paul and Brian would have had anything to do with what happened to George?" I asked.

"I can't see how," Phil answered.

"Have there been any rumors around town about who might have hurt George?"

"Nothing I've heard about, but most of the gossip has been focused on Brian killing the coach. Nobody believes Mr. Kleb did it," Sam answered.

"I don't think so either, but I do believe George's assault and the coach's murder happening the same day can't be a coincidence. Do either of you know anyone who George might have hung out with?"

"I've never seen him with anyone but Frankie Tate," Phil answered as Sam nodded in agreement.

"I'm planning to talk to her today."

"I thought you weren't going to get involved in anymore investigations." Phil said.

I was able to avoid answering him when I heard the semi-truck pull in to pick up the seed pallets. Phil and Sam got up to load the semi. "I'm going to leave for town," I said, "if either of you needs anything, let me know."

"We will, see you tomorrow Carmen," Sam said.

I drove into town thinking about Paul and Karen. I hope Paul wasn't involved in Brian's accident, but I could picture a scenario where somehow Brian was the one that hurt George and Paul went after Brian. The coach could have happened to come across Brian and Paul fighting and tried to help. That scenario didn't make sense as I couldn't imagine Paul being the type of person to kill someone, unless it was an accident, although maybe he thought he'd killed Brian too. But once he found out Brian was alive, why not confess, as defending the coach and George would be thought of as excusable. I gave up for the time being deciding I didn't have enough information yet. I dialed Marcy to find out how she and Charlie were doing.

"Hi Carmen," she said answering on the first ring.

"I wanted to check in. I heard they arrested Mr. Kleb."

"I think we both know it isn't possible Mr. Kleb did this. I've been trying to get the sheriff to let me in to talk to him. But he keeps telling me Mr. Kleb won't talk to me."

"He must be covering for someone," I agreed with her.

"I'm scared he's covering for Charlie. The sheriff said our vehicle was there and someone saw Charlie. That can't be; he doesn't even have a license."

"What does Charlie say?"

"He won't talk to me. He's scared silly by all of this. I don't know what to do."

"I can't do it today, but I'll try to stop by the Sheriff's Department tomorrow morning and see if the sheriff will talk to me, or maybe I can talk to Mr. Kleb at least."

"That would be great. Let me know what you find out."

"I will," I said as I hung up. At the same time it dinged as a text came in. Nick needed me to pick up some oil for the tractor. I had just enough time to swing by the auto supply store before picking up Edna. Jessica was going to meet us at the cabins.

Edna was standing in the window of her bakery, waiting for me when I pulled up. I saw her wave goodbye to her helper as she walked out the door and climbed into my pickup.

"Whew, what a day!" She said as she buckled her seat belt. Edna ran her bakery out of the main floor of her house. She never turned down the chance for an outing; I imagine living in the same building made it hard to separate herself from her work.

"Busy?"

"Not so much busy, as it was one of those days where if something can go wrong it will," she said as she settled back in the seat.

"I know the kind of days you are talking about, but enlighten me as to what a bad day in a bakery entails?" I asked her.

"The morning started off by sleeping through my alarm, which I haven't done in ten years. Once I got down to the bakery I spent twenty minutes trying to find my yeast. My new high school helper can't get my organization plan figured out in the pantry. Then I was in such a rush, I spilled ten pounds of flour on the floor. Then . . ."

"Alright, alright," I said laughing, "you win. It was a bad day."

"Are you excited for your first guests?" Edna asked me.

"Yes. It feels a touch unbelievable at the moment. I hope it isn't a bust. I'll be working until I'm eighty to pay off the loan if it doesn't work."

Edna snorted, "You're just like me; you love what you are doing, and you won't retire until then anyway."

"Thanks for the vote of confidence."

"It will be fine. How many people have contacted you about renting the cabins so far?" Edna asked.

"We're booked up already in April and May, and even a few other dates the rest of the summer."

"I'd say that's awesome considering it is only the beginning of November. So why are we doing one party of guests this weekend if you don't have anyone else until April?"

"They are an elderly couple Dad knew that have bought quite a bit of seed from us over the years. When they heard about the cabins they called. They wanted to stay this fall as they are avid birdwatchers. I gave them a reduced rate and told them that they would be our guinea pigs. They were happy to oblige as long as it didn't snow. Mother nature is cooperating with no snow in the foreseeable future." I pulled up in front of the first cabin where Jessica was already waiting.

"Have you been here long?" I asked her as we got out of the pickup.

"Only a few minutes, I was peeking in the windows trying to see what they looked like inside."

"That reminds me, here is a set of keys for each of you," I said as I handed them keys.

"What is the plan for tomorrow?" Jessica asked after tucking her set of keys in her coat pocket.

"The Gruber's will get here around 3:00 p.m. tomorrow. I explained to them that they are on their own for supper. How do you two want to do this? Do you each want to pick a day to deliver the other's food or be responsible for your own?" I asked them.

"They didn't want to be interrupted once they got here, correct?" Jessica asked.

"Correct. They said they'd prefer to have it all there when they show up. They will be leaving late Sunday afternoon."

"I think it will work best for me to deliver the food. Edna doesn't have any help in the mornings. I timed how long it took me to drive out here. It was seven minutes one way. If Edna can get the bakery items to me in the morning, my staff can cover me for the approximate twenty to twenty-five minutes it will take me to deliver the food, stash it, and get back to the restaurant. Can we go in and see what the set up is inside?" Jessica asked.

"We can," I said as I unlocked the door and we walked in.

"This looks great Carmen," Edna said. "I'd have no problem staying here."

That was high praise from her as Edna likes her creature comforts. The cabins did look nice. I had put up forest green gingham-checked curtains that matched the bedspreads and tablecloth on the little kitchen table. The small bathrooms had been decorated in a wildlife theme, with deer and bear as the décor on the shower curtain and bathroom rugs. The walls were knotty pine and I had even splurged on hardwood floors.

Jessica was busy opening the few cupboard doors there were, looking at the dishes and silverware and checking out the size of the fridge. After she was done she said, "You thought this out well. What time do you think I should get the food here by tomorrow?"

"You have some leeway tomorrow as they won't be here until 3:00 p.m., but I think in general you should aim for 8:00 a.m. I should add a question about time for food delivery to my checklist when people reserve a cabin."

"You shouldn't give them an open-ended time; it has to work for us. When they want all the food up front it won't be a problem, but when they want it delivered every day it should be a set window of time," Jessica said.

"You're right. I'd tell them between seven and eight, and if they want to sleep in, they'll have to take the food ahead of time," Edna suggested.

"That sounds good," I said making a note on my phone. Is there anything else either of you can think of?"

"I can't—how about you Edna?" Jessica asked.

"No. I'll try and help you out with food delivery also. I'm trying to hire another person. If it ever happens I'll be able to share in the duties, but so far I haven't had any applicants."

"It's getting harder and harder to find help. Have you found anyone to clean the cabins?" Jessica asked me.

"I haven't looked yet. I'm hoping to get a couple high school kids next spring when we are up and running."

"Good luck," Edna laughed. "I think you'll be cleaning them yourself."

"True, but with any luck Kirk will be here and I can dump them on him," I said smiling. By that time we had wandered back to our vehicles.

"I better get back to town," Jessica said. "James and I are planning to catch a movie tonight. I'll be at your bakery tomorrow around eight to pick up your stuff Edna."

"It'll be ready," she said.

We waved to Jessica as she turned her vehicle around and drove towards town.

"Are you ready to go also?" I asked Edna.

"I am," she said as she got into my pickup.

"I'm sorry this got so late. I know you don't have a lot of extra time in the afternoons," I said as I started up the pickup.

"It was fine. I'm looking forward to this. It's not much extra work, and it's an easy way to pocket another couple hundred dollars a week."

"I hope so. I'm glad you and Jessica wanted to do it. Homemade food is a plus for my advertising. Is your bakery going well? I know I don't get in there enough, but I do support you by buying the items you have at the convenience store."

"It's going well, other than the occasional shoving match," she laughed.

"What do you mean?" I asked her.

"Last week Tom Hartz stopped in, you know the guy that runs the lumberyard, he must not be a big fan of Brian Bozeman either. He started to bellow at him the minute he saw Brian. He charged over to Brian and started yelling at him."

"What was he yelling about?"

"I have no idea. There was enough noise from a mixer I had running that I couldn't make out the words, but it must have been something extreme, because the next thing I know Brian is shoving Tom, then Tom stumbled and fell down. Of course, Brian being Brian couldn't help but add insult to injury and he laughed at Tom. Poor Tom looked so humiliated sitting there on his bum, if it wasn't for the fact he started it, I almost felt sorry for him. If looks could kill, Brian wouldn't have made it out the door alive. The worst thing was they both left without buying anything." She chuckled and leaned back against the seat with her eyes closed.

"You should tell the sheriff this," I said.

"Why on earth should I?" She asked, opening her eyes and looking at me.

"Didn't you hear what happened to Brian?"

"No; what?"

"Did you know Coach Janning?"

"That's the guy they are inducting into the Hall of Fame next week." She answered.

"Yes, they found him dead next to Brian who was recovering from a blow to the head."

She looked stunned and said, "I guess that explains why the cake the school ordered was cancelled. They never gave me a reason. But if Brian killed Coach Janning, who knocked out Brian?"

"The sheriff says the evidence found at the crime scene proves it was impossible for Brian to have killed the coach, but he doesn't know who the real target was, Brian or the coach, and which one was simply in the wrong place at the wrong time. Adding another monkey wrench, Mr. Kleb has confessed to both killing the coach and knocking out Brian," I said waiting for her reaction.

She didn't disappoint, "Good grief, that frail little old man who's always in the library?"

"That's the one. George, the man who works for Jessica was assaulted the same day. He's unconscious in the hospital right now."

"Wow. I guess I haven't been paying too much attention to the gossip around town. But if Mr. Kleb confessed why do I need to talk to the sheriff?"

"I believe he confessed because the sheriff was trying to interrogate Marcy's son, Charlie. I think Mr. Kleb is so loyal to Marcy he confessed in a misguided attempt to help."

"That doesn't make any sense. He must have had some reason to believe Charlie did it, if he confessed for him. Otherwise why confess?" she asked.

"You know, I never thought of it that way. I wonder why he thought Charlie was responsible. You know on second thought, I think I'll use your story as another reason to stop by the Sheriff's Department tomorrow. I was planning to go anyway."

"Are you investigating again? Last time didn't go so well for you," Edna reminded me.

"I know, but Marcy asked me to help. So far I haven't been able to do much."

"I'm not sure what you can do when someone has confessed."

"I don't think the sheriff believes Mr. Kleb did this anymore than I do. Maybe he'll talk to me. I'm also hopeful he'll let me talk to Mr. Kleb."

"Good luck," Edna said as I pulled up in front of her bakery. She got out of the pickup, waved, and I changed direction to Frankie's house.

When I parked in front of Frankie's house I could see Melanie had been correct about the pet grooming business. There was a van decorated with cats and dogs, a phone number, and the words Frankie's Mobile Pet Grooming on it parked in her driveway. I made note of the number and entered it into my cellphone contacts for the next time Wizard tangled with a skunk or rolled in something disgusting. I knocked on the front door and Frankie answered. She was no more than five feet tall with vivid red hair. She had lost weight since I had last seen her six months ago at Judith's Dental Office.

At first she smiled when she saw me, then frowned and said, "I imagine you're here about George." This town was too small to keep my investigating inclinations secret. "You may as well come in."

I followed her into a living room filled with pet cleaning supplies and equipment.

"Sorry for the mess," she said as she cleared a spot for me to sit on the couch and she sat opposite of me on the top of a box that looked like it was a case of dog shampoo.

"Not a problem. I know you're working on getting your business going. Good luck with it by the way."

"Thanks," she said looking tense. "How did you find out about me? We haven't even told his family."

Deciding not to share who told me I answered, "Someone told me they saw you together, I decided to take a chance it was true. I won't tell anyone."

"Doesn't matter at this point, his sister knows now, nothing was going to keep me away from him in the hospital."

"Do you have any idea who might have assaulted George?"

"I don't know who did it but I might know why it happened." She replied hesitantly.

"Why didn't you go to the sheriff if you think you know something?"

"George trusted me with something, and I didn't want to betray his trust. The doctors say he's showing signs of waking up and I was going to wait and get his permission."

I decided to be honest with her. "Have you heard what happed to Coach Janning and Brian Bozeman?"

"I heard the coach was killed, but between worrying about George and starting this business I haven't paid any attention. Why?"

"I think whatever happened to George has something to do with the murder of the coach. Did George have anything to do with the coach or Brian that you are aware of?"

At first she shook her head.

I pushed her, "A murderer is walking around free right now, and if you know something that helps to identify who it is, I think you owe it to George to share."

She considered for a few minutes and then said, "George had proof the coach cheated to win the regional championship game that gave the team the state tournament berth. He was mad when the town decided to induct him into the Hall of Fame; he even called the coach and told him not to come."

"Obviously the coach wasn't too upset by it, as he showed up. What proof did he have?"

"The other team's coach had cheated on his wife and somehow Coach Janning found out. He threatened to tell the man's wife unless he threw the game. George overheard and recorded it. George was a little slow in school and the teachers let him record their lectures with a small handheld video recorder."

"That can't be important enough to beat someone up or kill anyone." I mused.

"I think there was more to it than that. George wasn't interested in exposing the coach; he was more upset by the coach coming back to town. He didn't want him here for some reason."

"So you think the coach may have assaulted George?" I asked.

"I don't know. I don't want to accuse anyone, but it certainly ties George and the coach together. I don't know how Brian factors into this, unless he somehow found out too."

"Will you tell the sheriff about this?" I asked her.

"I will Carmen, and thanks for stopping by," she said grudgingly. "I've been wondering if I should call the sheriff or not. Subconsciously I knew I should, but I didn't want to disappoint George's trust in me."

"I understand." As I let myself out the door of her house she was already calling the sheriff.

When I arrived home I was greeted by the smell of fried walleye. Dad was putting it on the table along with a bowl of coleslaw when I walked in.

"It smells amazing. Is there enough to share with me?"

"I was hoping you'd get home in time to eat it when it was warm," Dad said.

I grabbed myself a plate and was sitting down when my cellphone rang. I was tempted to ignore it, but when I saw it was Edna I answered. "Hey, what's up?"

"I thought I better tell you I remembered another person who had a run-in with Brian," she said.

"Who?"

"This was the day before Brian's fight with Tom."

"I had no idea your bakery was such a hotbed of intrigue," I joked with her.

"This wasn't in the bakery. It was after I closed for the evening and I was walking to the grocery store for some milk. I saw Chloe Johnson and Brian get out of his pickup. She was hanging on to him pretty tight and to be honest he looked irritated with her. He tried to pull away and walk back to his pickup but she wouldn't let go. I decided to turn around and pretend I was walking the other direction so they wouldn't know they had a witness. I took a couple steps the other way when I heard a crash. I turned around and Chloe must have thrown something at his pickup. Brian raised his arm like he was going to hit her, then dropped it and walked back to his pickup. I heard Chloe yell 'you're going to pay for this Brian Bozeman, just wait and see.'"

"That is interesting. I'll be sure to pass this along to the sheriff also. He may want to talk to you too."

"He knows where to find me," she said and hung up.

Dad looked up and asked, "What was that about?"

I sat down to eat and told him what Edna had said about both Chloe and Tom, my visit with Frankie, and I also filled him in on my plan to stop by the Sheriff's Department tomorrow. We finished eating, cleaned up the kitchen, watched some television, and turned in for the night.

CHAPTER TWELVE

Blue vervain has been used as a medicinal herb for treating headaches, cramps and fevers, but it can interfere with blood pressure medication.

I WOKE UP ON THIS LATE OCTOBER FRIDAY morning excited to welcome our first guests to the cabins, but first I had to stop by the Sheriff's Department to find out if Sheriff Poole would even talk to me much less share any information about the investigation. He might be more willing to share information if I provided him with a few more suspects and everywhere Brian went, he left a trail of people mad at him. Based on what Frankie told me I was sure the coach was responsible for George's injuries. I was beginning to believe far from being a man in the wrong spot at the wrong time, the coach had been meeting with Brian for a reason. Someone who was fed up with Brian, and there were many, must have witnessed the coach and Brian fighting and it became the last straw and they attacked Brian. The coach was a witness and got killed. It was too bad whoever it was didn't succeed in killing Brian; I shook my head as the evil thought crossed my mind. I also recognized if I was any kind of a detective I would have talked to Brian by now. I had to admit to myself that I was avoiding it; there was a part of me that continued to be intimidated by the man.

Dad was sitting at the kitchen table reading the newspaper so intently he didn't hear me when I walked in the kitchen. "What is so fascinating in the newspaper?"

"It's an article about Mr. Kleb being arrested for the murder of Coach Janning and the assault on Brian."

"I'm surprised the sheriff allowed any information to be printed."

"If I'm correct in reading between the lines, Sheriff Poole doesn't believe Mr. Kleb did this anymore than you or I do. I would guess he allowed the article with the hope a witness might come forward. He makes a point of asking if anyone was in the vicinity the evening of the murder, or if anyone knows anything, to please contact the Sheriff's Department."

"If he has requested the public's help it will make my goal of talking to him this morning go better," I said.

"Do you have anything factual to contribute?" Dad asked me.

"No, but I'm going to float some other possible suspects by him, and see if he'll tell me why he was so interested in Marcy's son Charlie."

"The article doesn't say anything about Charlie, but as he's a minor I suppose it wouldn't."

"I'm sure not. Also, after Mr. Kleb confessed, Marcy said the sheriff dropped all interest in Charlie. But if I want to talk to him this morning I need to get going. Don't forget the Gruber's are checking in this afternoon if you want to be there."

"I'm planning on it. It's been a while since I've seen Roy and Sue."

"They're supposed to call me when they get as far as Parkville. That will give me time to come home, pick you up, and meet them at the cabin site. See you later." I grabbed a couple of granola bars out of the cupboard, filled my coffee cup, and took off for town.

Ten minutes later I was pulling up in front of the Sheriff's Department. I was glad to see no other cars parked in front. Sheriff Poole might be more apt to talk to me if there were no witnesses.

I was surprised to see the sheriff sitting in the dispatcher's spot. He looked at me and grimaced when I walked in. He made a show of looking at the calendar on the wall and said, "I'm surprised it took you this long to stop by. Let me guess, you don't think Mr. Kleb did it?"

"As a matter of fact, I don't, and you can't make me believe you do either," was my response to him.

He stared at me for a few moments, and said, "You're right. I don't. But I can't do much when he keeps insisting he did."

"Did he tell you why he supposedly did it?" I asked.

"He said he was upset by the way Brian was treating Marcy and wanted to help her. It turns out Mr. Kleb is dying of cancer and he said he decided to get rid of Brian for Marcy and Coach Janning showed up at the wrong time."

"That's ridiculous. There is no way frail, tiny Mr. Kleb could have overpowered both of those men."

"I agree," was the sheriff's response.

"How is Mr. Kleb doing? Is he able to get treatments while he's in jail?"

"His doctor told us he quit taking treatments a couple weeks ago. Mr. Kleb said the horrible side effects from the chemotherapy weren't worth living a few months longer, which I can understand. He doesn't have any family left alive, so why be sick and miserable just to add a bit more time to your life. But I don't like him being in here for sure. He should be comfortable in his own home."

"What can we do to make that happen?" I asked.

"First of all there is no we, and second of all, that's what my deputies are out doing right now. They are trying to find anyone who might have seen something. The problem is it happened after most businesses were closed for the day and they were in an alley behind the hardware store. There wouldn't have been any reason for someone to have been back there to see anything. I've questioned Brian twice now and he is sticking with his story that he was finishing up work, and the next thing he knew he was waking up and the coach was dead."

"Mr. Kleb must have confessed because he thinks Marcy or Charlie has something to do with the murder."

"I agree. I'm almost positive Charlie was there, but the lawyer wouldn't let me talk to him. I have you to thank for that," he said looking at me with raised eyebrows.

"Why do you think Charlie was there?" I asked avoiding that statement, wondering how long I was going to be allowed to sit here asking questions.

"Their personal vehicle was seen at the site, and Marcy was at the library where plenty of people saw her. Charlie would be the only other person with access to the vehicle; I only wanted to ask him some questions."

"Couldn't someone have stolen it?" I asked.

"It's possible, but it was back at their house when Marcy got home. She admitted they have one set of keys for it, and they were kept on a key rack in the house."

"He's only ten. How could he have driven a vehicle there?"

"You know as well as I do, having a license has nothing to do with being able to drive. He's tall for his age, and his teacher admitted she'd heard him telling the other kids how his dad was teaching him to drive. But," and he held up his hand to stop me when he saw I was going to say something, "I don't believe he did any of this, but he might have seen something. However my chances of questioning him are gone now, both because of the lawyer, and Kleb confessing."

"You could have told Marcy you didn't suspect him and you just wanted to talk to him."

"I admit I could have handled it better, but what's done is done. So was there anything else you needed?"

"I was hoping you would let me talk to Mr. Kleb," I said trying to distract him.

"That isn't going to happen, not only because I won't let you, but Kleb won't talk to anyone. Marcy even tried."

"Have you considered any other suspects?"

"As I understand it, that's a wide open field, as more than one person in this town hated Brian. Is there anything else? My dispatcher should be back from her doctor's appointment soon, and I'd just as soon not have her see me talking to you. I got enough grief from various people in town for my not listening to you when I thought Jessica had killed her brother. I don't need the town thinking you are involved in this murder investigation, too. I can solve this without your help."

"I do have some alternative people for you to consider besides Mr. Kleb and Charlie," I told him knowing I was getting on his nerves.

"Who did you have in mind?" The sheriff asked with a big sigh.

"Marcy's brother, Steve, had no love for Brian."

"I'm aware of that. We talked to him. He saw Brian when he left the hardware store and said he saw the coach arrive as he was leaving. He claims he was on the phone talking to his hardware supplier trying to modify an existing order to replace items they had on hand instead of waiting for the back ordered ones."

"That should be easy enough to verify."

"You would think, however the salesman took off yesterday before we got a hold of him for a fishing vacation at a remote Alaskan resort where cellphone reception is sketchy and we haven't been able to reach him."

"But easy enough to prove or disprove when the guy gets back," I said not willing to give up.

"I agree. He's not high on my list, but he is on it. You got anyone else?" He asked; eyebrows raised again.

"Brian was harassing Paul Olson, he wanted the coaching position. Maybe Paul found out Brian hurt his brother-in-law George."

"Based on what Frankie told me over the phone, after talking to you," he glared at me obviously mad that I had talked to her first, "it's more likely Coach Janning is the one that beat up George."

"Tom Hartz and Brian got into an argument in Edna's bakery a few days ago. You can talk to Edna if you want."

"Hmmm," the sheriff wrote his name down, "anyone else?"

"Edna also saw Chloe Johnson get into an altercation with Brian."

He raised his eyebrows at me again. I don't know if he thought it made him look taller, but I was beginning to be very annoyed with those eyebrows. "Yes, Edna saw them together. She saw Chloe get upset with Brian and threaten him when he didn't respond like she wanted."

"Threaten him how?" The sheriff looked a little more interested.

"Edna heard Chloe yell at Brian that he was going to pay for this."

"It sounds like I need to have a visit with Edna. I wish we knew for sure who the actual target was. We know the coach died first so Brian couldn't have killed him, but that doesn't clarify who the actual target was. Although I'm starting to believe the coach was the actual target, and whoever it was knocked Brian out hoping he'd be blamed."

Starting to see the sheriff's logic I made up my mind it was time to stop avoiding it, I needed to talk to Brian. The door opened and the dispatcher walked in, giving us a questioning look.

The sheriff said, "If you don't have anything else to tell me, you are free to go."

"I don't," I answered thinking it was smooth of him to make it sound like he requested me to come to him. I wondered if I should be bothered, then decided it didn't matter. I looked at my phone which had been on mute. I was surprised to see it was already 10:00 a.m. and there was a missed call from Nick. I called him back when I got in my pickup. It rang a few times, and he answered sounding out of breath.

"I'm sorry. Did I catch you at a bad time?" I asked.

"No. I forgot to stick my phone back in my pocket and of course I was on the other side of the building when I heard it ring."

"I'm returning your call."

"Are you going to be in town at any point today?"

"I'm in town right now, what can I get you?"

"Could you swing by the auto parts store and pick up a battery for the tractor. I had to jump it again this morning, which shouldn't be happening when the temperature isn't even below freezing yet. I'm sure it's a bad battery and not something else. I figured I'd start there anyway."

"I'm trying to remember when we replaced it last. I think it's been a couple years, so it very well may be. I'll pick up a battery."

"Thanks Carmen, and by the way, would you be interested in going out to eat tomorrow night?" He asked sounding nervous.

"Like a real date?" I questioned him feeling warm inside.

"I'd like it to be," Nick answered, "unless you aren't ready for that yet?" His voice trailed off."

I thought for a few seconds and said, "I'd like to very much. What time and where?"

"There is a new Mexican restaurant in Parkville I heard about from Sam. Do you like Mexican food?"

"I love it. Jessica told me about it also. We've been meaning to try it."

"Did you want to invite her and James with?" Nick asked with less enthusiasm.

"It would be fun, but," I paused then said, "I think it would be good for us to have an actual date, just the two of us."

"That sounds great to me." Nick said his voice much more cheerful. "Does 7:00 p.m. work to pick you up?"

"See you then," I said thankful no one could see my goofy grin. "I'll pick up the battery and drop it off after dinner. I need to go over to Marcy's right now."

"Sleuthing again?" he asked.

"After talking to the sheriff it appears Charlie may have at least been in the vicinity that night. I'm hoping Marcy will let me talk to him and with any luck Brian will be around too. It's time he tells the truth about what his involvement is."

"Good luck and I'll see you later," Nick said and hung up.

The auto parts store was on the way to the library, so I decided to stop there first to pick up the battery. When I walked in, Mr. Fenmore was standing at the counter talking to Art, the owner of the auto parts store. "Hello Mr. Fenmore, hello Art."

Mr. Fenmore stepped aside and Art said, "What can I help you with Carmen?"

I told him the battery size I needed and when he left to check if he had one in stock, I turned to Mr. Fenmore. "I didn't mean to interrupt. I'm in no hurry."

"Oh, I'm just here visiting. Art puts up with an old man looking for a way to pass the time."

"You can't be that bored, Billy, and the bowling alley must keep you busy," I said with a smile.

"They do, but I find myself with too much free time when Billy is at school."

Art came from the back room carrying the battery, "you're in luck. This is the last one we have on hand. I was telling Mr. Fenmore about Mr. Kleb confessing. He hadn't picked up a newspaper yet. Nobody in town can believe it."

"I don't think the sheriff does either," I said.

"Are you investigating again?" Art asked looking worried now.

"Marcy asked me too. She wants a divorce and can't get Brian out of her life until this mess is cleared up."

"It's not complicated to me," Art said. "Brian was a bully who liked to get his way. The coach is dead and no one else was there except Brian. He should be in jail. The coach didn't deserve this."

Mr. Fenmore harrumphed. I turned to look at him.

"I happen to know Coach Janning wasn't an angel. It saved the world a lot of trouble when he died," he said and he hurried out the door.

"He has a lot of animosity for Coach Janning. Do you have any idea why?" I asked Art.

"No clue," he replied.

I shrugged and decided Mr. Fenmore definitely needed to be talked to soon. "Thanks for the battery," I said as I walked out of the store carrying it. It was now almost 11:00 p.m. I decided to call Marcy and ask her if now was a convenient time to stop in. She answered on the first ring.

"Carmen, I'm glad you called. Have you found anything out yet?"

"I was going to stop by the library and ask you if I could talk to Charlie." She didn't answer right away, so I went on, "I also want to talk to Brian if he's home. It's time he tells the truth, the sheriff doesn't believe his story either."

Marcy snorted, "Imagine that, Brian not telling the truth. You can question him anytime you want, but he's at work today. However I'm not sure Charlie should be bothered with this anymore."

"Marcy, the sheriff doesn't think Charlie had anything to do with this, but he does believe Charlie was there and he might have seen something. Would you please let me talk to him?"

She capitulated with a drawn out sigh, "Charlie didn't go to school today, why don't you meet me at my house at 11:30. I can get away for an hour at dinner."

"Are you okay with me doing this?"

"No, but I know you're trying to help. Charlie won't talk to me either. I know something is bothering him. Better you try and talk to him than the sheriff." She hung up.

I instantly started to regret this, but was committed now, wise or not.

CHAPTER THIRTEEN

Minnesota was once home to eighteen million acres of native prairie with only a little over 1% remaining.

I HAD DRIVEN AROUND TOWN AIMLESSLY, wasting time before I pulled up in front of Marcy's house at 11:30 p.m. I sat in my pickup, wondering how to go about this. My experience with children was limited to dealing with my twenty-three year old brother, Kirk, who wasn't the most mature person around, but was far from a child. Marcy must have noticed me as she stepped out on her porch and looked at me, wondering I'm sure why I hadn't moved from my pickup yet. I took a deep breath and opened my door.

"I don't know about the wisdom of this," she said to me as I walked up the porch steps.

"You and I both, but we need to find out if Charlie knows or saw something," I said as Marcy stepped aside and let me walk in the house.

"Do you know if Brian ever had anything to do with George?"

"Why? Do you think he truly had something to do with his assault?"

"No, but George had evidence the coach cheated to win his big championship game. I think Brian knew about it too. I'm also making conversation to avoid going upstairs."

Marcy laughed at that. "All I know is Brian found it funny George was a cook. Brian teased George when he was the football manager in high school and I believe he planned to keep on in adulthood, as in his archaic thinking mind, a man should not be cooking. What did I ever see in him?"

I had no reply to that. Marcy shook her head, took a deep breath and said, "Charlie is upstairs in his room. It's the only room upstairs with a closed door."

"Does he know I'm coming?" I asked stalling.

"Yes, I told him," she said picking at her sweater nervously.

"Did he say anything?" I asked wondering if he had objected in any way.

"No, he just looked at me and went back to his video game."

Great, I thought to myself, it was bad enough I didn't have a clue how to connect with a kid, but if he was into video games, I was going to have even less of a chance finding anything in common with him. I had zero eye-hand coordination and never could understand video games. I'd always preferred being outside. I took a deep breath, walked up the stairs, and knocked on his door.

"Hey Charlie, can I come in?" I heard some shuffling noise, but there was no response. I knocked again and the door opened a crack. I looked in and met Charlie's eyes. I gently pushed the door open, walked in, and sat down on a bench next to his bed.

He took off his headphones, muted the video game, and said, "Hi," in a soft voice, all without looking at me.

"What kind of video games do you like to play?" I asked trying to find a way to be less intimidating to him.

"Super Mario and Avengers are my favorite." He said looking a little more at ease.

"Do you get high scores?" I asked.

"I'm not the best. My mom limits the amount of time I get to play."

"Did your mom tell you why I wanted to talk to you?" I asked him.

"Yeah, she said it's about the night my dad got hurt." He said as he looked at me, his eyes looking sad.

"Were you there? Did you see what happened?" I asked him with a little too much insistence, as he looked down and shifted away from me. "I'm sorry Charlie, but it would be very helpful to tell us if you saw something." He started to shake his head, and I said, "You won't get into any trouble," I said hoping I wasn't lying to him. He didn't say anything, so I continued, "You know who Mr. Kleb is don't you?"

He nodded, continuing to stare at the floor.

"Did you know he confessed to killing that man and hurting your dad? Do you think Mr. Kleb would have done something like that?"

He shook his head but kept looking down, while he fingered the buttons on his shirt.

"I don't think he did either. I believe he thought he saw you there and is trying to keep you and your mom from getting into trouble. I don't think you did anything either, but you do need to tell us if you saw something. It would be a big help to Mr. Kleb."

He made eye contact with me again and said, "I wasn't supposed to have left the house."

"Why did you?" I asked trying to hide my piqued interest at his words.

"My friend Billy had the newest Super Mario video game he was going to lend me. We were going to meet by the library and he was going to bring it to me there."

The alley behind the hardware store would have led straight to the back of the library. I nodded and asked, "Why did you drive, why not take your bike?"

He shrugged his shoulders and said with a gulp, "I was mad at my dad," and then the words started pouring out of him. "Dad was supposed to pick me up after he was done at work and take me to buy the video game. He said no son of his was going to be borrowing video games. But he never came, and I knew Billy only had until 7:00 p.m. as he had to be home before that, and I wanted to play that game real bad. Susie Martin was making fun of me in school because I didn't have any new video games. I told her I was getting the new Super Mario game that night and she didn't believe me. I had to get it and play it so I could tell her about it at school the next day. I waited and waited for my dad. I started to get mad. Dad never comes when he says he will." He started to cry. "Billy said he could meet me at the library, but he had to be home by seven or his grandpa would be very mad at him. He lives a couple blocks from the library, but it would have taken me too long to walk there, so I decided to drive. Dad had been teaching me and I knew where the keys were. I drove super slow and I was real careful. I went through the alley so no one would see me, but when I got close to the hardware store I saw my dad's work pickup. I knew he'd see me if I drove past, so I parked it, and ran the rest of the way to the library."

"Did you see anything?" I prodded him trying to be gentle with my question.

He wiped his nose on his sleeve, took a deep breath, and nodded. "When I came back from the library I was curious why dad's pickup was there, but there wasn't any equipment or construction noise. So I snuck over trying to see what was going on and I accidently kicked an old can that was lying on the ground. I heard footsteps so I ducked behind a garbage can that was in the alley and hid behind it. I thought it was dad coming and I knew I'd be in big trouble. But no one came and then it was quiet until I heard a thud, so I peeked around the garbage can. I saw someone running away. When it was quiet again I moved out from behind the garbage can and I saw a guy lying in the cement. I started to walk over to him but I heard another noise so I got scared and ran away." He started to cry hard and said, "If I hadn't been so scared maybe I could have helped. Maybe that man wouldn't have died."

"Oh Charlie, you did the right thing. The noise you heard could have been the killer. They might have hurt you too."

He slowly stopped crying and looked at me. I knew he hadn't considered the idea that he might have been in danger. I asked him, "Did you recognize who was running away?"

"No, at school I'm getting called the son of a murderer, but my dad wouldn't kill anyone. Do you think I did the right thing by leaving? Some kids say I'm such a baby, and I guess I am." He started to cry again.

I bent down on the floor and hugged him. "No Charlie, you were very brave and wise. I'm sure you saved your father's life. If you hadn't been there I'm sure whoever was would have killed your dad too. You were very brave." I heard Marcy come in the room and I moved aside so she could hold her son. She must have been standing by the door listening.

She kept murmuring to him, "I love you Charlie. It's okay."

I gave them a few minutes until Charlie's tears subsided to a sniffle. "Charlie can you tell the sheriff what you told me?"

He looked at his mom and she said, "You aren't in trouble, but it might help Mr. Kleb."

He said, "I don't know who it was, but I don't think it could have been Mr. Kleb. He has to use a cane to walk and this person was running."

Marcy looked at me and said, "I'll take him over to the Sheriff's Department right away."

"I'm going to take off now," I said. She nodded and I walked out thinking poor Charlie, that little kid had a lot on his plate. As I drove to the shop to drop off the battery for Nick I thought about what Charlie had said. Charlie's testimony should at least get Mr. Kleb out of jail. It didn't do much to answer the question of who was supposed to have been killed, as I couldn't imagine someone was trying to get rid of both Coach Janning and Brian, but I suppose stranger things have happened. I know the coach was killed first, but Brian being knocked out could have been incidental; maybe the coach was the target. A couple people said Brian indicated something good was going to be happening to him and if it was good for Brian it wouldn't be good for anyone else. Maybe the coach was in on it. Mr. Fenmore indicated that the coach wasn't the great guy everyone thought. Nick happened to be in front of the shop when I pulled up to drop off the battery. He was standing staring at a tire on the front driver's side of his pickup.

"Is something wrong?" I asked when I got out of the pickup.

"The passenger side front tire was flat yesterday, so I took it off, found a nail stuck in it, and patched it. Now this tire is flat. I'm trying to figure out where I would have been driving that I would have picked up so many nails."

"Could it have been at your place?" I asked.

"I doubt it. I park in the same spot every day. I can't think why there would be a bunch of nails now, and I haven't been anywhere out of the ordinary here on the farm." He shrugged his shoulders. "I guess it doesn't matter; it needs to be fixed either way."

"Where do you want the battery?"

"You can set it by the shop door. I've got the tractor in the storage shed; I'll take it over there when I'm done here."

I set the battery down, turned around and took a moment to enjoy Nick's profile as he bent over looking at the tire. He turned and caught me staring. I could feel my cheeks getting red.

"Like what you see?" he asked smiling.

"Yes," I said. "I always enjoy looking at the grass fields," I answered avoiding the question.

Nick laughed. "We'll talk more about this tomorrow night," he said with a wink.

"I'd better get to the seed plant," I said, not sure how to respond as I continued to blush.

"Are you going to be back this way later?" Nick asked as I got in the pickup.

"I'm not planning to. After I check in on Sam & Phil I'll be going to the cabins to welcome our first guests."

"That's right; I forgot they were coming today. Good luck and Carmen, I'm looking forward to tomorrow night," he said looking at me smiling, and then turned back to his tire.

I could hear the mill humming along when I walked in the seed plant. Phil was standing by one of the chutes watching the flow of the seed. "Any problems?" I asked when I joined him.

"So far, so good," he answered.

"Will this seed lot last the rest of the day?"

"It should; we'd have to be very lucky to get done today."

"Okay. Is Sam around?" I asked.

"Yep, he's in back fighting with the shrink wrap machine. Don't tell him I told you but he bumped into it with the forklift earlier today."

"Is it broke?"

"No, it got a little bent on one side, he's straightening it now."

"I'll go take a look." I found Sam in back with the welder heating up a piece of metal on the shrink wrap machine and then pounding the metal back in place with a hammer.

"Crap, you caught me," he said when he finished and took off his welding helmet.

"I'm pretty sure I would have seen it either way," I said with a smile. "Accidents happen. I remember you having to fix up the mess I made when I ran into a conveyor with the snow blower."

"That is true," he said, "but I'm so good, I question that you would have noticed."

I laughed, "That's true. I don't have a lot of time; I have to check in our first cabin guests, but I wanted to see how cleaning the prairie blazing star was going."

"I got enough cleaned for the customer. I was starting to get the shipment ready when this fiasco happened. Once I get the shipment ready I may take off early today if that is okay?"

"Not a problem. Do you have something fun going on?" I asked Sam.

"No, I'm caught up, it's Friday, and instead of you wasting your money paying me to do nothing; I thought I'd go home."

"Now that's my kind of employee, have a good weekend." The Gruber's had called earlier and were on time for their 3:00 p.m. arrival. It was getting close to that time so I hustled out of the seed plant, waving to Phil as I went by. My phone rang; it was Dad.

"Hi Dad, I'm running late but I was just coming to get you."

"That's alright. Karla needed some help so I can't go with you to see the Gruber's."

"Okay. Is something wrong?" I asked.

"Nothing serious, a bull got out, and she needs help rounding it up."

"You're starting to be a regular cowboy," I laughed. "Good luck."

As I hung up I heard Dad say, "I don't want a cowboy hat for Christmas."

I chuckled, glanced down at my clothes, wiped off some dust, got into the pickup, looked in the mirror, ran a comb through my hair, and drove out to the cabins. The sun was now shining bright, making the fifty degree day feel a lot warmer. It was a perfect fall day for the Gruber's to enjoy the prairie, although it was too bad the wildflowers were done blooming. I hadn't checked for a few days, but the last time I'd looked at the forecast it sounded good for the weekend, high 50's and sunny. It should be a perfect weekend for them to spend time birdwatching and hiking.

I greeted the Gruber's, showed them the cabin and food, and helped them with their luggage. I left them my cellphone number and made sure they knew they could call me anytime. I told them it sounded like they'd have beautiful weather for the weekend, and they both gave me a funny look, but I continued with my spiel and told them I would be leaving them alone to enjoy the peace and quiet. They appeared quite happy with everything and as I left they were heading out the door, binoculars in hand. I waved and pointed at a small six-point white-tail buck standing near one of the other cabins. They stopped and stared and I continued out to the main road. My phone rang as I sat at the stop sign waiting for a semi truck to go by before I pulled out on the highway.

"Hi, Marcy, how did it go at the Sheriff's Department?"

"The sheriff wasn't very happy we hadn't let him talk to Charlie before. I do have to say I was impressed with how he handled Charlie."

"Did he release Mr. Kleb?" I asked her.

"Yes. It turns out Mr. Kleb did see Charlie running from the alley when he was walking home from the library and he assumed the worst. When he heard about the incident he figured Charlie had tried to protect me from Brian. He said since he was dying of cancer, he decided to take the blame."

"Had he seen anyone else?"

"Unfortunately, no, but he did say he'd seen Mark, one of Brian's bosses arguing with him that morning when Mr. Kleb walked to the library."

"Mark from MM construction?"

"Yes. But it could have been anything. I know Brian isn't the best employee."

"Thanks for calling but I'd better get going if I want to try and catch Mark. I'll talk to you later Marcy," I said and hung up.

Their receptionist was already gone for the day when I walked in the office of MM construction, but Mitch stuck his head out of his office. "Carmen what are you doing here?"

"Is Mark around? I would like to talk to him if he is."

"Sure he's in my office, come on in." He gestured for me to come down the hallway. "Have a seat," he said when I walked in; Mark was sitting in the other chair.

"Sorry to bother you guys."

"Not a bother," Mitch said. "We're not accomplishing anything. It's turning into a lazy Friday afternoon. The sheriff notified us our job site wasn't a crime scene anymore, but there wasn't much point in starting up this late in the day."

"That's why I'm here. Mr. Kleb said he saw Mark arguing with Brian the morning of the murder."

Mitch looked surprised, while Mark appeared confused and then he said, "Mr. Kleb. Isn't that who they arrested?"

"Yes, but it turns out he was covering for Brian's boy Charlie. He'd seen him run from the alley and thought he might have had something to do with hurting his dad."

"That's kind of crazy," Mitch said scratching his head.

"It's a long story, but anyway he's been released." I looked at Mark, "Do you remember what you were arguing about with Brian?"

Mark continued to look puzzled as he thought, and said after a short time, "I remember now, he was strutting around that morning telling me Coach Janning's Hall of Fame induction ceremony was going to be very helpful to him. I asked him what the heck he was talking about. He told me, 'everyone around here thinks the coach is such a great guy, but I know better and I'm going to expose him. I'll be a hero again in this town.' I have to admit he annoyed me with his smug attitude. Coach Janning was my coach in high school and you couldn't have asked for a more decent guy. He cared about all of us guys, even helped us with our homework."

"Did he say what he thought Coach Janning had done?" I asked wondering if my hunch was correct and Brian knew about the cheating.

"No, by then I was so frustrated with him, I just laughed and asked him if Coach Janning had robbed a bank, or what it was he thought the coach had done. Brian shook his head, smiled and said, 'you'll find out when everyone else does.' I lost my cool and told him he'd better shut up and get back to work. Then I left."

"How come you didn't say anything to the sheriff after Janning and Brian were found?" I asked Mark.

"I thought about it, but I heard Kleb was arrested so I didn't worry anymore about it. I assumed the coach was there trying to talk some sense into Brian, and Kleb had some issue with them both, but I'll give the sheriff a call right away," Mark said.

"Thanks guys, sorry to bother you. I won't take up any more of your time."

"Good luck with your investigating," Mitch said as I walked out.

I got in the pickup and my stomach growled. I was craving pizza. I looked at my phone, surprised to see it was 6:30 p.m. I called Dad to find out if he had anything ready for supper. When he said no, I told him I'd order a takeout pizza from the bowling alley. He said to get two. Karla was there also. I called in an order for a taco pizza and a pepperoni pizza. While I waited, I drove back to the alley to look at the crime scene. I got out and looked around. I could see the mess in the cement where they had to take out Coach Janning's body. Nothing stood out to me other than to acknowledge at this time of night it was indeed very quiet back here. There were a couple of apartments above some of the stores, but most looked abandoned with boarded-up windows. I was sure the sheriff would have interviewed people if anyone lived in them. I checked my phone for the time and left to pick up the pizzas.

CHAPTER FOURTEEN

Milkweeds are the only host plants for monarch butterflies.

DAD AND KARLA WERE SITTING IN THE KITCHEN when I got home with the pizzas. They had set out plates, silverware, and glasses along with some carrots and chips. I noticed Wizard wasn't at his usual spot begging under the table.

"Where's Wizard?" I asked.

Karla grinned as Dad answered, "He is locked in Kirk's room."

"What did he do now?"

"He's been behaving well the past couple days, or at least better than his normal, so when I left to help Karla I didn't pay attention that he wasn't around, I assumed he was sleeping somewhere."

"This doesn't sound good—what did he get into?" I asked, dreading the answer and hoping he hadn't destroyed anything valuable.

"He somehow managed to get the pantry door open and decided to have a little fun with potatoes, rice, flour, and a box of Cheerios. Basically everything that was on the floor of the pantry he decided to tear open and spread over the kitchen floor. Thank goodness he didn't make it any farther than the kitchen. It took me forty-five minutes to sweep it up."

Karla couldn't hold her laughter any longer. She got herself under control and said, "You should have seen his face. I was scared he was going to have another heart attack."

"I might have to admit he's a bad dog and Kirk isn't to blame." I said chuckling as I set the pizzas on the table and realized I hadn't seen Tabitha either this morning or now.

"Have you seen Tabitha today?" I asked Dad.

"She's been busy hunting. She's got a squirrel stuck in the lone tree by the garden shed. You might have to coax her away at some point. I don't think either her or the squirrel has eaten or drank anything all day."

I peeked out the window, and sure enough I could see a calico tail sticking out from behind the garden shed twitching back and forth. I grabbed some milk out of the fridge and sat down at the table with Dad and Karla. There wasn't much talking as we stuffed our faces.

Dad asked after we had finished eating, "Did you get the Gruber's checked in? Sorry I couldn't come with you."

"It was for the best, I was running late and wouldn't have had to time to swing by and pick you up anyway. Yes, they arrived right on time at three. I showed them around and gave them my number if they needed anything." Abruptly changing the topic I asked, "Have either one of you ever heard anything negative about Coach Janning?"

They looked at me puzzled. "Why would you ask that?" Karla questioned me.

"Frankie said George had proof Coach Janning cheated to win his regional championship game. I think Brian knew it also. Yet it doesn't feel like it would be anything important enough to kill someone over. There must be more to it."

"I just remember most of the high school girls having crushes on him. We didn't have many young teachers and I think his youth and good looks were a novelty. He was married, although his wife died young. If my memory is any good, he moved away from here about the same time she died. It would have been devastating for the Hall of Fame ceremony to be interrupted with a cheating claim, which I'm sure Brian knew."

"How do you know so much about the high school?" I asked her.

"When my husband Bill was alive he used to substitute teach in the high school. If you are looking for suspects, Steve, Marcy's brother had quite a temper. There wasn't a day my husband taught he didn't come home with some story about Steve either slugging someone, or getting detention. To be fair it was over fifteen years ago, and I've never heard anyone say anything about Steve having problems as an adult." She paused, and went on to say, "But Marcy, Charlie, and Brian haven't lived here the past ten years, and maybe he was trying to help Marcy get rid of Brian and the coach caught him." She shrugged her shoulders. "James played football for Coach Janning. You could talk to him, but I've never heard him say anything negative either."

"The sheriff isn't sure if the coach or Brian was the target. If it wasn't for Brian being the better candidate to get murdered, I'd be starting to think the coach was the target. After all, if Brian was your main objective and the coach's death was an accident, why not finish off Brian?" I asked.

"Maybe the coach got in the way, they got interrupted by something and whoever it was had to leave before they could make sure Brian was dead," Karla suggested.

I shrugged. "I don't know, but at least Marcy is okay, and both Charlie and Mr. Kleb are off the hook. I've been avoiding it, but I need to talk to Brian and see if I can get any truth out of him. The sheriff isn't having any luck and he's convinced Brian knows more than he's saying. I wish George would wake up and tell us who hurt him. I think his assault has to have something to do with the coach's murder."

"Why don't you give James a call? He's home tonight. Maybe he'll remember something about the coach." Karla suggested.

"I agree; high school football cheating doesn't feel important enough to kill someone over."

I looked at the time; it was eight. "I think I'll run over there and talk to him instead of calling." I got up and started cleaning the table, Karla helped while Dad relented and let Wizard out of Kirk's room. I opened the door and Tabitha came running. She must have decided the easily accessible food in the house was a better option than trying to catch the squirrel. It was a nice evening, so I decided to take a four-wheeler over to James' house. I grabbed my gloves out of my pickup, checked the gas in the four-wheeler, put on a helmet, and took off. It was cold, but it felt good to drive fast across the field to James and Karla's houses and not think about anything for the couple minute drive to their farm. Unlike me, James had moved out and built his own small house next to Karla's. He did spend most of his spare time at Karla's to help keep her from being lonely, but with her and my Dad spending time together I think James was enjoying more time in his own house. Whenever Karla felt the time was right, the plan was for her to move into the little house and James would get the big old farm house. I'm guessing it wasn't that far away, as I was sure he'd be proposing to Jessica before too long. I would bet Karla would offer her home pretty fast, with the hope of grandchildren filling it. The lights were on in James' house so it appeared he was in and not out in a barn somewhere. I left the four-wheeler next to his pickup and walked to the front door to knock. He must have heard the four-wheeler as he opened the door before I got my hand up to knock.

"Hey Carmen, what brings you over?"

"I'm not interrupting anything am I?"

"No, I just finished eating and Jessica is doing inventory at the restaurant tonight. Come on in, what's up?"

"You know Marcy asked me to look into this whole business with Brian and Coach Janning?"

"Yeah, but I thought it was over. Didn't Mr. Kleb confess?"

"He did, but he's been released. He says he confessed because he thought he was protecting Marcy and Charlie."

"Oh. That was nice of him; stupid, but nice."

"He's dying of cancer, so it was a noble gesture. He thought Charlie had something to do with it because he saw him in the vicinity the night of the murder."

"So are there any other suspects?" James asked.

"I'm starting to believe Coach Janning was the real target. Mark Carboot told me Brian may have known something bad about the coach and was planning to tell everyone at the induction ceremony. Frankie told me George had proof the coach cheated to win the championship game. I think Brian knew too. Maybe he assaulted George trying to get the proof George had. But I don't believe cheating to win a high school football game was something worth killing anyone over. Have you ever heard anything negative about the coach?"

James had led me into his small living room and we sat down on the couch. "Boy, I don't know. The team I was on lost most of our games, but I don't think that would cause anyone to kill him." He laughed. "He had his big success the year after I graduated."

"Did he treat everyone okay?"

"Yes, he was that rare coach who was able to please the parents with playing time for all the kids, and the players respected him too."

"What about George? I know he was a manager on the team."

"I can't imagine him having an issue with the coach. When coach caught Brian picking on George he would discipline Brian."

"There has to be something."

James thought for a few seconds and said, "I find it difficult to believe the coach would have anything too nasty in his past." He got up from the couch and asked, "Would you like something to drink?"

"A Coke would be nice."

"Ice?" He asked as he walked into the kitchen.

"Sure. What about Chloe Johnson?" I hollered at him in the kitchen.

"What about her?" He asked me when he came back and handed me a can of Coke and a glass of ice.

"Edna saw Chloe and Brian arguing about something. I'm reaching at straws, but can you think of any reason she might know what Brian was up to? I can't see her being interested in Brian in a romantic way; she's too much of a gold digger for him."

James laughed, "I think Jessica might be rubbing off on you. Chloe's not that bad."

"You better not let Jessica hear you defend her or you'll be in big trouble. Or do you kind of enjoy two women fighting over you?" I nudged him with my elbow.

"Maybe so," he laughed again. "But in all seriousness, other than a vague remembrance of Chloe being a football cheerleader I don't know of any connection between the two, but I haven't kept up with Chloe's life, on purpose." He shrugged.

Deciding to change the subject I asked, "How about you and Jessica? Things appear to be going well. I've never seen her happier."

"She makes me happy too. In fact I could use your opinion on something." He walked out of the living room towards his small office nook, grabbed something out of a drawer, and carried it back to me. "What do you think of this?" He handed me the small box.

I opened it to find a beautiful square cut diamond surrounded by smaller diamonds. "It's beautiful. Is this what I think it is?" I asked. "Are you going to ask Jessica to marry you?"

"I plan to. Do you think it's too soon? We've only been dating for about two months, which isn't long, but we've known each other forever. Do you think it's too soon?" he asked again.

"I think Jessica will be ecstatic, but you do know it's her dream to get married in the winter?"

James looked stunned, "That would mean a wedding in the next couple months or wait a whole year."

"That would be correct." I laughed at him.

"I'm not sure I'm ready for a wedding that fast."

"I think this is a topic you need to discuss with her not me. I'm just preparing you an actual marriage ceremony may be sooner than you were thinking."

He shook his head and said, "You know what; it doesn't matter. I want her to be my wife and if it happens in a few months or if it's in a year, I don't care. Most important is that she says yes."

"Don't worry, that's not going to be a problem," I said. "When are you planning to pop the question? Soon I hope, as this good of a secret I won't be able to keep for very long."

"Not to worry. I know you. I don't plan on waiting too long. The weather is supposed to be unseasonably warm on Sunday, so I was planning to take her for a walk in the state park and propose at the beach where we used to swim as kids, but then I realized it is Halloween. I'm not sure I want to propose on Halloween, so I'm hoping the weather will hold until Monday. If it does I'm going to pack a picnic and take her out after work on Monday afternoon."

"That sounds perfect. Is there any chance of some rain in the forecast, last time I looked it was supposed to be nice all weekend?"

"Tomorrow the weathermen are calling for a couple inches," James answered.

"I hope they are correct, we need the moisture. Although I just finished checking our first guests into one of our cabins and I told them the weather was supposed to be beautiful for the weekend. No wonder they gave me a funny look. Oh well, it's so dry I can't feel too bad for the Gruber's as we need the moisture for spring."

"If we got a normal winter for a change, the spring might not be so dry," James said, "but it's been about three years since we've gotten any significant snowfall. Instead of lots of snow we get lots of wind. It's a continuous battle to move the snow, but it's not fresh snow, only moving the same snow from one side to the other."

"I'm thinking positive. We ordered a new snow blower and the Farmer's Almanac is calling for a cold winter with a lot of snow."

"Well if the Farmer's Almanac says it, it must be true," James said mocking me.

I laughed with him and said, "I better get going. Let me know how it goes with Jessica."

"I'm sure she'll get to you before I do, assuming she says yes anyway. Maybe I shouldn't ask yet. What if she says no; that would be awful," James said starting to look worried again.

"Trust me, she'll say yes. Besides, you don't have a choice, now that I know; I won't be able to keep it quiet anyway, so you might as well go ahead." I said with a laugh as I walked out the door. I could see headlights coming down the driveway when I got on the four-wheeler and started it. It was Karla's vehicle. I waved to her as I drove across the field. When I got home I could hear the television in the den. Dad was watching the news when I walked in. I sat down and watched the weather with him. James was correct; they were calling for rain tomorrow. There was a chance of up to two and a half inches.

"I hope we get the moisture," I said to Dad when the forecast was over.

"It looks promising," he said as he turned off the television. "Was James of any help?"

"No, like everyone else, he can think of nothing bad the coach might have done."

"I think Brian had to be the target," Dad said. "Either way, Marcy, Charlie, and Kleb are off the hook so you don't need to be involved anymore. Your last investigation almost got you killed. I'm sure the sheriff will come up with something."

"I know, but now my curiosity is aroused. But for now I'm going to bed, and pray we get rain tomorrow."

"My bedtime too," Dad said as he got out of his recliner. He stopped and asked, "Are you around tomorrow?"

"I have a date with Nick tomorrow night, but I'll be around all afternoon. Did you need help with something?"

"If it is a rain day, how about if we tackle the garage? It hasn't been cleaned out since your mother passed away and it would be nice to be able to get the riding lawnmower parked in it."

"That sounds like a good plan. Good night Dad." I went upstairs, grabbed my pajamas, and went to the bathroom to get ready for bed.

CHAPTER FIFTEEN

Due to its shallow flowers the nectar can be easily reached making Golden Alexanders an important plant for short-tongued bees.

SATURDAY MORNING DAWNED TO A CLOUDY cool day. It was starting to drizzle; looking like the weather forecast might be accurate for a change, I hoped the Gruber's were doing okay. I got dressed and hurried downstairs with Tabitha following me. I was hoping I was early enough to make Dad breakfast for a change. I was in luck, he was up but he hadn't beat me by much as there was no food cooking.

"Can I make us some French toast and scrambled eggs?" I asked him.

"That would be wonderful," Dad said as he opened the door to let Wizard in. Tabitha peered out the open door, opted to stay in, but turned and looked at me with scorn as if I was to blame for the rain.

"Sorry," I said to her. "You've had an abundance of dry weather to hunt. Right now we need the rain." She flicked her tail at me and ran up the stairs. Ten minutes later breakfast was ready and Dad and I sat down to enjoy it.

"Are we going to tackle the garage today like you planned?" I asked Dad when we finished eating.

"Might as well," he answered. "It needs to get done. I had hoped to wait until your brother got home, but it sounds like the recording is going slower than they planned."

"Did you talk to him last night?" I asked as I started cleaning up the kitchen.

"Yes, he called right after you left for James' house. He said it's going to be at least another week."

"Is he upset?"

"He didn't act like it. He wasn't expecting it to take this long, but he is happy with the music they are recording."

When we were finished cleaning up the kitchen I told Dad I'd go out to the garage and get started. He could join me whenever he was ready. I knew he liked to take a few minutes after breakfast to relax, read his newspaper, and drink his coffee. I grabbed an old sweatshirt from the entryway, slipped into some waders, grabbed a pair of gloves, and walked out to the garage. It was starting to rain a little harder now. With any luck by the time we were done in the garage, there would be actual puddles in the yard. I turned on the lights and looked around. Dad wasn't wrong, it was a mess. We'd managed to keep floor space open for the vehicles, but nothing else. Boxes and odds and ends lined the walls. I decided to start on the section I knew held most of my discarded stuff from over the years. The first box I pulled down had old elementary art projects stored in it. This box could go to the trash and I set it aside. I pulled out a tub from under the shelves. This was full of old softballs, tennis balls, deflated basketballs, and other miscellaneous sports items; another bunch of stuff that should be thrown away. I decided I'd better get a trailer hooked up to my pickup so we had someplace to put the garbage and I'd haul it to the county landfill when we were done. I went out the door, got the trailer hooked up, backed the trailer in the garage, unhooked it, moved my pickup out of the way, and closed the overhead garage door. I got back in the garage right on time as it started to pour in earnest. I had just dumped the tub of sports stuff in the trailer and set the tub aside to use for items I wanted to save when Dad walked in the garage.

"I didn't realize how much stuff has been stored in here," I said.

"It has been bugging me for a while, but I haven't wanted to tackle it by myself," he said taking off his coat and shaking water off of it.

"Today is a good day; it's a blessing Kirk isn't here. We'll be able to throw more without him." We both knew Kirk was a packrat. "I'll try and leave his actual tubs and boxes alone, but we should be able to get rid of a lot of junk. Where do you want to start?" I asked Dad.

"We'll finish with where you started. It's all your stuff right?"

"In this area, yes. I think there are only a few more boxes of my stuff." I pulled down another box and we got into a rhythm. I worked my way down the side of the garage, getting boxes down, Dad would get them opened, check what was in them, set aside any we wanted to go through later, and then I'd carry the ones with stuff we didn't want to the garbage trailer. While Dad sorted I'd go through the miscellaneous unboxed stuff. We got through half of the garage before it was time for dinner with eight boxes set aside for more thorough inspection.

"What should I make for dinner?" I asked him as we both stood and contemplated the progress we had made.

"I'd like to finish this today, so how about some quick cold sandwiches and chips." Dad suggested.

"Perfect," I said as we opened the door. I was happy to see it had continued to rain and I got my wish, as actual puddles had formed while we were working.

"It's nice to see the rain," Dad said as he stood next to me. I nodded in agreement then we covered our heads, ducked, and hustled for the house.

I grabbed some deli turkey, tomatoes, pickles, cucumbers, lettuce, cheese, and some mayonnaise out of the fridge while Dad got out some paper plates and a bag of chips.

"Are you planning on going out with Nick tonight?" Dad asked.

"Yes," I answered as I suddenly wondered why I hadn't gotten any calls all morning. I pulled my phone out of my pocket and saw I had somehow set it on mute. I was thankful I hadn't missed any calls from the Gruber's but Nick had left a message wondering if picking me up at 5:30 p.m. was alright. I answered him, hoping he didn't think I was standing him up as it had been three hours since he sent the text. I got a thumbs-up emoji a couple seconds later. He must have been watching his phone, making me feel bad. I'd explain it to him tonight. Dad and I ate quickly and Dad went out to the garage while I cleaned up. I grabbed a water bottle, filled it and whistled for Wizard. He needed to get out and could wander around in the garage with us. Dad had opened another box and was sitting on top of a tub looking at the box, shaking his head when I walked in.

"What is it?" I asked him.

"It's a box of newspaper clippings about you and Kirk. Your mother always planned to make scrapbooks for you two. I used to tease her that it would never get done. Your mother was good at many things but crafts were not one of them."

"I guess I have a legitimate reason for my lack of interest in crafts. Put it aside, I'd like to look through it more thoroughly sometime."

"I'll put it with the save boxes." Dad moved to the next box and I continued going through the stuff not in a box or tub. We worked for three and a half hours until Dad got up and stretched. "I think I've had enough," he said.

"Well you're in luck because I have one shelf left of what looks like old sunscreen, bug spray, and old hats and mittens left to go through. There's a few boxes left over there, but they are all Kirk's."

"We got through everything?" Dad asked in disbelief.

"We got rid of the garbage anyway," I said pointing at the pile of boxes we had left to go through at a later time. "Why don't you go in the house; I'll finish this last shelf and then I'll move the keep boxes over to the side so they are out of the way." I looked at the time on my phone. "Nick is picking me up at 5:30 p.m. which gives me an hour to finish up here and get ready."

"Thanks for the help today." Dad went inside with Wizard following behind him. I looked out the window. The rain had stopped, and the rain gauge showed two and a quarter inches—a perfect, much needed rain. I hoped it hadn't ruined the Gruber's weekend in the cabin. After I finished the shelf I started moving the boxes out of the way. I decided to take the one with the newspaper clippings in to the house with me. I looked around. The garage did look better. I'd sweep tomorrow. I picked up the box, turned out the lights and carried the box inside. Dad was relaxing in his recliner with Wizard on his lap.

"What are you going to do for supper?" I asked him feeling guilty for leaving.

"Karla invited me over, but I think I'll take a nap first."

"Are you feeling okay?" I asked him worried now.

"I'm fine, I can take a nap without anything being wrong," he winked at me.

"I know how long your naps can be, you better set an alarm or you'll miss supper." I teased him.

"Go get ready and out of my hair," he said smiling at me.

As I ran upstairs I mentally applauded myself for keeping the secret about James planning to propose to Jessica all day even though not telling someone was growing painful. I set the box down in my bedroom where Tabitha hopped on top at once. For some inexplicable reason cats are attracted to paper and boxes. I took a quick shower and then tried to fix my wet head of hair. I never had much luck with wet hair, when I used a blow dryer, it only got frizzier and curlier. I decided to leave it wet and put the sides up. I put on a pair of dress pants with heels and a light sweater. I wobbled a little as I started to walk out my bedroom door, changed my mind and went back to the closet for some flats. I wasn't used to walking in heels and falling on my face would detract from the look of heels anyway. I made it downstairs right as Nick pulled up. I started to say goodbye to Dad, but saw he was sleeping, so I opened the door and closed it as quiet as possible. Nick was already out of his pickup and checking to make sure he hadn't parked in a puddle for me to walk through.

"You look nice," he said as he opened the door for me.

"So do you." And he did, he had on a pair of black pants and a nice beige Polo shirt. I climbed in the pickup feeling awkward. It had been a long time since I'd been on a real date. We drove in silence for a couple minutes until I said, "Sorry I didn't get back to you sooner today. Dad and I were cleaning the garage and somehow my phone got set on mute."

"Did you finish?" he asked.

"Just about, we have a few boxes left. It's a good thing we have a garage, because if we had stored all that junk in the house, we would have been accused of being hoarders." Nick laughed, breaking the silence and we talked with no awkwardness the rest of the drive to the Mexican restaurant in Parkville. I was getting spoiled, eating out twice in one week. We pulled up to the restaurant and by the amount of cars in the parking lot it was going to be packed.

"I hope we don't have too long of a wait," Nick said. "I'm starving."

"I am too. I don't suppose you have a wad of cash to slip the hostess?" I asked joking with him.

"Sadly no, my boss is kind of stingy," he said as he took my arm and we walked into the restaurant.

"That was a low blow." I started to punch his arm, but stopped as I realized the waiting area was full and everyone was looking at us. Nick moved to the hostess desk and checked on how long the wait time would be while I found a place for us to sit.

"There is an approximate forty-five minute wait time," Nick said as he sat down next to me. "Can you wait that long?"

"I think I'll make it. But no judging for the amount of food I'm going to order."

"I would never," Nick said holding up his hands in surrender. "Should we move into the bar while we wait?"

"Good idea, we can get an appetizer." There were a couple of spots open at the bar and we grabbed them without paying attention to who was sitting in the stools next to them. I had just picked up the menu sitting on the bar to see what they had for appetizers when I heard a snide voice say, "Well aren't you two the cutest couple."

I looked over and saw Chloe Johnson sitting next to me. "Hey Chloe," I said unenthusiastically. It was unfortunate I didn't share Jessica's ability to be nice to all people. I turned to Nick, handed him the menu and said, "Do you see any appetizers you'd like?"

"What about me for an appetizer?" Chloe asked, bending sideways from her bar stool to insert her body in front of me in order to ogle Nick.

Nick ignored her, glanced at the menu and said, "How do jalapeno poppers and bean and cheese taquitos sound?"

Chloe sat back in her own stool when she realized she wasn't going to get a reaction from Nick.

"Delicious," I answered enjoying Nick ignoring Chloe. The bartender came over and Nick ordered the appetizers and a Budweiser. I decided to get a Coke as I'd gotten a little tired while we were driving and thought a shot of caffeine would do me good. Nick and I looked at each other; we were both uncomfortable talking to each other with all the listening ears sitting so close. His beer and my Coke came; we smiled at each other and took a drink. I remembered then what Edna had told me and I turned to Chloe. "I hear you and Brian Bozeman had a disagreement the other day."

"What are you talking about?" She asked with suspicion.

"Edna told me she saw you get out of Brian's pickup last week and the two of you had an argument," I said, apologizing in my mind to Edna for bringing her name into this.

"Oh, it was nothing. He was giving me a ride and made a rude comment," Chloe answered being evasive.

"I don't think so. It sounded to Edna like you were trying to get in on some business deal he had going, and he wasn't interested in sharing."

Chloe leaned over me again, making sure her cleavage was showing as she addressed Nick, "Why are you hanging around with this buzz kill? I could show you a lot more fun."

I didn't like her very much before, and the way she was acting had me disliking her even more, so I decided to keep pressing her. I raised my voice, "Should I tell the sheriff you and Brian had something going on? I'm sure he'd like to know if you have some insight into what happened between the coach and Brian."

She glared daggers at me, but she settled back onto her own stool and hissed, "You better not talk to the sheriff about me, and keep your voice down."

"You could tell me what was going on," I answered her.

She chewed on her lip while she considered what to tell me, I kept staring at her. She looked like she was debating with herself and said, "Coach Janning wasn't the fine upstanding citizen everyone thought he was."

"What does that mean?" I asked her, feeling like I might be getting somewhere.

"Why aren't you questioning Brian about this?" She studied me for a few seconds, and then laughed, "You're scared of him aren't you? Some detective you are."

"Did Brian have proof of the coach doing something?" I pushed her hoping she would verify what I suspected.

"I don't know what he had," she admitted. "He picked me up last week because he said he wanted to take me out."

"He is married, you know." I instantly regretted saying anything as now she might clam up.

She surprised me and continued, "He was the one who asked me. I wasn't trying to take him away from his wife. Anyway, he wanted to ask me if I was one of the girls who had a crush on the coach," she paused, "I told him we all did. No big deal."

"So why were you so mad at him?"

"I told him to leave the coach alone. He was only in town for a short time and didn't need to be harassed by Brian. When I suggested I was going to let the coach know Brian was trying to cause him trouble in case he wanted to leave town, Brian got weird, he grabbed my arm and told me it would be the last thing I did if I messed up his chance to fix things with his family. I imagine that's what Edna saw."

"And you backed off? That doesn't sound like you."

"To be frank, he scared me. I decided my life was worth more than getting on Brian's bad side. It looks like I was right. The coach must have fought back and died for his efforts. That's all it was, so it's nothing you need to involve me with the sheriff for." She grabbed her purse and flounced off.

I turned and looked at Nick.

"It's never boring around you," he smiled.

"I'm sorry," I said.

"Don't be sorry, you're trying to help Marcy. I admire you for sticking your neck out. You're a good person; nosy and not scared of putting yourself in danger, but a good person."

I felt myself blush, thankful the bartender showed up with our appetizers. We dug in and conversation stopped. Several people got called to their tables while we ate. After we finished the appetizers, I said, "Maybe the poppers were a bad choice for our breath."

"Is there a reason we need to worry about our breath?" Nick asked with an exaggerated leer.

I blushed and answered vaguely, "Maybe." We finished our drinks while we visited with a little more freedom now that we had some privacy. I was pleased we found a lot in common to talk about without even once discussing the farm. Our table opened up and we moved into the dining room without missing a beat in our conversation. It was an enjoyable evening and by the time we had finished eating I was surprised to see it was almost 10:00 p.m. and the restaurant was closing. Best of all, I had managed to keep from telling him about James planning to propose to Jessica. We walked out to his pickup, hand in hand.

"Thanks for the nice evening," I said to Nick as he opened the pickup door for me.

"I enjoyed it too," he answered, and then bent down to kiss me.

We stopped when we heard applause and looked over to see someone standing by the trash bin with a bag of garbage grinning at us. We laughed and got into the pickup.

As we pulled out of the parking lot, Nick asked, "Do you want to talk about it?"

"We've been talking all night, what specifically are you talking about?" My heart sank, thinking he was going to bring up his trip away, and while I would love to know what was going on in his personal life, I didn't want to ruin our evening.

I was relieved when he said, "The stuff you talked to Chloe about. Do you think it is possible Brian knew something about Coach Janning?"

"I do. According to Frankie, George had proof of the coach cheating, and I can see Brian using that to embarrass the coach if he knew about it, but it can't have been enough of a reason to kill someone."

"The coach may have assaulted George to get that evidence back, as he wouldn't have wanted the town to know about it." Nick said, stating the obvious.

"If only George would wake up and tell us. I'm positive it was either the coach or Brian, but there has to be something more." I responded feeling frustrated, knowing I had to talk to Brian. "I don't feel like I'm getting anywhere as most of the people I suspect could be involved are all people who hated Brian not the coach."

"Like who?" Nick asked.

"Marcy's brother, Steve, hated how Brian treated Marcy. Paul Olson from the theater had a reason to want Brian dead as Brian was trying to get rid of him as the football coach. Tom Hartz has no love for Brian, Chloe too as I'm sure she wasn't telling us the whole truth, even Mark Carboot was seen arguing with Brian."

"It sounds like you have quite a few possibilities," Nick said after pausing a few minutes.

"I know, but none of them make sense from the standpoint of the coach being the intended victim."

"Well, we know the coach was meeting with Brian, maybe whoever it was, hit Brian and when the coach showed up they killed him thinking they killed Brian so they had to kill the coach too."

"Doubtful. Steve said he saw the coach arrive and meet with Brian, so it would be awful poor timing to kill the coach for something with Brian present. Beat up Brian in the heat of the moment, but kill the coach too. I just can't see it." I thought for a few minutes and then blurted, "Maybe Coach Janning did beat up Brian, and whoever had a beef with the coach happened along and took advantage of the situation. I imagine if the coach knocked out Brian he wouldn't have been paying attention to anyone getting close to him. Either way, I know I'm being nosy but I want to know what Brian thought the coach had done or was doing. It has to be why the coach was killed."

"Does this guy have a first name? All I have ever heard anyone say is 'the coach.'"

I laughed. "If he does I've never heard it."

"So what's your next step going to be?"

"I've been avoiding it, but I need to talk to Brian."

"Would you like me to come with?" Nick asked.

"I would love it, but I need to face him on my own. I also need to talk to Mr. Kleb. He was there if he saw Charlie running away, and maybe he saw something or someone else."

"Don't you think the sheriff asked him?"

"I'm sure he did, but I doubt the sheriff will tell me, and in addition I don't want to aggravate him by asking. It'll be easier to ask Mr. Kleb myself. Mr. Fenmore has alluded to knowing something about the coach and I need to talk to Chloe again, but I doubt I'll get anything out of her until I have something to hold against her."

"Maybe you could get James to talk to her," Nick said with a grin.

"That would be a good plan if I want to lose Jessica as my best friend."

The drive home had gone by too fast. Nick pulled into my yard and parked in front of the house. Tabitha was waiting for me on the front steps and I could hear Wizard barking in the backyard. Dad must be home. "Tomorrow night is Halloween. Dad and I hand out candy at the seed plant."

"Why there?" Nick asked.

"We never get any trick-or-treaters here. We're too far off the beaten path. But the seed plant is closer to town at six miles and the locals have gotten used to us being there. We get quite a few kids, and we give away a good haul of candy to each kid. It's kind of fun if you want to join us?"

"I will. Is it okay if I contribute to the candy stash? I did buy some in case anyone showed up at my place, but I'm farther out of town than your place and if you don't get anyone, I doubt I will."

"Dad has a bunch already, but it never hurts to have more."

"I'll see you tomorrow," Nick said as we exchanged a long kiss goodnight.

I floated into the house, not even noticing Tabitha scurrying in the door ahead of me. Dad was letting Wizard in through the kitchen door, I said goodnight to him, and floated up the stairs.

CHAPTER SIXTEEN

A thick stand of switchgrass makes excellent winter wildlife cover because of its ability to remain in an upright position when covered with snow or ice.

I WOKE UP SMILING. I SPENT A FEW MINUTES lounging in bed thinking happy thoughts about last night before I realized there was no noise coming from downstairs. Dad must have left for church. On Sunday mornings he and Karla would have breakfast together at her place and ride together to church. I got up, took a leisurely shower, found an outfit to wear to church, then packed some clothes in a bag to change into as right after church I'd have to check the Gruber's out of the cabin and clean it. Dad had left a note on the kitchen table for me, saying he had fed Wizard and as the day was so nice he'd left him outside. Taking care of Wizard wasn't a lot of extra work, but it would be nice when Kirk got back to take over. I looked out the window; the puddles from yesterday had dried up emphasizing again how dry it was. I saw Wizard circling a tree that a chattering squirrel was in. I left him to it, and sat down to eat a bowl of cereal and some toast with peanut butter. I enjoyed having Dad around, but sometimes it was nice to have the house to myself. I worked on the crossword puzzle in the paper for a few minutes before checking the clock and realizing it was time to get going. I let Wizard back in, he had given up on the squirrel and was laying by the door panting from the exertion of squirrel hunting. I made sure he had water and left for church.

It was hard to believe it was Halloween as most years it wasn't uncommon to have snow on the ground and twenty degree temperatures. The kids were going to have a fun night not having to battle snow and freezing temperatures. Dad, Karla, James, and Jessica were already in a pew and moved over for me when I joined them. The pastor must have had a yearning to get outside and enjoy the unexpected nice fall day as his sermon was fifteen minutes shorter than normal. I had a few minutes to visit with James and Jessica before I had to change clothes in the bathroom and leave for the cabin. It was difficult to refrain from saying anything to Jessica, but James hovered close knowing how difficult it would be for me to say quiet.

Jessica said, "I know you are trying to sneak out, but you had a date last night and you're not leaving until you tell me some details."

I laughed and said, "All you need to know is it was a wonderful night. Besides, I don't have time to share any details as I have to go and check the Gruber's out of the cabin."

"I can help you clean when I'm done at the restaurant." she offered.

"No, you enjoy your day." I would have appreciated the help but I knew I couldn't let myself be alone with her or I'd end up spilling the beans about James' plan to propose. "Are you and James doing anything for Halloween?"

"He's going to help hand out candy at my house tonight. What about you?"

"Dad, Nick, and I are going to hand out at the seed plant, but I do need to get going. I'll talk to you later." The extra time to visit made me almost late to the cabin. I made up a few minutes by taking a shortcut that involved a pot-holed rough gravel road. I got there as Roy and Sue Gruber were putting a suitcase in their vehicle. I got out and ran to help them.

"Did you have a good visit?" I asked as I helped with another bag that felt like it was camera equipment.

"We did," Roy said with enthusiasm.

"It was so peaceful," Sue said. "We were too late in the year for a lot of many different varieties of birds, but with most of the leaves gone we got some fabulous pictures of eagles. We spent about an hour yesterday evening watching two elk and took a lot of pictures of them also."

"The rain yesterday didn't ruin the weekend for you?" I asked.

"Absolutely not," Sue replied. "I think all the wildlife were so thankful for the rain, we saw more than we would have as they were out and about enjoying the moisture."

"The first night we were here the wolves howled for part of the night. It was very eerie, but beautiful," Roy added.

"What is that beautiful, golden-brown tall grass? It glowed when the sun was setting," Sue wondered.

"There are a couple different species. I'm guessing you are referring to either big bluestem or indiangrass."

"Well, it was something to see, and beautiful when those elk came walking out of it. I can't wait to print out the pictures," Sue Gruber said, looking happy.

"I'm glad you enjoyed your stay. As our first guests I'd like to pick your brain for a couple minutes. Is there anything you can think of that would have made your stay more comfortable or worthwhile? And please, be honest, I want this to be an enjoyable experience for our guests."

They looked at each other.

"Please let me know if there is something," I said again.

Roy said, "I can't think of anything."

Sue offered, "The only thing I can think of was an extra blanket would be nice. I know you supply one for the beds, but an old one that could be used on the porch would be useful. It got cold last night after the rain and when we sat outside on the porch to watch the elk we got chilly."

"That can be taken care of easy enough. Is there anything else?"

"More of the delicious food," Roy said.

"Oh no, I'm sorry, wasn't there enough?" I asked feeling awful.

"Don't let him worry you," Sue laughed. "There was plenty, in fact the leftovers are being taken home for supper tonight. He's teasing you. But please tell whoever made the food it was delicious."

"I will pass it on. Is there anything else I can do for you?" I asked as I put their last bag in the car.

"Reserve us a spot next fall please," they both said.

I laughed, "I have your email on file and will send you some dates to choose from."

"That sounds wonderful," Sue said and they got into their car, waved, and drove away.

I walked back into the cabin and opened the windows to air it out a little with the weather so nice. It didn't take much time to clean as the Gruber's were very neat people. I stripped off the sheets, grabbed the towels and washcloths, bundled them up, and took them out to the car. I'd have to remember to get them washed and brought back out here in the next day or two. I scrubbed the bathroom and kitchen area, washed the floor, gathered up the garbage, locked the doors, and drove home. It was already 2:00 p.m. I had missed dinner and I was starving. As I sat at the stop sign before turning out on the main highway my phone rang.

It was Frankie and she excitedly told me, "George woke up!"

"That's wonderful news. Do you think I can talk to him?"

"I'll check with the hospital and get back to you."

"Great, and Frankie, you need to make sure he talks to the sheriff too."

"Believe me I will. I'll drive him there myself if I have to."

I called Jessica at once. Phyllis answered and said Jessica was busy. I convinced her it was important and Jessica wouldn't mind

being interrupted. I was correct; she squealed with joy and said
she'd head to the hospital right after work to see him. I cautioned
her to check with Frankie or Karen first, as Frankie was going to
ask the hospital when I could see him.

I had just put my phone back on the console in my pickup
when it rang again. "Hello." I answered, not looking at the caller ID
before I picked up.

"You mentioned that you'd like to talk to Brian," Marcy whispered. "I thought I'd let you know he's going to be home all day."

"I'll be there in five minutes." I turned my pickup around and
drove to Marcy's not giving myself any time to change my mind.
Of course that worked against me, as when I pulled up in front of
her house and saw Brian working on repairing the garage door I
realized I hadn't prepared any questions. I braced myself, got out of
the pickup, and walked up the driveway.

Brian saw me, put down his cordless drill and said, "What are
you doing here Carmen? Marcy is in the house."

"I came to talk to you, not her."

"Is that right, what could you possibly want to talk to me about?
Oh, let me guess, I've heard around town that you fancy yourself a
sleuth, so I imagine you want to ask me about the coach's murder.
You're too late, I already told the sheriff everything I know; you'll
have to go talk to him." He sneered at me.

"I already did, and he doesn't believe you told him the truth at
all. In fact it's looking more and more like you are the only person
with any reason to kill the coach. After all you've been running
around town hinting that the coach has something in his past that
you were going to expose," I said lying to him as he had succeeded
in getting under my skin as he always could. "I think you made it
up. What, were you jealous of all the girls having crushes on him
in high school, or was it that he was revered by the town while
everyone can't stand you?"

"You don't know what you're talking about." Brian stepped
toward me.

I held my ground and pushed, "Why don't you tell me what you know? You know you're bursting to let someone know what was so terrible about the coach, and now you won't be able to announce it at the ceremony and prove you were better than the coach."

He paused, and then unable to help himself he said, "I overheard George talking to the coach when we were fixing George's house. Apparently the coach cheated to win that championship game and George said he had a recording. I searched his house when I was working there alone one day and found it. He hadn't even tried to hide it, just had it sitting under his television with the rest of his junk. He even had it labeled. I was going to tell everyone at the induction ceremony." He stopped talking and looked at me, then said, "I do feel bad for taking it, as I'm sure the coach is who assaulted him trying to get it back and poor George didn't have it anymore."

"I already knew about the cheating but I don't think that's everything. You know something else too, don't you? Did you see anyone else when the coach was killed? Did you see who knocked you out? I hope you aren't trying to blackmail a killer."

"The last thing I remember was the coach hitting me. That's all I have to say Carmen. I heard George is awake; you need to talk to him. Chloe has a story to tell too, heck you might even want to talk to Paul Olson."

"Did you see who hit you?" I repeated.

"That's all I'm saying." He picked up his drill and walked in the garage.

Marcy had been sitting on the steps about forty feet away, waiting for us to get done talking. She walked up to me and asked, "Did you learn anything from him?"

"I'm not sure. He suggested I talk to Chloe, Paul, and George. Oh no, what time is it?" I asked.

"It's 4:30 p.m." Marcy answered.

"I have to get going. I need to change into my costume and meet Dad and Nick at the seed plant to hand out candy. I waved goodbye as I raced to my pickup. Frankie called as I was driving and told me I could meet with George tomorrow morning. I flew into our yard, startling Tabitha who had been sunning herself in the last rays of the late afternoon sun on a bench by the garage and raced into the house pulling off my clothes and changing into the witch costume I wore every year, as fast as I could. The one update I'd made this year was buying a new hat. Wizard had gotten a hold of last years. Thinking of him made me realize he wasn't around. Dad must have taken him with to the seed plant. I hope he remembered to grab Wizard's doggy devil costume. I had forgotten to look for it earlier and I didn't have time now. I made myself a peanut butter and jelly sandwich and took a few minutes to apply some green makeup to my face and hands, did a final check in the mirror, and rushed back out to my pickup.

Dad and Nick were handing candy to a family with a little cowboy and a Superwoman when I drove in. I laughed when I saw Nick's costume as I drove by and parked around the corner of the seed plant. I came in the back door and was greeted by Wizard wagging his tail and looking proud in his devil costume.

"It's about time you got here," Dad said taking off his Frankenstein mask so he could talk without his voice being muffled.

"As usual I got delayed. Most important Frankie called and told me George was awake."

"That's great news," Dad said.

"It is." I looked around. "It looks like Phil and Sam cleaned up or did you guys have to do it?"

"It was all picked up and swept when we got here." Dad answered.

"Have I missed many kids?" I asked.

"No, that was the first car," Dad answered. "Nick brought lots of candy too, so be very generous when you hand it out."

"Will do," I said as I adjusted my hat.

Nick walked up to me and said, "You should have added a wart, the green paint isn't enough to make you sell the witch look."

"Wait till you get to know her longer," Dad said walking by us on his way back to the door to watch for kids.

"Thanks Dad," I yelled after him. He ignored me and kept walking.

"It's clear you have no insecurities about your appearance." I said looking over his costume which consisted of a white sheet wrapped around him, green rubber gloves, black rubber boots, and he'd made his hair stand straight up with a streak of green color running through it. "What are you supposed to be?" I asked laughing.

"Hold on." He ran to the front of the building and came back holding a beaker which he held up and said, "Now what do you think I am?"

I cocked my head and stared at him for a few seconds and a light bulb went off in my brain, "A mad scientist."

"Correct, although I'm disappointed you had to have assistance to figure it out," he said with a grin.

"I think I was blinded by the green hair." We heard the squeal of kids and Dad made a groaning sound. "It sounds like we're up," I said as I grabbed a bowl of candy and cackled my way to the front while Nick walked beside me yelling, "Eureka!"

We had a steady procession of vehicles for the next four hours. It was a good thing Nick brought candy as I don't think we'd ever had this many kids before. We must have pulled some from neighboring towns as I didn't think we even had that many kids living in Arvilla. When it slowed and we hadn't had a vehicle for twenty minutes I looked over at Dad who was sitting in a chair eating the last candy bar and at Nick whose hair was no longer sticking straight up. "I think it's safe to lock the door and head home. We can set the bucket, which only has a couple handfuls of suckers left, outside and they can help themselves if there are any stragglers."

"That sounds good to me," Dad said. "I think next year you can do this by yourselves. It's getting to be a bit too much work for me."

Nick looked at me worried, "Don't listen to him," I said. "He says that every year, and then he's the first one to start planning it again." I sat down to help myself to a mini box of Dots I had saved for myself.

Nick started to shut off the lights. I finished my last Dot candy, put the chairs away and swept up the gravel that had been drug in the door by the kids coming in and out. I grabbed the bucket of suckers and walked to the door with Dad. He got into his pickup and left. Nick joined me after shutting off the last light. I locked the door and set the bucket where it was visible, but high enough to keep it away from any animals that might wander by.

"That was fun," Nick said.

"Tiring; but yes, it is fun." I answered leaning on him, dislodging my witch hat.

Nick caught my hat, looked at me and said, "I may have kissed a witch or two in my life, but never one that admits to it."

I laughed and said, "Well I guess you don't need to kiss this one."

"I think I will anyway." He bent his head, kissed me and if I would have had curled up witch boots my toes would have matched the boots.

"That was nice," I said when we stopped.

"Yes it was," he sighed and held me close.

I pulled away with reluctance. "I'd better head home."

I kissed Nick goodbye and we both got in our pickups and drove away. Dad was already in bed when I got home. I took a quick shower, getting rid of the green on my face and hands, and fell asleep the minute I hit the bed.

CHAPTER SEVENTEEN

*Native prairie plant seeds can lie dormant for more than fifty years,
until the soil and climate conditions allow the plants to grow.*

THE ALARM WAS NOT A WELCOME SOUND when it went off
Monday morning two hours earlier than my normal time to
get up, but I wanted to make sure I had enough time at the seed
plant before I went to talk to George at the hospital. I shocked
myself when I managed to make a breakfast that would be waiting
for Dad when he woke. True, it was just frozen caramel rolls that I
got from Edna's bakery, but I did have to rush downstairs and stick
them in the oven before getting dressed, which was an accomplish-
ment at that time of the morning for me. I made sure I had enough
to bring to Phil and Sam and was packing them in a container
when Dad came in the kitchen.

"Something smells good," he said going straight to the coffee pot.

"Caramel rolls were calling to me this morning; hard to believe
my body wants more sugar after feeding it so much last night," I
answered.

"Are you going to the seed plant right away this morning?" Dad
asked.

"Yes, the seed plant was all cleaned up, so the guys must have finished the blue grama and the prairie blazing star on Friday. It's time to get started on the leadplant." I enjoyed cleaning leadplant, but this year would be a little tricky as with the drought, I'd been reluctant to use any herbicides for weed control in case I damaged the crop. The roguers, our summer hand weeding crew, had gone through the field but wild buckwheat came out of nowhere right before harvest. It would take time and some lost crop to get the mill set correct. "I'm free this afternoon if you need help with something," I told Dad.

"I was hoping since cleaning the garage went so well, we could get to the little garden shed next. I'm having dreams of a decent garden this coming summer, and I need to take stock of what we even have."

"I can help you. You're not going to require my help for the actual garden are you?" I hated gardening with a passion. You wouldn't think someone who raised grasses and wildflowers would be so against gardening, but I despised it. I liked planting the garden and I liked eating the vegetables, but all the things that came in between, like watering, weeding, harvesting, and processing the vegetables were not anything I enjoyed.

"Don't worry, it will be my own project," Dad answered with a smile.

"Okay. I'll be home for dinner and we'll work on it after that." I grabbed my container of caramel rolls and walked out the door.

When I arrived at the seed plant I grabbed the seed cleaning notes to see what we had done last year for mill settings. I tried to write down the settings each year; they could vary from year to year, depending on the growing conditions, but it gave me starting point. It was nice to work without anyone here, while Phil and Sam were excellent, it went faster if I had no distractions. All I had left was to turn on the mill when I heard a noise and looked out the window. It was Sam driving in pulling a wagon of seed. I opened the overhead door for him and he backed up to the conveyor.

"I thought I beat everyone to work," I said to him when he got out of his pickup.

"I couldn't sleep and decided I might as well load a wagon of leadplant."

"Perfect timing, the mill is ready," I told him. We got the seed moving into the conveyor, turned on the mill and as it ran I watched the flow, grabbing a handful of seed every so often and checking to see if any weed seeds where coming through, I also checked the waste wagon to make sure too much good seed wasn't getting cleaned out. I stopped the mill a couple times, made some adjustments, and by the time Phil showed up the seed mill was running smooth.

"Good morning Phil. I put some caramel rolls by the front door for you whenever you'd like one."

"You never told me that," Sam said in mock outrage.

"Sorry, I forgot. Go help yourselves."

"Thanks," Phil answered. "How long have you been here?"

"An hour or so, I won't be around much this morning so I wanted to make sure the mill was running for you. Sam also came early and loaded a wagon of seed."

"How does the seed look? I know this is one of our more high value crops and with the drought I wasn't sure what kind of quantity you'd get."

We sold seed based on pure live seed rather than bulk. Sometimes the seed quantity of your harvest could be a lot, but once you start cleaning it, you find out that a lot of it is dead. "It looks okay. I'd estimate it at about 80% of last year's crop, which isn't too bad for the growing season we had." We spent the next hour doing a few minor tweaks and got two forty pound bags cleaned and sewed up. Some crops were faster than others at cleaning, but leadplant went slow. Sam left to load another seed wagon for us after eating two of the caramel rolls.

I checked my watch and decided I'd better get going if I was going to meet Frankie at the hospital in Parkville. I said goodbye to Phil and snagged a caramel roll for the drive.

I met Frankie in the lobby and she told me the sheriff was here too, but she and George had told him they wanted to wait until I got there so George would only have to go through it once. I wasn't looking forward to the sheriff's reaction to that. We rode the elevator up together. "How is he?" I asked her as we walked down the hallway to his room.

"He's got a terrible headache, but otherwise doing well; the doctors expect he'll make a full recovery."

"That's wonderful!" I responded as we walked in George's room. The sheriff was standing next to George's bed, arms crossed, glaring at me as I sat down in one of the chairs on the other side of the bed. George looked so bedraggled with a pile of bandages swathing his head I couldn't help but hug him, shocking both of us.

"I'm so glad you are okay."

"Thanks Carmen, so am I." He winced as he resettled himself on the bed.

The sheriff cleared his throat, "As touching as this is, I've waited long enough. What happened to you?"

George focused on the ceiling and said, "As you know, I'm a shy person. I enjoy being around people, but I'm not good at interactions. Anyway, I became the manager of the football team and other than a couple of the guys giving me grief, Brian in particular, I enjoyed it. The coach was a great guy which was why I was so shocked by what I witnessed one night when I stayed late after practice, taking advantage of the quiet locker room to get some homework done." He shifted in the bed again. "When I left I heard voices under the bleachers. I wandered over there to see what was going on. I was curious when I saw Coach Janning talking to the coach of the team we were playing that week for the championship game to go to state. I crept closer and was astounded when I heard them talking about the upcoming game. I don't why, intuition I guess, but I started my tape recorder and caught Coach Janning threatening to tell the other coach's wife about his affair unless he made sure they lost to us on Friday night. I had hoped what I witnessed was wrong, but when we as the underdogs easily won that Friday, I knew the coach had destroyed any admiration I had for him. Callie Fenmore, Billy's mom, was my best friend at the time." He looked down at his hands, "That's kind of a lie, she was my friend; I wanted to be her boyfriend, but she, like most of the girls had a crush on the coach. Being selfish I told her what the coach had done, hoping she would lose her adoration of him and think of me as a boyfriend. It didn't work."

"She didn't believe you?" I asked interrupting him.

"She believed me, it just didn't matter. The coach's wife had just died, making him even more attractive to teenage girls as he grieved."

"This is a nice story, but who came in your house and assaulted you?" The sheriff asked making it clear he was getting impatient.

George sighed and said, "The coach shocked everyone and resigned after the football season, I assumed he wanted a fresh start after losing his wife, but then about a month after he was gone, Chloe Johnson and Callie found me. Callie was pregnant and the coach was the father. Callie and Chloe were cheerleaders and at the banquet they held for the team after winning the championship, Callie stayed to help the coach clean up and he gave her a ride home, as they were neighbors. I don't know if the coach was grieving, if Callie threw herself at him, or a combination of both, but for whatever reason they slept together. I assumed that was what made him resign, he was getting out of town before anyone found out what he had done, or maybe Callie told him about my recording. Anyway when the girls told me about the pregnancy, they swore me to secrecy and asked me to keep the recording safe. Callie was going to raise the baby herself and didn't want anyone to know who the father was."

"Why did she want it kept a secret?"

"For two reasons, first the coach had always wanted kids and he and wife were unable to have any. Callie was sure the coach would demand custody; she knew when he left after they had sex that she meant nothing to him. She wanted to raise her child and didn't want to risk losing it."

"He wouldn't have dared; she was a minor and he took advantage of her."

"She had just turned eighteen when it happened. She was also scared her parents wouldn't let her keep the baby if they knew the coach was the father. Her father hated the coach, she never knew why, but he is a stern man and she was convinced his dislike of the coach would make him force her into giving the baby up for adoption. They asked me to keep the recording safe to use as blackmail to ensure if the coach ever returned to Arvilla he could be forced to leave. Callie didn't want him to ever encounter her child and recognize him either by appearance or by figuring out the child's age. Callie gave birth to Billy, died in the car accident, and her parents took over raising Billy. They are a happy family and the only parents Billy has ever known. So when I heard the coach was coming back for the induction ceremony, I called him to tell him about the recording and suggested he not return. It didn't work, and what was worse he saw Billy at the corn maze Sunday and did put two and two together; they both have the same dimple. I'm sure he recognized himself in Billy. He came to my house that night, angry. He demanded I give him the recording and told me he was going to pursue custody of Billy. He was furious he'd had a child all these years that he hadn't known about. I couldn't find the recording, he didn't believe me, we struggled, and he's the one that hit me on the head with my serving dish." He stopped and touched his head. "The sad thing was; I did feel sorry for him. I would be mad too if I had a child out there somewhere that was being kept a secret from me."

There was silence in the room as we digested George's story until George said, "Frankie told me the coach is dead. Do you know who did it?"

"Not yet," the sheriff replied.

George paled; the sheriff noticed and asked, "Do you know who killed him?"

"I'm not positive, but if you have no other motive, Chloe was the only other person who knew the coach was Billy's father. Maybe she was protecting the Fenmore's?" He quit talking clearly dismayed at the thought of Chloe being responsible.

"It's something to consider, but we aren't sure if Brian or the coach was the actual target. I will be talking to her though." The sheriff looked at me and said sternly, "I will be talking to her, not you."

I held up my hands. "I understand, but just so you know if I run into her somewhere I won't be able to help myself. Also, you should know Brian told me he took the recording from George's house."

"It would have been smart of him to have mentioned that to me," the sheriff said shaking his head. "Please make sure you don't accidently run into Chloe on purpose." The sheriff started to walk out the door then turned and said, "Thank you for your time George, I'm glad you are doing better."

George was looking tired. I said, "I'd better get going too. Dad wants some help cleaning out a shed. For what it's worth, the evidence from the crime scene supports Brian's insistence that he didn't kill the coach, but who knows who else he might have told about the recording. Chloe isn't the only suspect; Brian told me I should talk to Paul Olson about the coach too. Do you have any idea why he would say that?"

"I have no idea." George responded.

I hugged George again, and left. In need of a friendly conversation I called Nick on the way home.

"How is George?" He asked when he answered the phone.

"Okay; and you don't have to give me grief about sharing information with the sheriff as he was there also." I proceeded to tell him what George had shared with us. I finished up with the sheriff's warning that I stay away from Chloe. I must have been talking fast as when I stopped I had to take a big breath and I heard Nick laugh.

"That was a lot of information in one burst but it sounds like the sheriff is trying to retain some semblance of control over the investigation," Nick said. "He doesn't know you well yet does he?"

I laughed and said, "I guess not. I better hang up; I'm on my way home for dinner now."

"Okay. I'll talk to you later," he said as he hung up.

Dad was eating a peanut butter and jelly sandwich when I walked into the kitchen. "Are you sick?" I asked him

"What do you mean?" he asked puzzled.

"A peanut butter and jelly sandwich is not the normal kind of dinner you eat."

"Oh," he laughed. "It sounded good for some reason. I think I'm stuffed from all the candy I ate last night and the caramel rolls this morning. Next year remind me to not eat so much candy."

"You say that every year," I told him as I prepared my favorite food in the world, over easy eggs and toast; quick and delicious.

"How did the visit with George go?" Dad asked.

Once again I related what George had told us.

Dad surprised me by saying, "I can understand wanting to get to know a son you never knew you had, but to pursue custody and rip a ten year old from the only home he's ever known, well maybe the coach dying wasn't such a bad thing." Then he shook his head and said, "Forget I said that, murdering someone is never justifiable. Are you ready to clean the shed?"

I cleaned up the kitchen and joined Dad and Wizard by the shed a couple minutes later. Dad had opened the shed door and it looked like a rake that was lying by his foot had narrowly missed hitting him when the door was opened. I peeked in and was stunned by the disarray of gardening tools inside.

"What happened in here?" I asked. We weren't the neatest people in the world, but not being able to walk into our buildings wasn't normal.

"Kirk," Dad answered and shook his head. "While I'm thankful he stepped up and did take care of most of the yard maintenance, I had no clue this was his idea of putting things away."

We emptied everything out of the shed. Along with a couple push mowers and weed whackers, we also found several bags of split-open potting soil, many broken handles, hoes, shovel and rakes ends with no handles, and even a couple bags of rotting leaves.

It took us the rest of the afternoon to finish cleaning the shed. When I called for Wizard I wasn't surprised when he came running from where I had stashed the bags of rotten leaves. He had found a way to get into one of the bags as he was covered with leaves and when I picked him up, he had the pervasive smell of mold emanating from him. "Oh crud, is there anything this dog doesn't like to roll in? I wish Frankie's mobile pet grooming business was operational."

"I'll get the water running in the bath tub," Dad said walking towards the bathroom.

I followed him holding a squirming, happy dog until I crossed the doorway of the bathroom and Wizard realized what the running water meant. I closed the door quick with my foot before he could escape from my arms. Dad grabbed him and put him in the tub. Of course my phone picked then to ring.

It was the sheriff letting me know he hadn't found Chloe yet. I got the feeling he was checking on me to make sure I wasn't hunting for her too. Wizard had calmed down in the tub so I left Dad washing him and walked out of the bathroom, closing the door behind me.

"Was there any other evidence found at the scene you haven't told me about?" I asked taking advantage of the sheriff calling me.

"There was a fingerprint on a board that was found lying by Brian. It may have been used to conk him on the head but it didn't match anyone in our system, which isn't surprising, unless they were employed by the government or been previously arrested. If we ever come up with a suspect we could check the fingerprint against that person, but other than Mr. Kleb we haven't had any other suspects to check it against. It could also just be a board too, there was nothing forensically tying it to Brian or the coach, plus there was a stack of lumber there. Who knows how many people might have handled the boards."

"The fingerprint didn't match Mr. Kleb."

"No. I didn't expect it too; it gave us another good reason to turn him loose."

"It doesn't sound like much progress has been made," I said dejected.

"I wouldn't say that," the sheriff said. "We now have a possible reason why the coach may have been the target; we know the coach was aware of the recording. We know Brian had it, which I guess is the reason why both Brian and the coach were at the same place. It would help if Brian was capable of telling the truth."

"I agree, and thanks for calling sheriff."

"I know you won't stay out of it, so I won't try telling you again to stay away from Chloe, but keep me informed if you find anything out."

"I will. Thanks again." I said smiling at the sheriff's contradiction of himself. Dad and a clean Wizard came out of the bathroom. While Dad fed Wizard I cleaned up the bathroom. I decided to swing by the shop and see if Nick needed any help. Sam and Phil must have been okay at the seed plant as there weren't any missed calls from them. I realized as I drove to the shop that I'd been so busy I had forgotten about James proposing tonight. He got a nice day for his plan to propose outdoors. I couldn't wait to hear from Jessica.

CHAPTER EIGHTEEN

Different species of grasshoppers and caterpillars feed on blades of Indian grass,
providing important food sources for upland game birds and song birds.

NICK WAS WALKING OUT OF THE shop when I pulled up. I rolled down my window and asked, "Are you done for the day?"

"Yes." Nick walked up to my pickup, "Do you want to catch a bite to eat somewhere?"

"Sure, where should we go?"

"How about you hop in my pickup? We'll go through the drive-through at the Dairy Queen and then over to the park in town to eat. It's a nice evening and I've been stuck in the shop all day."

"It has been quite a day," I agreed. I got in Nick's pickup, but when we pulled up to the Dairy Queen we were dismayed by the amount of cars in the drive-through lane. "Should we go somewhere else?" I asked him.

"Let's try the grocery store. I could go for some of their fried chicken. They have a good selection of sides in their deli don't they?"

"They do, and their potato salad is awesome. Sometimes the chicken sells out, but it is early. Let's try it." I called Dad to tell him

I wouldn't be home for supper, but I could bring him something later if he wanted.

"Did he want anything?" Nick asked when I hung up.

"No, he's going to Karla's for supper," I answered, "but he did say Kirk will be home sometime Friday afternoon."

"They finished their record?"

"I guess so. We should have some sort of party for the band on Friday night. Would you be available?"

"Sure, do you want help with anything?"

"I need to think about it some more and see if Jessica can help with food." Thinking of Jessica made me remember her and James again. It's fortunate we were eating at the park in town and not the state park or we'd run into them. It was killing me not to tell Nick but I decided it wasn't my news to share and I'd better keep quiet. I continued, "I think if I can pull something off, maybe you could help by getting Kirk out of the house in the late afternoon once he's home so I can decorate."

"That might be difficult, it's not like we have much in common that he won't be suspicious if I try to get him to do something. Why don't you do it at the shop? I can work on cleaning it up this week."

"That would work better. I'll be able to help too."

By then Nick had arrived at the grocery store and parked. There weren't many people in the parking lot which was a good sign. There were only two people ahead of us in line at the deli section and from what I could see there was plenty of chicken left. Paul Olson got in line behind us. I debated with myself and then turned around.

"Hi Paul, It was good news to hear George was awake and okay."

"It was. Karen was so relieved."

Deciding it wasn't my place to tell George's story to his brother-in-law I changed the subject, "How is the football season going this year, it must be playoff time?"

"It hasn't been the best season, we might get past our first play-off game, but I don't expect we'll get much farther."

"It was terrible to hear what happened to Coach Janning. Did you know him well?"

"No," he answered looking nervous.

"I was talking to Steve Crumpet the other day," I lied, "and he was telling me about the damage that was done to his house from the wind storms. Don't you live close by him? Did your house have any damage?" By this time Nick was looking at me strange, no doubt wondering what I was up to.

"Yeah, we lost some shingles, and a tree limb went through a window."

"Did you have MM construction fix things too?"

"Yes. They did most of the repairs on our street."

"Did Brian cause you any problems?" I asked.

"No, when I found out he was working for them I made sure I was gone whenever they were at my house. I didn't want any dealings with him."

"You don't like him too much do you?"

"I don't think anyone does, other than Marcy, and I heard even she was sick of him and thinking about getting a divorce. Why are you asking?"

"I heard Brian knew something about the coach and he was going to use it to discredit him at the Hall of Fame induction ceremony. When I talked to him about the coach he indicated you knew something about the coach also. I guess I'm trying to find out if Brian knew what he was talking about or if he was trying to divert attention from himself to you?"

Paul looked panicked and then ignoring my question said, "If Brian were dead I could understand questioning me, after all he was a pain in my butt. I had to go to the school board to get him banned from the football practices. Not that it's any of your business but I was on my way to an escape room with my kid and a couple of his friends that night. I remember as I'm also a paramedic and I had my phone on mute during the evening so I missed the call."

He sounded genuine, and the fact he wasn't in town the night of the murder meant I had to remove him from my mental list of suspects, which made sense as I was going to have to give up on thinking Brian was the target and Paul had no interaction with the coach I was aware of. "I'm sorry for bugging you," I apologized.

Paul started to turn around, his shoulders dropped; he turned back to me and said, "I may as well tell you, I'm sure you'll find out anyway. Coach Janning was married to my aunt. He didn't treat her well but as I said before I was with my son that night. Brian has always been a jerk, and I'm confident he killed the coach even if the sheriff doesn't think so."

It was our turn at the deli counter. I apologized again to Paul, and Nick and I moved up to the counter to place our order. We ordered their eight piece chicken special with two sides. I selected potato salad and Nick chose coleslaw. After getting our supper handed to us, we turned to leave and Paul caught my arm.

He said, "If the sheriff is correct and Brian didn't kill the coach, Steve did have some sort of a past with the coach. I don't know what it was about, but I remember him being furious at the coach when we were in high school. In fact he hit the coach one time and was suspended from the team for two weeks. I never could figure out why the coach even let him back on the team. Maybe you should talk to him, he hated Brian too."

"Okay, thanks Paul. Good luck with the rest of the season."

While I was talking to Paul, Nick had grabbed silverware and napkins for us and asked "Do you think we should get some paper plates too?"

"I'll go find them if you want to grab us something to drink. There are small refrigerators by the checkouts. Would you get me a bottle of water while I find the plates? I'll meet you at the checkout." We parted ways. I found the plates and caught up with Nick as he was starting to pay.

"I'll get this," I said.

"Nonsense, call me old-fashioned, but I'm hoping this counts as a date and I pay for dates."

"Take him up on that," the girl running the checkout till said, "the guys my age expect everything to be Dutch treat."

I sighed, "Okay, I will."

I was quiet on the drive to the town park.

"At least you can cross a name off your suspect list," Nick offered, breaking the silence when we arrived at the park.

I sighed and replied, "I guess so." His comment snapped me out of my stupor. There were a few people walking around, enjoying one of the last nice fall days, but the picnic tables were empty. We sat down and hungrily dug in to the food.

"You were correct. The potato salad is awesome," Nick said.

"Eating here at the park was a good idea also," I mumbled through a mouthful of chicken. A puppy on a leash got away from a little girl who had been trying to walk it and came bounding over.

As she came running up to us I asked her, "Can I give him a piece of chicken as long as there isn't any bone in it?" It was hard to ignore the cute squirming body wagging its tail in front of me.

"That would be nice of you, but I'm not sure I'll be able to get him away from you if you do," she answered in a high pitched voice.

"We're finished anyway," I said, as I gave the pup a generous chunk of white meat, as we had plenty, due to Nick and me both preferring dark meat. We cleaned up our mess while she tried to pull the puppy away. He lost interest in us once we stuffed it all in the garbage can and they took off running across the park.

"Do you want to go for a walk?" Nick asked grabbing my hand.

"Yes, it's been a busy day. It would feel good to unwind for a bit. Dad has been on a cleaning spree as of late," I said and told him how we'd cleaned up the garden shed today. "All the cleaning turned out to be smart as we got rid of a lot of junk before the hoarder, Kirk, gets home." Nick laughed when I told him about Wizard getting into the rotten leaves. I did my best to avoid all talk of murder and focus on Nick and me, although I did check my phone discretely a couple times to make sure I hadn't missed a call from Jessica. We ambled around the park talking until it was too dark to see and then we walked back to the pickup.

"I hadn't realized how cold I got," I said when we got back into the pickup and Nick cranked the heater up.

"It appears winter is on its way," Nick said. "This will be my first winter here and I'm hearing lots of stories about how cold it can get from the locals. I'm not sure I believe them."

"What have you heard?" I asked while smiling, knowing no one would be lying to him, maybe exaggerating a bit, but not lying.

"Minus forty degrees Fahrenheit." Nick shook his head and said, "I don't want to believe that."

He looked so forlorn I couldn't help but laugh at him, "It isn't an everyday occurrence, but yes we have stretches of wind chills that cold for a couple weeks at a time, but the actual air temperatures are more like minus ten to minus seventeen. But again, it goes in streaks, we have plenty of winter days in the teens and twenties which is when we do most of our fun winter activities like snowmobiling, snowshoeing or ice fishing."

"I guess I'll have to get used to it, as I don't plan on moving anywhere else, unless there's a chance you'd like to move someplace warmer?" he asked.

I felt my cheeks turn red and then looked at him and said, "No, I guess if you're interested in me, you'll have to tolerate the cold."

"I'll get used to it," he said as he took my hand and held it the rest of the way back to the shop so I could get my pickup.

We kissed, and I left for home happy that Nick and I had been able to get away for some time together. The more time I spent with him, the more involved my heart was getting. Then I realized, who was I kidding? I had fallen hopelessly for him. Yes, I was bothered by him withholding things about his personal life from me, but as everyone kept telling me, I knew deep down he was a good, decent man and he would share when he could. Dad was letting Wizard in from the backyard when I walked into the kitchen. Tabitha must have just come in also as she was busy eating her dish of food. Wizard came over to me at once and started to jump up on me, which was strange as he normally didn't have this much affection for me. I was sure it was due to the smell of the puppy on me. After realizing I wasn't going to lift him up on my lap he gave up. I sat there a few minutes until I couldn't take it anymore and decided I had to tell someone, and as Dad was here, he got to hear about James planning to propose to Jessica tonight. Of course Karla had already told him, yet I was impressed I managed to hold it in as long as I did.

"It's going to get cold tonight," Dad said when we stopped talking about James and Jessica.

"Which reminds me; I'd better get the heat lamps plugged in for Clyde and the feral cat." I started to go back outside.

Dad stopped me when he said, "I did it when I got home from Karla's. It won't freeze tonight but you might want to pick up another heated water dish for them tomorrow. I couldn't find our old one anywhere, and I don't remember seeing it when we cleaned the garage."

"If my memory is correct, I think it quit working at the end of the winter last year, and I threw it." I said as I pushed Wizard down when he tried to jump on me again.

"Did you and Nick have a good night?" Dad asked.

"Yes."

"It looks like the chicken was good," Dad said smiling at me.

I looked down and realized I had chicken crumbs all over the front of my coat. "Nick could have said something, instead of letting me walk around the park all night looking like this. But it explains why Wizard is suddenly in love with me." I took off my coat and put it in the laundry room realizing the dirty laundry was overflowing.

"It looks like I'd better get a couple loads of laundry done tonight."

Dad peeked in the room and said, "It did get out of control. I can do it tomorrow."

"I'll do as much as I can tonight. I'm not tired and I'm hoping Jessica will call."

"I'm tired," Dad said. "I think I'll watch some television and if I fall asleep in the chair, just leave me."

"What about your neck?" I reminded him, knowing how sore he had been the last time he spent the night in his chair.

"I'll have to deal with the pain; sometimes it feels good to fall asleep in my chair."

Wizard followed him into the living room no doubt looking to enjoy Dad's lap. It was one of his favorite places to sleep. Tabitha joined me in the laundry room. She loved to sleep on top of the piles of clothes. I gave her a gentle shove, telling her, "I don't need cat hair on my clean clothes." She gave me a dirty look and went up the stairs no doubt to spread hair on my bedspread. I sorted the clothes and ended up with five piles. I stuck the first load in and then wondered what to do with myself while I waited. I decided to go upstairs and get the book I had been reading. When I reached my bedroom, to no surprise Tabitha was tucked up in ball on top of my bed, I gave her a kiss on her head and noticed the box of newspaper clippings I had saved from the garage. I decided to look through it while I waited for laundry. I carried the box back downstairs, put it on the kitchen table and pulled a garbage can close so I could throw away any clippings I didn't want to keep. It looked like they were from mine and Kirk's high school years with the most recent on top as most of them were clippings about Kirk. I set them aside for him to look at when he got home. I had forgotten most of the stuff Kirk and I had been involved in. Drama club, band, choir, and track for Kirk. Mine consisted of FFA, debate, knowledge bowl, and a few random clippings of my sad attempts at different sports. There were quite a few clippings of the published school board meeting minutes. Mom had been on the school board for a short time. I started to read through them wondering if there was ever any mention of Coach Janning. I heard the washing machine stop so I got up and put the load in the dryer and started the next washing machine load. I went back to the board meeting minutes and decided to arrange them in chronological order. It was interesting reading all the drama that a school dealt with over the years from teacher suspensions, hiring's, and parent complaints. I'm glad I had never been interested in being on the school board, which was logical as one should have a child in the school system to be on the school board. My next load finished. I checked the clock; it was late, almost 11:00 p.m. I wasn't tired and no word yet from Jessica, so I put in another load and kept reading through the minutes. I was starting to feel tired, and almost missed it the first time I read it, but then I stopped and read it again. There had been an incident the coach brought to the board concerning one of his players. He had found the player in possession of alcohol in the locker room; what's more the player was selling it to other underage players. When the coach confronted the player he was hit in the face, which is why law enforcement was brought in. The incident had been resolved, but the coach wanted the board to be aware of the situation. I'm sure the board minutes couldn't contain a minor's name but it had to be Steve. I imagine this was what Paul had referred to. I checked the other school board member names to see if anyone was alive or living around here to talk to them. Two were deceased but I was surprised to see Mr. Kleb's name as a school board member. I hadn't realized he and his wife had moved here that long ago. Maybe I could get on the school board some day as he wouldn't have had any kids in the school either. I decided I'd try and catch him at the library tomorrow. I put the clipping referencing the coach in an envelope to give to the sheriff. I threw the rest of them in the garbage where they joined my high school achievements or lack thereof. I stuck Kirk's pile on the dresser in his bedroom, finished another load of laundry, and looked to see if Dad was in his recliner yet. He must have moved to his bedroom at some point in the evening. Wizard was in his dog bed in the living room. He opened one eye at me as I tried to get him to go outside one more time. He wasn't interested, closed his eye, and curled up even tighter. I gave up, shut off the lights, and went upstairs to bed wishing Jessica would have called.

CHAPTER NINETEEN

Wild lupine is the sole host plant for the endangered Karner Blue butterfly.

DAD WAS GONE BY THE TIME I got up Tuesday morning. As I was pouring a bowl of cereal, I noticed a note he had left by the coffee pot. One of his buddies had suffered a heart attack in the middle of the night and his wife had called early this morning to ask Dad if he could check on their house and pets as they were at the hospital in Grand Forks, ND. That was too bad, it wasn't someone I was familiar with but I remember Dad mentioning him over the years. I think they had done more together as couples when mom was alive. Tabitha must have gone out with Dad when he left as I could see her outside watching the bird feeder, behind a flower pot thinking she was hidden. She came running when I opened to the door to let Wizard out. While he was taking care of his business I made sure they both had food and water, then let him back in after I had dressed. I looked around to make sure there was nothing sitting out that Wizard could destroy, picked up the envelope I had set aside for the sheriff, grabbed my keys, and took off.

I was a couple of miles from town when my phone rang. I checked the caller id before answering on the hands-free mode, it was Jessica at last. "Hello," I answered excited for what I knew she was going to tell me.

"James asked me to marry him!" she shrieked.

"Did you say yes?" I asked knowing full well she would have.

"Of course," she answered and proceeded to tell me all about it as I drove the rest of the way to town.

I didn't tell her I knew ahead of time and enjoyed listening to her as she told me all the details. When her words slowed, I interjected with an enthusiastic, "I'm so happy for you!"

"Thanks Carmen, I'm so excited and to make things even better George will be back next week! I need to get back to work, but I couldn't wait any longer to tell you about James and me." She hung up right as I pulled up in front of the Sheriff's Department.

The sheriff was in and the dispatcher took me right back to his office.

"Good morning Carmen," Sheriff Poole said as he looked up from a stack of papers on his desk. "We got a break in the case."

"That's great, what did you find out?"

"One of our deputies who's been here a while remembered we had Steve Crumpet's fingerprints on file from some of his youthful indiscretions."

"Wouldn't that be in a sealed juvenile file?" I asked interrupting him.

"It would have been had it ever gone to court, but the charges were dropped. We compared the fingerprints from the board found at the scene and he is a match."

"I thought you decided the fingerprint wasn't too great of a clue, as anyone could have handled those boards."

"Anyone from the lumberyard or MM construction," the sheriff said.

"It was a project on Steve's property. He could have many legitimate reasons to have handled the board plus I thought he had an alibi," I said wondering why I was defending him so hard when I thought he may be a suspect also.

"We haven't been able to verify his alibi yet. He's getting picked up as we speak and it may be he can explain about the board, but it's the first real lead we have, so I'm going to pursue it. What brings you by this morning?" he asked.

"Talking to Steve does tie in with what I was bringing you this morning," I said as I handed him the envelope. "It's a newspaper clipping of a board meeting where the coach explained to the board why he called law enforcement to deal with one of his players. I suspect it might be Steve. I'm going to talk to Mr. Kleb; he was on the school board when this happened. I want to see if he remembers this and if he can verify if it was Steve or not."

"Where did this come from?" Sheriff Poole asked.

I explained we had been cleaning and came across a box mom had kept newspaper articles in while she was alive. I went on, "You might want to question Paul Olson too. He is the one who told me about Steve and the coach having problems. Maybe he'll remember more if you talk to him."

"I'll talk to them both after I get done with Steve, if I need to."

As I left I passed a deputy escorting Steve into the building.

I decided to walk over to the library. I was confident Mr. Kleb would be there as Marcy had indicated he spent most of his days there. The library board had done an excellent job making the library such a welcoming place. I know there were many senior citizens that took advantage of the library as a social outing and took in many of the programs the board and she had started. Even Dad would go on occasion to hear a speaker or catch up on all the newspapers from around the area. Mr. Kleb was sitting at a table with a couple of other men quietly playing some sort of card game. I walked up to their table and waited until they had finished their hand. It looked like a serious game of Pinochle.

I tapped him on the shoulder. He hadn't seen me come in and was startled. "Can I interrupt your game for a bit, and ask you some questions?"

I didn't recognize the other men, but one of them looked up

and said, "It's okay by me, I need a restroom break anyway." The other men nodded in agreement.

Mr. Kleb followed me over to a couple chairs in a far off corner so we wouldn't disturb anyone with our talking.

"Is something wrong Carmen?" he asked.

"Dad and I cleaned out our garage a few days ago, and I came across a newspaper clipping my mom had kept from her time on the school board. I'd show it to you but I just came from dropping it off with the sheriff."

He was looking at me with curiosity. "I remember being on the board with your mother for a short time; what would the sheriff need school board minutes for?"

"It turns out Coach Janning had an altercation with one of his players causing law enforcement to be involved and he was at the board explaining it. I was wondering if you remembered the incident and if so, do you remember who the player was?"

He was quiet for awhile; I kept silent and let him think.

After a few minutes he said, "My memory isn't what it used to be. I think it was Marcy's brother, Steve. If I remember correctly he hit the coach. Does this have something to do with the murder? I know Marcy and Charlie aren't going to be able to get away from Brian until this is all cleared up, but I hope her brother isn't involved."

"Is that what made you confess to the murder, trying to help Marcy?" I asked.

"I'm sure the sheriff told you I'm dying."

"Yes, I'm so sorry."

"It's okay; I've lived a good life. I'd be lying if I didn't say that I'm scared of the pain. So far my medications are keeping the pain under control, but they tell me that won't last much more than another month. I'm trying to enjoy the time I have. When I saw Charlie running down the street that evening and then the next day when I heard what had happened I assumed Brian had killed the coach and somehow Charlie had fought with his dad. I wanted to protect Marcy and Charlie. I should have put two and two together when I had just seen Billy a couple blocks before. Those two boys are best friends and were being typical kids. They were only acting furtive because they had snuck out of their houses to meet each other."

"I knew Charlie snuck out to meet up with Billy, but what makes you think Billy had done the same?"

"I met up with his grandpa when I was close to my home. He was rushing around looking for Billy. He was very agitated, and said Billy had never snuck out before. Not like my cousin's two kids," Mr. Kleb said and laughed softly. "They must have ducked out of the house at least once a week when they were growing up. It about drove their parents crazy. Anyway," he stopped to catch his breath. "I'm sorry I don't remember more."

"You did great, I was almost positive it was Steve, and you helped confirm it," I said as I got up from the chair and then helped Mr. Kleb up. He was unsteady so I held his arm as we walked back to where he was playing cards. I said goodbye and walked out of the library.

I decided to take a few minutes and stop by to congratulate Jessica in person. The restaurant was quiet when I walked in. It must have been the lull between breakfast and dinner as there were only a few people in the restaurant lingering over their coffee. Jessica was sitting with Frankie and George in a booth. George's head was covered in a few less bandages than when I saw him earlier in the week.

"Good morning Jessica, George, and Frankie. It's so good to see you out of the hospital George. I didn't think they'd release you so soon."

He looked up and smiled, "They let me out this morning. I'm supposed to be home resting, but I talked Frankie into stopping by here first."

"We'd better get going now though," Frankie said as she helped George up.

"Thanks for the omelets," George said, "sure beats hospital food."

As they started to walk towards the door Jessica said, "I can't wait for you to come back to work George, but don't push it. I want you to make sure you are one-hundred percent recovered first."

George nodded and waved.

"Let me see your ring," I asked Jessica as I sat down in the booth next to her, the smile on her face even broader than normal. "Do you have a wedding date set?"

"No date set yet, but for sure next summer some time."

"I thought you wanted a winter wedding?" I asked astonished.

She giggled, "I did, but James acted so panicked, I decided a summer wedding would be beautiful too. It gives me more time to plan anyway, which he may regret. You will be my maid of honor won't you?"

"Of course, I'd be honored," I said. We spent the next few minutes talking about possible places to hold the wedding until I said, "I do need to get going, but I wanted to stop in and say congratulations again. Oh, yeah, I forgot to tell you Kirk and his band are coming home Friday and I want to have a surprise congratulations party for them. Could I hire you to provide the food?"

"You don't have to pay me Carmen. I'd be honored to do it." She answered in typical Jessica fashion.

"I'm paying, besides it won't be easy as we are hosting it at the shop and you'll have to haul all the food. Do you have any thoughts on what you could provide that wouldn't be too difficult?"

"Off the top of my head, I'm thinking spaghetti. Would that be alright?" she asked.

"Whatever is easiest for you will work for me."

"What would be easiest is if you held the party here. I've got the banquet room in back and then I wouldn't have to transport any food," she offered.

"That would be appreciated, if you're sure it's okay with you. I'm going to pay you for the food and to rent the room though, and don't even try to refuse me."

She laughed and said, "Okay. What time?"

"I haven't got that far in my planning yet." I thought for a moment and said, "how about seven—does that work for you?"

"It's fine by me. You should talk to Edna about making one of her three dimensional cakes." Jessica suggested.

"I will, maybe she can do a guitar. I'll give her a call."

People were starting to come in the restaurant for dinner and Jessica said, "I better get back to work."

"Same here, congratulations, and thanks again," I said and gave her a hug before I left.

I stopped by the shop to see Nick, but he was up to something as he met me outside, and wouldn't let me inside the shop. I continued on to the seed plant, where I spent the rest of the morning and early afternoon helping Phil work on the leadplant and clean the little mill to get it ready for the small crop of purple coneflower we'd be cleaning next. Sam was gone loading a wagon. Phil and I finished around two and by then we were both starving. He had a dinner with him, but I decided to go home and grab a bite to eat.

Dad was home sitting on the front steps petting Clyde. Wizard greeted me by barking and running around in circles.

"How is your friend Alfred doing?" I asked him

"He's doing okay. He'll need to have a couple stents put in. He was fortunate his wife was home and was able to get him to the hospital quick."

"That's good news. What's happening with their pets?"

"I'll check on them again tomorrow. Their son should be here from Iowa by Thursday morning. Alfred's wife and son will alternate back and forth with at least one of them always being at the hospital. He should be there about two or three days."

"Is something else wrong?" I asked as he sounded melancholy.

"No, it just brings back memories. I was fortunate too, many aren't."

"I see." Dad was correct, we had been fortunate when he had his heart attack. It had been a long, scary, couple of weeks, but he had made a remarkable recovery.

I sat down next to him on the steps where we sat in silence until my stomach growled.

"Did you miss dinner today?" Dad asked with a smile.

"Yes. The leadplant cleaning is going well. We got the small seed mill cleaned up and ready to start the purple coneflower. By the way, do you have any idea what Nick is up too?"

"No. Why?"

"He wouldn't let me in the shop to see what he was doing. When I got to the seed plant, Phil said Sam had been there earlier helping him before he loaded seed."

"No idea," Dad said.

My stomach growled again, I stood up, "I need to get something to eat."

"I made a frozen pizza for dinner; there are some leftovers in the fridge."

"What kind?"

"I made a garlic chicken alfredo pizza."

"That sounds delicious." Dad followed me into the kitchen and sat down while I preheated the oven and put the pizza on some tinfoil. Once the oven was heated up, I stuck the pizza in, set the timer for eight minutes, and poured myself a glass of milk. I grabbed a plate and sat down next to Dad.

"How is your investigation progressing?" Dad asked.

I told him about Paul's connection to the coach, my suspicions of Steve being responsible for the murder of the coach, finding the newspaper clipping, and the visit to the sheriff, and how he had already zeroed in on Steve.

"Do you think Steve killed the coach?" I asked Dad, "Because it doesn't feel right to me. Why kill him now? High school was over fifteen years ago. He is hot-headed, which if Brian was dead, I think Steve would be the prime suspect, but I can't buy him killing the coach."

"Maybe it's as simple as he did try and kill Brian and when the coach showed up for the meeting with Brian, he witnessed Steve knock out Brian and Steve in turn killed him." Dad suggested.

"Possible I guess; we only have Steve's word for it that he saw the coach show up to meet with Brian. He could have been lying, but then why not finish off Brian?"

"He got interrupted by someone else." Dad offered, shrugging.

"Paul Olson told me the coach didn't treat his aunt very well. Did you ever hear anything about that?" I asked Dad.

"No, but your mom and I didn't run in the same social circles as the coach."

The timer went off. I inhaled the pizza, and finished off my milk. "I'd better get going. I want to see if I can find out what Nick is up to. Are you going to be home for supper?" I asked Dad.

"I'm planning to be. Karla's going to pick me up later this evening. She's been making some hotdishes and we're going to stick them in the freezer at Alfred's house, so they have some ready-made food when they get home from the hospital."

"I'll take care of supper for us and if I have enough time I'll make a batch of cookies you can take with too."

"Thanks Carmen."

I double checked to make sure I had chocolate chips on hand and put out some butter to soften before I left. Both Nick and Sam's pickups were at the shop when I arrived. Sam must have come back here again after getting the seed loaded. I parked so they couldn't see my vehicle and opened the door to the shop as quiet as I could, and saw both of them grinning like fools next to a neatly-organized wall display of tools.

"Wow. That is amazing," I said startling them both.

"You're lucky we were finished," Nick said, "or I'd be mad you spoiled the surprise by sneaking in."

"I'm not complaining, but what made you decide to do this?" I asked.

"I couldn't take it anymore," Nick answered, "every time I needed a tool I had to dig through three different tool boxes, as no one, including myself, is able to put anything back where it is supposed to go. This way everything has a place and the tool shape is outlined so you know where to put it back."

"It's awesome. Thanks a lot, both of you. It could be a challenge to keep it up," I laughed.

"Exactly what I told him," Sam agreed. "I'd better get over to the seed plant; I have to work on getting some pallets of leadplant together if Phil has enough seed cleaned."

"Thanks Sam. Tell Phil I'll be there in a little bit."

Sam nodded and walked out.

"This is awesome," I said again to Nick. "Thanks."

"It wasn't hard and I'm waiting for parts so I had the time. I assumed you'd want me busy instead of drawing pay for sitting around."

"I do have to constantly hound you to work harder," I said although I knew better, as Nick never wasted time. "Are you planning on bowling with us again tomorrow night?" I asked him.

"I am. I'll have to meet you there. Phil wants me to swing by his place tomorrow after work and help him install a new washing machine. It shouldn't take long, but I wouldn't want both of us to be late if something goes wrong."

"That's nice of you to help Phil, but don't be late or Jessica will be mad. Tomorrow night is the first night of the league tournament and she's on a mission for our team to win the championship and put an end to the reign of Chloe's team. I believe they've won the last three years in a row. Although Chloe may not be there, the sheriff has been trying to talk to her and hasn't been able to locate her. If she is there, I'm going to question her for sure. The sheriff warned me off looking for her, but I can't help it if she shows up where I am," I said with a grin. "Anyway, don't be late or you'll have to deal with a rare dangerous creature—an angry Jessica."

"I'll do my best, but Phil's wife may feel like clean clothes take precedence over bowling."

I laughed, "You tell Donna she can wash her clothes at my house if things don't go well, because we need you bowling."

"I'll be sure to let her know," he said with a grin.

"I better get moving. I'm going to make a quick stop at the seed plant and then home to come up with a supper for myself and Dad. You're welcome to come over if you want, around 6:30 p.m. if that works."

"I'll take you up on that. I was planning on a frozen pizza."

"If I don't get moving, that may be all you'll be getting for supper at my place too."

"Fine by me, it's the company I'm coming for anyway," he said with a smile that melted my heart.

"I'll see you later." Phil had the leadplant flowing through the mill with no problems when I stopped in, and the little mill was busy with the purple coneflower. With both mills running, Phil was busy. We had a small five acre field of purple coneflower and it shouldn't take an entire day to clean the seed. I did change one setting and was only there a short time, but was shocked to see it was almost five-thirty by the time I left. As I drove home I pondered what I could make for supper that would be fast and decided on tacos. I could see Dad and Wizard taking a walk out in the field when I got home. I set the table and started thawing hamburger, as Dad and Nick walked in the door at the same time. As I cooked I simultaneously mixed up a batch of chocolate chip cookies. I was up and down several times baking cookies as we ate, but by the time Karla showed up I had five dozen ready to go. Dad and Karla left to deliver the food, leaving Nick and I to clean up the kitchen.

"Thanks for inviting me over," Nick said as he put the leftovers in the refrigerator.

"I'm glad you came." We spent the rest of the evening sitting side by side on the couch talking and watching Wizard and Tabitha play. When both animals were bored they did manage to get along well. Karla dropped off Dad and when he got in the house Nick got up from the couch.

"Thanks for supper and the nice evening," Nick said. "I'd better take off. I'll see you tomorrow." He gave me a kiss and left.

"Did you have a nice evening?" Dad asked grinning from ear to ear.

I ignored his grin and gave him a short answer, "Yes. Did you get all the food delivered?"

"We did. We also took their dog for a walk." Dad yawned and said, "I'm going to bed."

I was surprised to see it was 10:30 p.m. I shut off the lights and went upstairs to bed also.

CHAPTER TWENTY

Bison contribute to the prairie ecosystem as their small pointed hooves turn up the soil aerating it and allowing it to hold more water.

WEDNESDAY MORNING I WAS EATING scrambled eggs for breakfast when my cellphone rang. Tabitha who had been tormenting Wizard by playing with his tail glared at me for interrupting her fun as Wizard moved when the phone rang. I grabbed the phone and saw it was Marcy.

"What's up Marcy?"

"The stupid sheriff arrested Steve this morning when he was on his way to open up the hardware store."

"I know Steve got called in for questioning yesterday, but what led to them arresting him this morning?"

"I don't know. I wanted to go to the Sheriff's Department but Steve asked me to open his store instead. He opens at seven so I'm stuck at the hardware store for him until his employee gets here at eight. Once his employee is here I have to go home and get Charlie ready for school. I can't believe Steve is worried about the store when he's been arrested for murder. Is there any way you can stop by the Sheriff's Department and find out what is going on?"

"I'm on my way."

I left a note for Dad, ran out to the pickup, realized it was very cold, and went back to grab my thicker winter coat and left again. I got to the Sheriff's Department fifteen minutes later.

"Can I talk to Sheriff Poole?" I asked the dispatcher.

"Let me ask." She left me standing there and came back looking surprised.

"He said you can go on back, he's in his office."

When I walked in the sheriff greeted me with a smile on his face. "What's going on?" I asked not trying to hide my suspicions.

"I figured Marcy would call you to come," the sheriff said.

"Do you honestly believe Steve killed Coach Janning?" I asked.

"I'm not sure. This whole thing is a mess with not knowing who the real target was—the coach or Brian. I've got Steve locked up for the time being while we check out his story."

"What is his story?" I asked, curious what Steve had said.

"He admits he was there and said after work he planned to confront Brian and threaten him into granting Marcy the divorce. He picked up a board that was laying there and started to walk up to him but then he saw the coach coming so he dropped the board and left."

"It sounds plausible, after all Brian never said anything about seeing Steve."

"Doesn't mean he didn't sneak up behind him and knock him out and the coach interrupted him," the sheriff stated sounding discouraged.

"Somehow I don't believe Steve would have left Brian alive." I said.

"I know; that's what is troubling me. He also claims he saw Chloe's white SUV there. In the meantime we are also waiting for verification of his alibi, the call to his supplier, whenever he gets back from his fishing trip. Chloe will be questioned also."

"Do you have any other proof Chloe was there besides the presence of a white SUV? After all, a lot of people in this town own one."

"No. I'd like to know where she is though—we haven't been able to locate her and her name keeps popping up."

"What am I supposed to tell Marcy? She's the one who asked me to come over here."

"Tell her the truth. Steve is being held on suspicion of murder while we track down his alibi."

As I stood up to get on with my day I asked, "Will you let me know how it goes with Chloe when you find her?"

The sheriff surprised me by saying he would. Before getting in my pickup I dialed Marcy's number.

"What did you find out?" She asked when she answered the phone.

"Not a whole lot, they have a fingerprint of his on a board they believe was used to kill Coach Janning and they are checking on his alibi. Are you going to be okay?"

"No, I'm not, but I'm on my way to work at the library right now. It might calm me down some, but when I get a break I'll be on my way over there to give the sheriff a piece of my mind. Thanks for trying to help Carmen."

"You're welcome. I'm sorry I couldn't do more." I hung up, got into my pickup, and drove to the seed plant. Sam was getting the paperwork ready for another leadplant shipment while Phil continued running both mills. Phil looked up when I walked in and said the coneflower was almost done.

"Did you remember to save twenty-five pounds of leadplant for our mix orders?" I asked Sam.

"I did," Sam answered. "I put it in the mix room."

"Thanks." I decided to spend some time in the mix room doing inventory and getting it organized while Phil finished the coneflower. There was less coneflower than I'd thought as I had only been working for a half hour before Phil came to tell me he was done.

"You finished fast," I said. "We couldn't have gotten too much seed."

"It's a lot less than last year for sure," Phil said. "The leadplant will be done soon also."

We spent the rest of the morning cleaning the mill. We had to clean the mills after every crop as there could be no contamination between seed types. We finished around dinner time and walked over to the break room where I was hoping there was something in the fridge I could scavenge for food. I was in luck and found a frost-bitten chicken TV dinner that was in the freezer portion above the fridge.

"Is this either of yours?" I asked them.

"Not mine," Phil said and Sam shook his head. "It must be left over from the roguing crew this summer."

"It doesn't look promising," Sam said as I scraped ice off the box.

"It's better than nothing," I said sticking it in the microwave. While it cooked I found myself a plastic knife and fork and went out to my pickup to grab my water bottle. The microwave timer went off as I walked back in to the break room. I was surprised to find the dinner wasn't half bad.

"Do they know anymore about who killed the coach?" Phil asked.

"They arrested Steve Crumpet this morning but I don't think the sheriff is convinced he's guilty."

"It wouldn't surprise me," Phil said. "I heard Steve has a temper, but it is tough to believe he would kill someone."

"Do either of you know Chloe Johnson?" I asked.

"Doesn't she own the grocery store?" Sam asked.

"Yes."

"Why are you asking about her?" Sam wondered. "If the sheriff arrested Steve, you don't need to look into this anymore."

"I'm just wondering about her connection to this. Her name keeps coming up."

Phil contributed, "The only thing I know about her is she is good friends with the Fenmore's. I think she used to know their daughter, Billy's mom, and when she passed away Chloe kind of stepped in as a surrogate daughter to them."

"I guess she has a few nice bones in her body," I said in surprise.

Sam laughed, "I don't think she's evil unless she sets her eyes on your man."

"What would you know about that?" I asked.

"I don't have any experience with it, but ask Phil," he said laughing.

Phil was sitting there with red cheeks and said, "Let's just say Donna doesn't let me go in the grocery store by myself anymore, which is fine by me. Women like Chloe make me nervous."

"Do I get to ask what happened?"

"No you don't, and that's all the more I'm going to say."

Sam and I laughed. They picked up their trash and went back to the seed plant. I took a few minutes to clean the break room before going to the shop. Nick was pounding on a tire when I walked in and hadn't heard me. I went back to the door, opened it, and slammed it shut this time.

His body jerked as he turned and saw me. "I wasn't expecting anyone, you startled me," he said looking embarrassed at getting caught off guard.

"Sorry. What are you working on?"

"I need to get this tire off the rim, there's a hole in it somewhere but the lug nuts are stuck."

"Let me see if I can help." I went over to the new tool rack and picked out a wrench and between the two of us we got the wheel off.

"Thanks," Nick said when he came back from dragging it over to the door.

"I can drop it off in town on my way home if you help me get it in the pickup."

Nick and I got the tire on our portable hoist, pushed the hoist and tire out to the pickup, and loaded it in the back. I started to walk away but remembered I hadn't told Nick about Jessica and James. "I forgot to tell you Jessica and James are engaged."

"That's awesome!" Nick exclaimed. "Have they picked a wedding date?"

"Jessica said sometime next summer, but no definite date set yet. I'll see you later at bowling." I waved and drove to town arriving at the tire shop right before closing. They unloaded the tire and I continued towards home. As I drove I remembered to call Edna and talk to her about a cake for Kirk's party. She was excited to try her skills at creating a three dimensional guitar and I spent the rest of my drive home convincing her to accept payment.

CHAPTER TWENTY-ONE

Prairie dropseed tolerates dry conditions with very low water needs and is great for planting on top of a berm or in a rain garden.

ONCE HOME I FOUND I HAD PLENTY OF TIME to cook supper before I had to be at the bowling alley. I had the unrealistic hope if I ate a filling supper I wouldn't be as tempted to eat a bunch of junk food tonight.

Dad and Wizard walked in the door, "I was wondering where you two were."

"We've been out walking again, trying to get in as many as possible before it snows and it's too deep to walk on the path." Dad sniffed and asked, "What smells so good?"

"I threw together a stir fry."

"That sounds good." Dad said.

We tried to sit down to eat, but I soon realized I had forgotten to feed both Wizard and Tabitha as Wizard planted himself between myself and the chair I was going to sit in, and Tabitha was on it. Dad snickered and started eating while I filled their dishes. The kitchen was silent as we ate. While we cleaned up the kitchen I told him about the sheriff arresting Steve. Dad was surprised but not disbelieving as he knew how much Steve hated Brian.

"I wish I felt more confident about Steve being responsible."

"Why don't you?" Dad asked.

"It makes sense if Brian was the target but I'm not sure he was." I said with a sigh.

"I thought you found out Steve and the coach had an altercation in high school?"

"They did, but getting suspended from school can't be a grudge worthy of killing someone ten years later." I answered.

"Who else do you think might have killed the coach?" Dad asked.

"I thought maybe Paul Olson as Brian had been harassing him and when I found out the coach treated his aunt poorly it appeared he had motive to get rid of either Brian or the coach, but he has an alibi. Tom Hartz from the lumberyard certainly hates Brian and had confrontations with him, but there is no way he would have killed the coach."

"What if the coach saw him attack Brian?" Dad offered as an explanation.

"No, he truly loved the coach, causing me to cross him off my list. For a brief time I even considered Mark Carboot as he wasn't very happy Mitch hired Brian, but again the coach is dead, not Brian." I said exasperated. "I'm not giving up though; I have to talk to Mr. Fenmore and Chloe yet. Mr. Fenmore wasn't a fan of the coach and Chloe knows more than she's saying. It would make so much more sense if the sheriff was wrong and somehow, evidence to the contrary, Brian killed the coach." I stopped talking as by now I had gotten myself worked up and was pacing around the kitchen.

Changing the subject, Dad asked, "How are the plans going for your brother's party on Friday night?"

"I've been working on it. I did talk to the other band member's families during my drives between the Sheriff's Department and the seed plant." Dad looked at me and raised his eyebrows in a question. "Don't worry, I'm using the hands-free app when I'm driving," I continued, "Jessica is letting us host it in her restaurant along with providing the food. I'm going to insist she let us pay her for it all. The hardest part will be getting Kirk and the other band members to the restaurant. I'm not sure what ruse will work. I did ask Nick but he thought Kirk would suspect something as they don't know each other well and he would find it strange Nick was asking him to do something the same day the band got back."

"Let me work on that," Dad volunteered. "I'll figure something out."

"I'm planning on talking to Jessica tonight at bowling to finish planning the food."

"Don't get too fancy; you know your brother's favorite food is pizza."

"I know. Jessica thought maybe spaghetti."

"That sounds more like Kirk. What about a cake?"

"Edna is going to try making one in the shape of a guitar. I thought maybe it would be too much like a kid's birthday party cake, but she assured me it would be cool looking and I trust her judgment."

"She's a great baker," Dad agreed.

I checked the time, "I'd better get going or I'm going to be late." I ran upstairs, changed clothes, and put my hair in a ponytail. It was the first night of the tournament and I didn't want any hair to fall in my face and mess up a throw. The rest of the season was fun, but there was something about tournament time that brought out the serious bowlers in all of us.

I got to the bowling alley at the same time as Jessica and James, and we all walked in together. Nick showed up as we were putting on our shoes, greeted me with a kiss in a rare for us public display of affection, and congratulated Jessica and James on their engagement.

"How did the wash machine installation go?" I asked him trying to recover from the kiss while Jessica and James grinned at me.

"It went well, and even better, Donna served me delicious

lasagna for supper. I may be too full to bowl." He answered rubbing his stomach.

Jessica heard him and said, "You better be kidding. It is tournament time, and I'm expecting everyone's best bowling."

"Who knew she was this competitive?" Nick asked and we all laughed.

Nick proved he was kidding about being too full to bowl as he had the best game of all of us and we easily won our first game, giving us a breather before we played our second game. I volunteered to go get us something to drink.

Mr. Fenmore and Chloe were having what looked like an angry animated discussion when I walked up to the counter.

They stopped when I approached. Chloe looked at me and said, "I've been out of town for a few days and when I got back I heard from the gal who was watching the grocery store for me that the sheriff is looking for me. I imagine Miss Detective knows why."

"He has some questions for you, yes," I answered.

"You and the sheriff think I killed the coach. You guys are trying to railroad me and it's not going to work." She took one last look at Mr. Fenmore and flounced off.

So much for my chance of questioning her I thought to myself.

"Could I have three waters and a Coke please?" I asked Mr. Fenmore.

"Sure." He appeared distracted, but went to get the bottles.

"Have you known Chloe a long time?" I asked him when he came back with them.

"She was my daughter's best friend. After my daughter died she stepped in to help with Billy and check in on my wife and me. I know she acts tough, but she has a good heart."

"I guess I don't see it very often. Her catty side is all she shows to my friends and me."

"She's jealous of what you guys have."

"What do you mean?"

"You are a close group of friends. Chloe's never had a friend other than my daughter, Callie, who died ten years ago and she's lonely." He handed me my change.

I'd been meaning to talk to Mr. Fenmore for days. Since he was being so amiable I decided to ask him about Coach Janning. "I'm sorry for bothering you about this, but a couple of times you insinuated Coach Janning wasn't such a great guy. Would you care to share why you feel that way?"

Mr. Fenmore didn't answer.

I said, "Paul Olson told me the coach didn't treat his wife well. You were his neighbor, did you witness that? Is that why you didn't like him?"

"What would Paul know about that?" Mr. Fenmore asked.

"The coach's wife was his aunt." I replied.

"He would have known then." Mr. Fenmore debated for a few seconds and said, "We were neighbors, let's just say I came to know him as a different man than he presented to the rest of the town, which is all I'd like to say about it. The man is dead after all."

"The sheriff arrested Steve Crumpet this morning for the murder."

Mr. Fenmore's eyes jumped back to me and he said, "Why would Steve kill Janning?"

"They think he was fighting with Brian and the coach got in the way. Steve says he didn't do it, but he did say he saw Chloe's vehicle there." I answered.

"Nonsense," he said. His eyes went to where Chloe was sitting with her team, and then he looked back at me and said, "I have no idea what may have led to his death or who did it. All I know is Coach Janning was not a man that should be honored or admired by this town." He left me and walked away to assist another bowler.

I went back to our table alternating between feeling mad that Mr. Fenmore knew a lot more about Coach Janning than he was sharing and feeling crummy about how Jessica and I had been treating Chloe all these years. Sure, she deserved it; she'd never been nice to us either. But we should have recognized she didn't have any true friends.

I got back to our table and as I handed out the beverages Jessica said, "I figured out what to serve for Kirk's party."

"What did you decide on?"

"My grocery order got messed up this week. Instead of spinach for my breakfast omelets they sent shredded lettuce. I can use the lettuce for a taco bar which would be perfect for Kirk and his band. I can use my salad bar set-up for all the taco fixings and put the taco meat in a soup kettle warmer. Everyone can help themselves and we can enjoy the evening too, other than refilling containers as needed."

"Great idea and I know Kirk and his band enjoy tacos. I'll come over early and help you chop up everything. Dad and I are paying you for the food along with the room." She started to object and I cut her off, "don't even argue." She started in again, but I held up my hand with a determined look on my face.

Laughing, she said, "Okay, okay. I'll give you a bill."

I made a mental note to add more money to whatever amount she gave me as I knew she'd never bill me for the full amount. It was time for our next game. This one was closer. It didn't help matters when I slipped and threw a gutter ball. Thankfully Jessica and Nick carried James and I as he was having an off game also. In the end we prevailed by one pin, putting us one game away from the league championship game, both of which would be next Wednesday. In celebration we ordered nachos and mozzarella sticks. I saw Chloe visiting again with Mr. Fenmore which reminded me to share what Mr. Fenmore had told me about her.

Jessica was the first to respond, "I feel awful."

"To be fair, she hasn't gone out of her way to be nice to us either; remember how she acted towards James," I reminded her.

"I know, but I also know James, and deep down I know I had nothing to worry about."

"You have that correct, my fiancé," James interrupted her and put his arm around her.

"I should have recognized she acts that way because she's trying to get attention," Jessica said frowning.

"We all should have," I said.

"Wait a minute," Nick interjected, "I didn't have any problem with her. I kind of enjoyed her flirtations."

Jessica and I looked at him stunned.

He roared with laughter and James joined in. I mocked hitting him and he pulled me close to him and gave me a kiss, shocking me again with the public display. "You're not even close to funny," I told him finally putting all doubts aside and acknowledging how happy Nick made me feel.

"I think I'll invite her to our next book club meeting," Jessica said.

"You might want to wait on that. The sheriff thinks she may have something to do with the murder or at least knows something about it."

"I heard Steve was arrested, so why is the sheriff considering Chloe?" James asked.

"Steve claims he saw Chloe's vehicle at the crime scene and Edna witnessed Chloe and Brian fighting." I explained.

"It wouldn't surprise me at all if Steve is responsible," James stated.

"What do you mean?" I asked him. "I know we all suspected if it had been Brian who was killed Steve would be a good suspect, but it was the coach."

"I'd forgotten about it until I heard he was arrested, but I saw Steve and the coach in an argument at the corn maze. They were shoving each other. The coach backed off and walked away, but I could tell Steve was furious."

"I'd better let the sheriff know. Do you have any idea why they were fighting?" I asked.

"No idea. But I assumed the sheriff had figured it out when he arrested Steve."

"Perhaps I misjudged Chloe again; I was convinced she had something to do with it."

"Maybe she does," James said. "Steve is single, and Chloe has dated most of the single men in this town. It could be she knows something about Steve and is scared of him. Everyone knows he has a temper."

I looked at my phone and saw it was just about 10:00 p.m., too late to call the sheriff tonight, but I was going to call him in the morning.

Jessica grabbed the last mozzarella stick and said, "I hate to break this up, but I better go. Breakfast prep at the restaurant comes early."

We all agreed it was time to go, and stood up.

James and Jessica got in his pickup, waved, and drove away.

Nick walked me over to my pickup. He must have been able to tell where my mind was as he asked me, "Do you think it is possible Steve killed Coach Janning?"

"I hope not for Marcy's sake. She and Charlie are going through enough without her brother going to jail for murder." I stopped and forced myself to focus on Nick, "Enough of that; are you going to make it to Kirk's party on Friday night?"

"I'm looking forward to it, but have you figured out yet how to get Kirk to show up at a surprise party?" he asked.

"Dad said he would take care of it. Kirk will be more receptive to Dad suggesting something than anyone else."

"Are you planning to have the band perform any of their music?" Nick asked.

"Dad and I never thought of it, but it is a good idea, except I'm not sure how to get their equipment there."

"Do they keep everything in their van? I suppose not, they wouldn't leave it out in the cold," he answered himself.

"As a matter of fact they do. Kirk parks it in our heated garage at home."

"Does he leave the keys in it?"

"No, but I know where the spare is."

"After your Dad gets him out of the house, I'll stop by and drive it over to the restaurant. The instruments won't be set up, but they will at least be there."

"That would be great; if they aren't set up the band have an excuse if they don't want to play. Thanks Nick."

"My pleasure, I'd better get going myself," he said giving me a kiss, and without an audience it was one I felt better about returning whole-heartedly. He waited until I got in my pickup and started it before walking back to his. I drove home with a smile on my face. The house was dark. Wizard must be in Dad's bedroom and Tabitha was sitting on the kitchen floor waiting for me. She followed me upstairs.

My good mood lasted through breakfast Thursday morning which was helped by the scrambled eggs and bacon Dad had made. Dad finished his coffee and said he was going over to pick up Karla, as they were planning to attend a presentation on cattle vaccines by the local veterinarian the library was hosting. After he walked out the door I remembered I had to call the sheriff. I waited fifteen minutes until 8:00 a.m. before I dialed the number it was now my misfortune to know by heart. The dispatcher answered and I asked to be connected to the sheriff. I had been on hold for a few minutes when the sheriff answered.

"I haven't talked to Chloe yet if that's why you're calling," were the first words out of his mouth. "We haven't located her yet either."

I held off from saying they couldn't have been looking too hard as she was at bowling last night.

"I called about Steve," and I proceeded to tell him what James had told us about the coach and Steve arguing.

"You don't think Chloe did it do you?" he asked.

"I think she knows something, but I'm not convinced she's a murderer." I finished by saying, "I think you should at least find out what the coach and Steve were arguing about."

"I'll talk to him," the sheriff said and hung up.

I grabbed my pickup keys and walked out to my pickup. My good mood disappeared when I realized the sheriff's deputies wouldn't be picking up Chloe any time soon, as she was waiting for me by my pickup.

CHAPTER TWENTY-TWO

In North America grasslands are called prairies, on other continents the same land is called savannas, grasslands, and pampas.

CHLOE HAD BEEN PETTING CLYDE but looked up as I approached. She was not the tight clothes fitting, inappropriate dressed Chloe I was used to; instead she had on loose gray sweatpants and a sweatshirt. She looked at me with red rimmed eyes when I got close to her.

"Morning," I said, wondering why she was here. "Are you alright?"

"No," she said. "It's been a long couple of days." She gave a big sigh and said, "I didn't kill the coach."

"I don't think you did either, but the sheriff thinks it's a possibility."

"Tell me something I don't know." Her snarky tone returning, but going away just as fast when she said, "But I think I know who did."

"Why don't you come inside and we'll talk." She nodded and we walked to the house where Wizard greeted her with his tail wagging and a toy in his mouth. Jessica would view that as a betrayal, but Wizard for all his evil ways was a good judge of character, which again made me believe we had been judging Chloe too harshly.

She sat down at the kitchen table, looked around, and said, "How quaint."

Then again, if I was going to try and be friendlier towards her she may be best handled in small doses. "Would you like something to drink?" I asked.

"A glass of water would be nice."

"Coming right up." I grabbed a couple of ice cubes and filled a glass with water. I handed it to her and sat down. "So who do you think did it?"

She took a big drink, set the glass down, gave Wizard a couple of pats and said, "I always wanted a dog."

"What's stopping you?"

"I'm too busy and with nobody but me in my household, a dog would be left alone too much. I hoped to get one when I married some day, but that doesn't look to be in my future. I've made too many bad dating choices."

"That doesn't mean it can't yet happen," I told her.

She looked straight at me, "In this small town, not likely. I've got a certain reputation, not undeserved I do understand. It's tough to change who you are in a small town."

I was silent for a few minutes thinking, and said, "You may be right, but people could be persuaded to think different if you made an effort to change."

"It never seemed worth the effort when I was younger, now," she shrugged her shoulders, "now it would be nice. It would be easier to move, but my business is here, and I don't have much faith anyone is interested in buying a small town grocery store. So . . ." her voice trailed off.

"Jessica and I are willing to get acquainted with a new you," I said when she didn't start talking again.

She laughed at that, "You maybe, but Jessica hates me."

"You gave her good reason as the minute she and James started dating you decided James was worth going after. But Jessica is the most forgiving, kind-hearted person I know. You should come to her book club meeting next week."

"If I'm not in jail, I might consider it."

I acknowledged her statement and said, "So why don't you tell me what you know to ensure jail doesn't happen." She sat in silence and I decided to give her a nudge, "It was Steve wasn't it?"

She looked up, "Steve, no. At least I don't think so. He's got a temper the same as Brian. It would be poetic justice if it was him."

"But you don't think so."

"No." She took another big drink of her water, and said, "Callie Fenmore was my best friend in high school. Like you and Jessica are. I don't even remember how we met, but somehow we did, even though we were in different schools. We were like sisters and did everything together. My home life wasn't the best so I spent a lot of time at their house. I can't tell you how many times I wished her parents were mine. I was desperate to be noticed in high school. Extracurricular activities were combined between our two schools and I wanted us to join something together. Neither Callie nor I were interested in the usual team sports so I talked her into joining cheerleading. She never wanted to be a cheerleader, she was way more reserved than I was and she thought parading around in those short skirts would be embarrassing, but she went along with it for me. It helped that like many of the girls from Arvilla she had a crush on Coach Janning too." She paused and chewed nervously on her lip. "I wish with all my heart I would never have talked her into it."

"What happened?" I asked when she stopped talking again, being careful not to move as to not disrupt her.

"The coach gave her a ride home after the end-of-the-year football banquet. He had been grieving his wife as she had died maybe a few weeks before the end of the season. The other cheerleaders kept making jokes about wanting to help him with his grief, but

Callie was serious. She was so kind-hearted and she truly felt bad for him. They were neighbors also so she saw him more than rest of us. Callie told me on the ride home he pulled into the alley behind his yard; he parked his car, looked at his house, and started crying. Callie hugged him and one thing led to another. She was so naïve, she thought they were going to have a relationship and was devastated when the coach ignored her, resigned, and left town. I think he couldn't deal with what had happened and left. After he was gone, Callie overheard Mr. Fenmore telling his wife, Alice, he was glad the coach was gone. He had witnessed more than one occasion of the coach being verbally abusive to his wife about not being able to get pregnant and how her sickness was all in her head. Between the coach leaving without a word to her and what her dad said about him, she was relieved he was gone. A month later Callie discovered she was pregnant. She knew if the coach found out, he would want the child, so she never told anyone who the father was. I know a lot of people around town thought it was George. I wish it would have been; he was so enamored of Callie."

"Did she consider abortion?"

"Never, she wanted that baby so bad. She was scared the coach would come back to town someday and maybe recognize the child so when we heard about the recording George had of the coach cheating we told George what was going on. We had what we thought was a brilliant plan; if we ever heard the coach was coming back for any reason, we would use that recording to blackmail him into staying away. I can't claim we were the brightest kids around," Chloe said with a grimace.

"You were doing your best. What did her parents do when they found out she was pregnant?"

"It did hurt Callie when her dad treated her like a slut who slept with some random boy, but they were starting to make their amends when she died in the car accident a few weeks after Billy was born."

"You never told the Fenmore's who Billy's father was?"

"I wanted to, many times, but Callie had made me promise, and I felt responsible for the whole mess because I was the one who forced her into being a cheerleader, which besides him being her neighbor, also brought her into closer proximity to him. Honoring her wishes was the last thing I could do for her. I think I was also instinctively protecting Mr. Fenmore. I'm not sure what he would have done to the coach if he had known and he had to be around to help Alice raise Billy. I did what I could, but I'm not great parent material."

"Is it Mr. Fenmore who you think killed the coach?" I asked her.

"I think so," she sobbed. "I was there when it came over the news the coach was dead and he had such an expression on his face. He said it couldn't have happened to a better man. I suspected then, but when I heard about Kleb confessing to save Charlie and I realized Billy and Mr. Fenmore where out the same night; I'm almost positive it was him. I've tried to talk to him, he won't come out and say it, but I'm sure he did. He did tell me not to worry if I was arrested, he would take care of it. I think he would confess to protect me, but only if I'm arrested. I don't know what to do. He's been like a father to me, and now I'm betraying him. Maybe it is best if I go to jail, after all my life isn't worth much; and Billy needs him."

"Let's tell the sheriff what's going on. It may not have been Mr. Fenmore, after all Steve was seen arguing with the coach and how would Mr. Fenmore have found out Billy was the coach's son?"

"That's true." She brightened a little.

"But the sheriff does need to know what you told me. Will you come with me?"

She nodded, finished her glass of water, and followed me out to my pickup.

"Are you okay to drive yourself or would you like to ride with me?" I asked her.

"I can drive." She dug out her keys and asked, "Do you think there is a real chance Steve did it?"

"I don't know, but for Billy's sake I hope it was someone other than Mr. Fenmore." I got in my pickup to follow her vehicle to the Sheriff's Department.

CHAPTER TWENTY-THREE

Dried stems from butterfly milkweed can be used to make ropes.

CHLOE GOT OUT OF HER CAR and made it to the door of the Sheriff's Department before I did. She waited by the door looking hesitant to walk inside. I smiled at her and opened the door, she looked at me but didn't walk in so I went first and she at last followed me inside.

The dispatcher looked at me in surprise and said, "The sheriff has been trying to get a hold of you. He's called your cellphone about five times."

I looked at her blankly until I realized I had put my cellphone on the charger at home in my bedroom and in the rush of the morning I hadn't even thought of it. "I didn't grab it this morning," I said, wondering how many other phone calls I had missed.

"I'll go see if he's ready for you, he's in his office." I saw her motion for an officer to watch us. It appeared the dispatcher was aware the sheriff had been looking for Chloe and she wanted to make sure Chloe didn't disappear.

Chloe sat down looking very nervous, "Are you doing okay?" I asked her.

"As well as I can be I guess."

The sheriff walked out a few minutes later and looked at the officer standing by us with his eyebrows raised. It was nice to see he looked at other people than just me that way. He motioned for us to follow him back to his office. As he sat down at his desk he stared hard at Chloe and said, "My officers have been looking for you all morning. Where have you been?"

She answered looking straight at him, "I didn't kill the coach or hurt Brian."

"If that's true, why are you here?" Sheriff Poole asked putting her on the spot.

"She has something to tell you," I interjected. "Will you please listen to her?"

He looked at me and I tried to tell him with my eyes to let her talk in her own way. He must have somehow understood as he turned, focused on Chloe, and said, "Go ahead."

Chloe looked at me, I nodded, and she haltingly started in on why she thought Mr. Fenmore may have killed Coach Janning. When she was finished the sheriff leaned back in his chair and said, "That's interesting, but Steve says he saw your vehicle when he left the hardware store that night."

"Steve is lying." Chloe stated. The sheriff's words nudged the defiant Chloe personality back in to existence. She crossed her arms and stared at the sheriff.

"Did he tell you why he was fighting with Coach Janning at the corn maze?" I interjected.

"He did. He claims he approached the coach to apologize for how he acted when the coach had him kicked off the team all those years ago. The coach wouldn't accept his apology and turned his back on him, which made Steve angry. He's embarrassed, but did admit he has a short temper and doesn't always control it well."

"That doesn't sound like a very good explanation." I said.

"I didn't think so either, but it doesn't mean it's not true." The sheriff replied.

"It wasn't me," Chloe insisted looking panicked.

"Can you prove you didn't kill the coach?" The sheriff pressed her, reluctant to give up on his theory.

"No, I was home, alone, that evening," she answered.

"Are you sure Steve didn't do it?" I asked the sheriff.

"His story holds up. His supplier got back from the fishing trip and verified he was on the phone with Steve." He held up his hand to stop my objection, "I know we don't have the exact timing of when things happened, but I believe Chloe here is the best suspect. You've admitted you and George are the only ones who even knew who Billy's real father was, and George was unconscious in the hospital at the time of the murder."

Chloe started crying and choked out, "It has to be Mr. Fenmore. I don't want to think it was him either, after all he's been like a father to me all these years, but I do know it wasn't me. He must have overhead the coach and Brian; he was out looking for Billy."

I was trying to console her when the sheriff's dispatcher walked in and motioned to the sheriff. She caught his eye and he excused himself. When he came back in the office Brian was with him and he said, "Brian wants to talk to me. When I told him I was busy with you people, he said it was alright if you listened in. What did you want to tell us?" The sheriff prodded him.

"You already know I found the recording that George had, and I'm sure you know I was planning to use it to expose the coach at his induction ceremony. What you don't know is that until the coach showed up at the construction site I had no idea he was Billy's father. I heard Steve was arrested for killing the coach. I figure I stirred up enough of a hornets' nest with my meddling and I couldn't let Steve be suspected of something he didn't do; at least I don't think he did. Then when I got here the dispatcher said you think Chloe may be involved also. She wasn't there that night, not that I saw. I did see Mr. Fenmore out of the corner of my eye right before I was knocked out. I don't know if the coach hit me or Fenmore, but I had witnessed Steve leave at the same time the coach showed up. Chloe was nowhere around."

We stared at him in amazement. I was thinking to myself, could Brian be a decent human after all?

The sheriff asked, "Was Steve on the phone when you saw him?"

"No; but he left. I did see Fenmore." Brian replied.

The sheriff said, "It doesn't mean Steve didn't come back, but based on what Chloe just told me, we better go visit Mr. Fenmore. Why didn't you tell me about this when I questioned you before?"

"I didn't want Fenmore to get in trouble, he's raising a boy, just like Marcy and I are. A boy needs a man in his life. I didn't think solving the mystery of who killed a man like the coach was worth a kid losing his father, but I can't let an innocent person be arrested." Brian said.

We left the Sheriff's Department and Chloe and I got into my pickup to drive to the Fenmore's house. She buckled her seatbelt and said, "Thanks by the way."

I looked at her questioningly.

"Thanks for believing in me, and thanks for coming with. I'm sure you have a hundred different things you'd rather be doing, not to mention I haven't been the nicest person to you and Jessica."

I nodded in agreement, "True, but to be fair we never made an effort to get to know you either. I'm hopeful we can start over when this is done."

She looked at me for a moment and said, "I'd like that."

It was only a couple blocks to the Fenmore's house. Alice Fenmore was backing out of their driveway when we drove up.

"What's going on?" She asked us when she rolled down the window of her car. "I was going grocery shopping but I can go later."

"That's okay Alice, you go ahead," Chloe said, "we need to talk to Mr. Fenmore, is he home?"

"Yes dear, he was dozing in front of the television. Make some noise when you go in so he knows it's you and doesn't get startled."

"We will; thank you Alice." Alice rolled up her window and waved goodbye. "I'm glad the sheriff isn't here yet, she wouldn't have left otherwise and if what I think happened is true, it is better she's not here," Chloe said. Alice drove around the corner just as the sheriff arrived. When the sheriff joined us we proceeded into the house after knocking on the door and stood in the entryway. I could hear a television on somewhere.

"Mr. Fenmore, It's me Chloe. Can I talk to you a bit?"

He came walking down the hallway, stopped when he saw us, and his shoulders slumped as he said, "You may as well come in."

He led us down a hallway lined with pictures of Billy at various stages of age, ending up in a comfortable decorated den. He shut off the television, sat down in a well-worn recliner and motioned for us to sit. "I imagine you're here about Coach Janning's murder."

"We are," Chloe said. "The sheriff believes I killed the coach, and I know I didn't, but I think you know who did. Will you tell us the truth?" Mr. Fenmore kept silent.

Chloe tried again, "Please help me."

He looked at her again, shook his head in sadness, and said, "All these years I was convinced Callie had a simple lapse in judgment. I thought she slept with some boy and didn't want to fess up. We tried to let her know we loved her, that the reason we wanted to know the boys name was so we could make him accept some responsibility, and if he was able, to force him to help out financially. The Mrs. and I felt he needed to do his part. Callie continued to maintain her silence. A couple weeks after Billy was born, I started hounding her again about giving me a name. It was the same night she was in the accident. I'll never forgive myself. I believe I made her so upset she was distracted. I've lived the past ten years feeling like I caused my daughter to die. Billy is the best thing that ever happened to us. I should have been happy about a grandchild and not worried about anything else." He put his head in his hands and stared down at the floor with his shoulders shaking.

"What happened the night the coach died?" I asked.

He took a breath and continuing to stare at his feet said, "Billy had snuck out to meet up with Charlie. Something about a video game, I didn't know that then, I just knew he wasn't in his room when he was supposed to be doing his homework. I left the house and started walking around town looking for him. His bike was here, so I knew he hadn't gone too far." He stopped again, and took deep breath. "I cut through the alley behind the hardware store and saw Brian talking to the coach. I decided to ask them if they had seen Billy. I slowed down when I got close as I realized they were arguing. They must not have seen me coming and when I got close enough to hear what they were saying you can imagine the horror I felt when I heard the coach tell Brian, that he didn't care about some recording, it wasn't going to keep him from pursuing custody of Billy. I stood there in shock until I heard Brian say to him, 'you can't do that to Billy or the Fenmore's. This is the only life he's known. What kind of man are you that you want to destroy your own son?' The coach got mad and shoved Brian. Brian shoved him back and the coach landed on his rump with his hands in the cement. He got up, grabbed a board, and hit Brian with it. Brian fell and didn't move. The coach shook Brian's shoulder and turned to start walking away," Mr. Fenmore paused and looked up at us. "I don't know what happened next, my mind went blank, and I saw red. I remember charging the coach and hitting him with all the fury I felt over hearing he was going to try and take Billy away from us. The next thing I knew the coach was on the ground not moving. I ran away, and a couple blocks later I found Billy. The next day I heard the coach was dead. I never intended to kill him." He started to cry. "I'm so sorry. I would never have let you go to jail for this. I was just waiting for Steve to say something as he was coming around the corner when I left, I was sure he saw me but he must not have."

Chloe went over and knelt beside him.

The sheriff cleared his throat and we all looked at him, "What did you hit the coach with?"

"I hit him with my fist, why?" Mr. Fenmore asked.

"Because the blow that killed him was from a board, you may have knocked him out, but you didn't kill him."

Mr. Fenmore looked up in wonder and said. "I didn't kill him?"

"I think it's a good thing I haven't released Steve yet," and Sheriff Poole turned and walked out of the house.

I left Chloe with Mr. Fenmore and followed the sheriff out. I caught him as he was getting into his Sheriff's Department car. "We have no real evidence, how are we going to get Steve to confess?"

"I object to the word we, but I don't imagine I have much choice. Hop in and we'll strategize on our way back to the department."

We discussed various ideas, most of which were disregarded. With no divine inspiration hitting us we settled on hoping Steve's anger would get the best of him.

The sheriff had called ahead and Steve and a deputy were waiting for us in his office. The deputy stepped out when we walked in.

"We know you killed the coach, Steve. Mr. Fenmore saw you." Steve started to deny it then must have realized it was pointless. The sheriff continued, "But we don't know why."

"You don't have any evidence to prove it, remember my alibi." He stated sounding sure of himself.

"I don't think it's going to be a problem to disprove your alibi. Brian told us he saw you when you left and weren't on the phone; I didn't think to ask where your supplier lives. He's in a different time zone isn't he?" The sheriff said surprising me with that insight. Steve started to look nervous.

"So why did you do it, jealous of the coach, couldn't stand it that he got you in trouble all those years ago?" I chimed in. "Or was it Brian you were after? Mr. Fenmore saw you, we know you came back; don't you want to tell us why? Did you leave Brian alive because you realized Marcy and Charlie needed him?"

That got Steve's attention, "Never! Marcy and Charlie don't need that jerk. I wanted him to go far away and when I saw the coach knock out Brian and then Mr. Fenmore come out of nowhere and knock the coach down, I saw my chance to get rid of both of them. I picked up the board the coach used on Brian and whacked him again when he was starting to get up. I figured Brian would be accused of murdering him, and problem solved. No more Brian and no more coach. I hated that man, what was the big deal about selling some alcohol? I had to spend a month in juvenile detention because of him."

Sheriff Poole called the detective in who had been listening at the door. Between the three of us and Mr. Fenmore placing him at the scene it should be enough to put him away for a long time. Poor Marcy and Charlie, maybe it would have better if Brian had been guilty. I sensed losing her brother would hurt more than if it had been Brian. I walked back to the Fenmore's and got in my pickup and drove to the shop. Nick and Sam looked up when I walked in. They saw my face; Sam excused himself and left while Nick listened as I told him the story.

"It sounds like you should go home and relax," he said after hearing the story.

I considered it for a while and decided, "No. I think it would be better if I worked." We spent the rest of the afternoon getting the new snow blower attached. Just in time too as when we finished and stepped outside to lock up for the day a light snow was falling.

Nick put his arm around my shoulder and we stood in the doorway enjoying the scene for a few minutes. The first few snows were always magical, but by the time you get to March you didn't want to see any more snow, ever. "Do you want to go for a drive and unwind?" he asked me.

"That would be nice. May I use your phone to call Dad and let him know what happened?" Nick handed me his phone but it turned out I was too late, the grapevine travels fast in a small town and Dad had heard all about it. Nick and I spent the rest of the evening driving around after we picked up some food. He listened while I sorted through my emotions. Eventually I relaxed and the connection between Nick and I evolved into something even more genuine as we enjoyed our time together, even discussing a potential future between us. It was eleven before he dropped me off back at my pickup.

"Thanks for the nice night. It was needed."

"I enjoyed it too." He gave me kiss goodbye, waited for me to get in my pickup and drive away before getting into his. I got home thankful Dad was in bed so I didn't have to talk. Wizard was zonked out in Kirk's room and Tabitha was waiting for me on my bed. I changed into my pajamas and fell asleep with a cat paw touching my head.

CHAPTER TWENTY-FOUR

The wildflower, Spiderwort, is being studied for its use in assessing an area's exposure to radiation as its stamen hairs change color when exposed.

I SLEPT IN FRIDAY MORNING AND ONLY WOKE UP when Dad came in my bedroom and told me Marcy was waiting downstairs for me. I changed into jeans and a sweatshirt, ran a brush through my hair, brushed my teeth, and walked downstairs. Dad and Marcy were having a cup of coffee at the kitchen table. They looked up when I walked in, and then laughed when I stumbled over Wizard.

"Do you need some coffee?" Dad asked with a grin getting up and pouring me a cup and handing it to me.

"Thanks," I said as I sat down. I took a long drink and looked at Marcy.

"I apologize for waking you up," she said, "but I couldn't wait any longer to come and thank you for your help, even though it wasn't the outcome I was expecting."

"I'm sorry," I said.

"It wasn't your fault; between Brian and Steve they made a mess of things."

"How is Brian?" I asked.

"I think he's grown up a little, seeing the outcome of his scheming humbled him. One positive outcome is he did agree to the divorce."

"At least something good came out of this." I said feeling terrible for her that her brother had committed murder.

"He knew he had enough to do to repair his relationship with Charlie without adding the stress of the two of us fighting over a divorce," she said.

"I wish there had been a better outcome for you," I responded knowing she was going to grieve the loss of who she thought her brother was.

"Thank you, it will take some time to come to terms with it," she said. "My parents had their difficulties with Steve, but he was always a super brother to me. Anyway," she stood up, "I wanted to say thanks. It meant a lot to me to have you, Jessica, and Melanie on my side through all this. It reassured me I made the right decision to move home."

I got up and hugged her goodbye. "Do you know what time Kirk is getting home today?" I asked Dad after Marcy left.

"He thought he'd get in around five. Is everything ready for the party?" Dad asked me.

"I hope so, I have to work at the seed plant this morning, but I'll be done by dinner and then I'm going to pick up some decorations on my way to the restaurant to help Jessica with the food and setting up the banquet room."

"What did she decide on for food?" Dad asked.

"We're having a taco bar. I'm planning to help her chop up the lettuce, tomatoes, black olives, and anything else she needs help with after the restaurant closes at two. Edna is bringing the cake over at some point in the afternoon also. How are you going to get Kirk and his band to the restaurant?"

"I'm planning to tell him Jessica needs help with some booths she needs replaced and if they will all help carry them out it shouldn't take but a few minutes. I think the guys will agree to that and of course their families will be there waiting."

"Nick is going to bring their van and instruments over in case we can talk them into playing, which reminds me I need to find the spare keys for it."

"They should be in the junk drawer," Dad said.

I got up, dug through the drawer, found them, and stuck them in my pocket. While I was up, I grabbed a yogurt and a spoon. I ate the carton of yogurt and said, "Before I leave for the seed plant I'm going to grab some nice clothes for the party as I won't get a chance to come home and change before Kirk gets here. I'll see you tonight."

"Let me know if you need any help this afternoon," Dad yelled after me.

I packed a bag, gave Tabitha, who had fallen asleep again on my bed, a kiss and rushed out the door. There was a light dusting of snow on the ground making the roads slippery on the drive to the seed plant. Phil and Sam had been having some problems with the most recent load of big bluestem. It was from a new field which had a few more weeds than we liked to see. It took a while, but we obtained a clean sample. I was going to lose a lot of seed with the setting, but it was worth it as I couldn't sell it if the weeds weren't cleaned out. Nick told me last night he was going to help me at the restaurant with setting up the banquet room so I text him I was leaving the seed plant, but I had to stop and get decorations first. I asked him if he wanted me to order him a sandwich if I got to the restaurant before him. He answered that he'd take a BLT and some fries. I found some streamers, balloons, a couple of congratulation banners, and some other little trinkets. It didn't take much time to pick up decorations so I had no trouble getting to the restaurant before Nick. I ordered for both of us and the food was just arriving when he came in the door.

"Thanks," he said as he sat down in the booth. "I got late because a guy stopped by looking for you to get a price on a seed mix. He saw the snow blower sitting there and had a thousand questions about it."

"It is a nice setup," I agreed. "You did a great job picking it out. Did you get his name and number for me to call him back about the mix?"

He handed me a piece of paper with a name and a phone number on it. "I told him it might be Monday before you got back to him, but if you have time to call before then, I think he'd appreciate it."

I had inhaled my sandwich in record time so I decided to call the guy back while I waited for Nick to finish eating. "That was a good sale," I said when I hung up. "He is planning on a dormant seeding and wants to pick it up Monday afternoon." I set a reminder on my phone to put a mix seed mix together on the computer this weekend so we could mix it on Monday morning.

Nick went to pay for our sandwiches while I ran out to my pickup to get the decorations. James was walking in the restaurant at the same time I was coming back in.

"I ran into Melanie when I parked my pickup. She said Steve murdered Coach Janning. How much did you play a part in that?" He asked.

"Not much, I can honestly say," I answered.

"Don't let her fool you." Nick told him.

"The sheriff already had Steve in custody without my help." I protested.

"Yes, but your questioning of people led to all the puzzle pieces being connected." Nick insisted putting his arm around my shoulders.

"I guess, but I don't think the sheriff would agree with your assessment," I said with a smile at Nick.

"Either way it's solved, and you didn't put yourself at risk," James responded as he grabbed a bag of decorations. "Let's get this place decorated."

Nick and I followed James back to the banquet room and spent the next two hours moving Jessica's salad bar cart into the room, setting up an area for the band to play, and putting up the decorations. Jessica closed the restaurant and she and I started cooking the ground beef and chopping vegetables. I gave Nick the van keys and the guys left. Nick was going to wait for my text to know when Kirk and the band were at the restaurant before bringing the van and James went home to get cleaned up. Edna walked in with the cake minutes after they left.

"Wow that is impressive," I said in amazement. She had shaped a three dimensional guitar out of cake and somehow managed to get it upright standing next to a microphone on a stand, with a single drum at its base. The name of Kirk's band was iced along the length of the guitar. "That must have taken you hours," I said to Edna.

"I won't deny it, but it was a fun project. I do have an ulterior motive as I'm hoping to get a picture with the band next to it and put it on my Facebook page. I'm hoping it will lead to more business for my three dimensional cakes."

"We'll make sure that happens," I told her and gave her a big hug. I turned when I heard the door open. Friends and family of the band started pouring in. Jessica and I finished the taco bar set up and I did a last check on the nacho cheese for the tortilla chips. James walked in carrying a cooler, and a few others jumped to help carry in the rest of the beverages. We got settled down and Jessica had hustled to the front of the restaurant when the front doors opened and we heard Jessica greet Dad and the band.

"Congratulations," she said. "Did the recording go well?"

"Awesome," I heard their excited answer. "What do you need help with?" They asked her. I sent a quick text to Nick letting him know the band had arrived.

"I appreciate your help. I know you are anxious to get home to your families. The booths are in the back room, if you could help carry them out here," Jessica said as she led them to where we were all waiting.

She turned on the lights giving us our cue, "Surprise!" everyone shouted.

The band was visibly startled, chaos erupted with everyone talking and congratulating them. I had been kept busy refilling food containers for about an hour when Kirk approached me and said, "I assume you're to blame for this." He gave me a hug.

"Don't forget Dad too, but everyone helped, I did very little."

"The cake is incredible," he said.

"I know. Please make sure Edna gets a picture of the band with it before it gets cut. Are you happy with the record you made?"

He looked serious for a moment, and said, "It was the hardest thing I've ever done, and yes I'm happy with it. Now it's a waiting game to see if the public likes it."

"I'm sure they will, me, probably not," I teased, although it wasn't a lie. I did not understand Kirk's hard rock music. Nick walked in the door along with Wizard who rushed in heading straight for Kirk. Kirk bent down, picked him up, and was rewarded with a pile of slobbery kisses. "I'm not sure bringing Wizard to the party was a wise decision," I said to Nick.

"I'm sure it wasn't, but he wanted to see his master," Nick said as he grinned.

Nick handed Kirk's keys to him and at the same time put his arm around me. "I brought your van over in case you guys wanted to play any of your music," he told Kirk.

"Thanks," Kirk said and shook Nick's hand as Dad joined us.

I looked at Nick with my family and at all my friends gathered; and with a grin appreciated the terrific life I had.

Tara Ratzlaff lives in the northwest corner of Minnesota (just about in Canada) with her husband of twenty-nine years, daughter, five fat cats, and one rescue dog who fiercely greets family, friends and strangers the same—as if she wants to eat them. Tara graduated from North Dakota State University with a degree in Civil Engineering and became the first female County Highway Engineer in the state of Minnesota. She retired early from her career as a Civil Engineer when she and her husband purchased a native grass and wildflower seed farm/business which they operated for over twenty years before recently retiring. With her daughter busy in college and the seed farm no longer keeping her busy, she decided it was time to pursue her dream of writing cozy mysteries. Her hobbies are reading (mysteries only, of course), long walks, swimming when the pool isn't frozen and being amused by the antics of her pets

Printed in the USA
CPSIA information can be obtained
at www.ICGtesting.com
LVHW032116110624
782961LV00010B/242